Now That You're Gone

Now That You're Gone

Julie Corbin

MULHOLLAND
BOOKS

HODDER

First published in ebook in Great Britain in 2014 by Hodder & Stoughton
An Hachette UK company

I

This Mulholland paperback edition first published in 2017

Paperback ISBN 978 1 473 65974 2
eBook ISBN 978 1 444 75402 5

Typeset in Plantin Light by Palimpsest Book Production Limited, Falkirk,
Stirlingshire

Printed and bound in Great Britain by Clays Ltd, St Ives plc

Hodder & Stoughton policy is to use papers that are natural, renewable
and recyclable products and made from wood grown in sustainable forests.
The logging and manufacturing processes are expected to conform to the
environmental regulations of the country of origin.

Hodder & Stoughton Ltd
Carmelite House
50 Victoria Embankment
London EC4Y 0DZ

www.hodder.co.uk

For Dad and Caroline, always.

Prologue

Every night since your death I've dreamt the same dream. We're ten years old and we're cycling along the track that leads to our house, yellow-flowering rapeseed head-high in the fields either side of us. I'm pedalling as fast as I can, my face redder than a raspberry. You're at least a wheel's length in front, sometimes more, but never less. For years I believe I can win, but I never do and you never let me. When we get home we throw ourselves onto the rug in front of the TV and watch the Saturday afternoon film, sucking on sherbet dabs and sticks of liquorice.

I wish I could wake up then, but I don't. The dream jumps time, fast forwards to the morgue. I'm in a lift. A woman stands beside me. We have plastic name badges on cord loops around our necks. The lift doors open, and we walk along a corridor. That's when my heart starts to race because there's a part of me that knows I'm dreaming and that I have to wake myself up. Now. *Right now.*

We go into a room. About five metres away there is a metal trolley. A body-shaped mound, covered with a sheet, lies on top. Adrenaline surges through me, demanding that I run, run, *RUN!* I try to lift my feet, but they're stuck to the floor. I try to turn my head, but my neck feels as if it's encased in cement. The trolley starts to slide towards me, and as it slides the sheet slips away from the face. At first the trolley's pace is slow and then it moves more quickly until it bangs up against my thighs.

Don't look. Don't look. *Don't look!*

I look.

It's you, Dougie. Your battered, bruised, part-blue, part-waxen flesh frames lifeless, empty eyes that stare up at me.

I scream myself awake, and into another day without you.

1. It Can't Be You

The exact moment your body was being pulled from the Clyde, I was driving to work. I was singing along to the radio – badly! You know me – I wouldn't win any prizes for my voice – but when the 80s' tunes get going, so do I. The sun was well above the horizon, and Edinburgh was in the distance, looking grand like she always does. I made it to work before the rain started, and two hours into the morning I had a second mug of coffee by my hand and was assessing an insurance claim. The policy-holder had made three substantial claims in as many years, and I was about to dig deeper into his story when Alec came into the room.

'Isla.' He cleared his throat. 'You need to come into my office.'

'Can I finish this first?'

'No. Come now.' His fingers tumbled through the change in his pockets. 'Don't ask me why, love. Just come through.'

My smile faltered because, well, you know Alec. He has difficulty with eye contact never mind terms of endearment, and he had never called me 'love', not even when Gavin had just left me and he found me crying in the loo. All I'd warranted then was a vague 'never mind' and 'you're better off without him', and he'd left me to quietly mourn the end of my marriage.

'What's wrong?' I said.

'The police . . .' He trailed off, throwing an arm out behind him. 'In my office.'

'Why?' I stood up slowly. 'Jesus, it's not one of my kids, is it?' Breathing was suddenly difficult. I shut my eyes and immediately felt dizzy so I opened them again. 'Please tell me it's not one of my kids.'

'No, love. It's not one of your kids.'

He took hold of my elbow and I walked alongside him into his office. I didn't think of you at that point, Dougie. Family names and faces pushed to the front of my mind – Dad, Gavin, Marie, Danny, Jess, Martha, Erik – but not yours. You could always take care of yourself. You'd spent twenty years in the Royal Marines. You had combat skills. And you had the reflexes of a man half your age. You were the last person I ever worried about.

Two police officers were standing by the window. The younger one had a sharp haircut and a body-builder's frame; the older one was lithe and balding. They introduced themselves, but I didn't hear their names or their ranks because when I saw the serious expressions on their faces my ears filled with a high-pitched ringing sound. 'What's happened?' I said too loudly. 'Is it Gavin?'

'Are you Isla McTeer?' the younger one asked.

I nodded.

'Would you like to take a seat, Isla?'

'Just tell me.'

'Isla,' Alec said. 'Why don't you sit down?'

'I don't want to.' I kept my eyes on the officers. 'Please just tell me what's happened.'

'Have you been in contact with your brother recently?' the younger one said.

'Yesterday.' I shook my head at him. 'Why?'

'We are sorry to inform you—' He stopped talking

and glanced at the older man, whose face was unreadable. 'We are sorry to inform you that the police in Glasgow have found a body.' His Adam's apple moved through a slow and deliberate swallow. 'We think it might be your brother.'

A silent scream tunnelled through my chest, but I held it there. Tightly. There was no letting it escape, because Dougie, how could it be you? I'd have known. I'd have felt something. You are my twin, for God's sake! We might not have been kids any more, but we were still closer than most siblings. 'No. No. Can't be. Can't be my brother. He's in good health. He's well.' I nodded my head. 'He's really healthy.'

'We understand that this is a shock for you,' the older man said.

I met his eyes and immediately flinched away from the sympathy in them. I stared across at Alec, hoping for him to voice loud denial. *'Dougie? Not a chance! There's the door! Fuck off and bother someone else.'*

But Alec said nothing. He was standing by the window, his head bowed, his hands joined in front of his stomach. His sorrow was palpable, and it ignited a panic inside me. I held onto the corner of the desk to steady myself. The ringing in my ears had stopped, but my heart had expanded to fill my ribcage and was beating fast enough to make me gasp.

'This morning, at seven-thirty, a barge operator noticed a body in the Clyde,' the younger officer said. 'When the body was pulled out of the water, there was a wallet with photo ID and a mobile phone in the jacket pocket.' He cleared his throat. 'Both items belonged to your brother.'

'No. No, no, no.' I gulped a couple of shallow breaths and clenched my fists by my sides. 'That can't be right.'

The younger policeman took a step away from me while the older one moved forward and steered me into Alec's chair. I focussed on the desk, on the familiar: photos of Alec's grandchildren, messy piles of papers, pens and clips and drawing pins, a rubber-band ball. I picked up the ball and gripped it in my hand.

'He needs to be formally identified, but the evidence would suggest that the man is your brother,' the older one said.

My mind clutched blindly for a reply, but I couldn't find any words to counter what he'd said. I squeezed the ball tighter.

'You don't have to do this on your own, Isla.' The older policeman was kneeling down in front of me now. 'Is there someone you would like to accompany you?'

I closed my eyes then. I closed them because I wanted the men to stop talking so that I could think.

We were twelve, on holiday in Skye.

'Come on, Isla!' You shouted.

I stayed on the bank and watched you dive into the freezing water, swim all the way out to the buoy and back again. One hundred metres or more. My heart was in my mouth.

'Mum will be mad!' I shouted after you. 'It's dangerous!'

Still you swam.

'It won't be Dougie.' I opened my eyes and stared the policeman down. 'He's an ex-marine. And a strong swimmer. He couldn't possibly have drowned.'

The older policeman pursed his lips and put a hand on my arm. I could tell what he was thinking – I was in denial. And he was right. I was. I was in so much denial that my whole body hummed with enough energy to send me off on a hundred-mile run, non-stop, taking me far, far away from a possible future that didn't include you.

'It won't be Dougie,' I repeated. I stood up and faced the three doubting men. 'We can go to Glasgow if you like. But it won't be him. If you'd met my brother you'd know that he's just . . . He wouldn't drown.' I shrugged my shoulders. 'He just wouldn't.'

I left the room to fetch my bag and my coat, but before I rejoined Alec and the policemen I locked myself in the loo and called your mobile. 'Just pick up, Dougie. Pick up.'

I willed your voice on the other end of the line, but there was no answer and then I remembered that the policeman had said your mobile was in the dead man's pocket. I was momentarily deflated, felt myself begin to plummet back down into a quicksand of panic. You weren't one for losing your things, and you were too canny to have anything pinched, but there could always be a first time. Of course there could. You weren't infallible! Just because the police had your phone and your wallet, that didn't mean that the dead body was you. And when I got to Glasgow I would see that that was true. Some other poor sister had lost her brother. Not me.

Before I left the bathroom I called your landline, twice. And twice it went through to your answering machine. 'This is Douglas McTeer, private investigator. Please leave a message and I'll get back to you as soon as I can.'

'Dougie! It's me,' I said, the first time. 'Call me as soon as you get this. There's been a terrible mix-up. I need to know you're okay. Please call me.'

And the second time, 'Dougie, it's me. For fuck's sake! What's going on? Call me. Call me now!'

All the way to the morgue, I had myself convinced that it wouldn't be you. I sat in the back of the police car and the two policemen sat in the front, wipers full on, clearing raindrops the size of elephant's tears from the windscreen. For most of the journey I kept my eyes closed, visualising you walking, talking, laughing, and full of life, as if my thoughts alone could keep you alive.

We arrived at the morgue just as office workers were braving the weather to buy some lunch. Umbrellas were blowing inside out and coats were being held close to bodies shrinking inwards against the rain. We parked at the entrance and went inside a drab grey building lodged between two red-brick Victorian ones. My two escorts left me there and someone else, a woman this time, had me sign myself in at reception. She introduced herself, but I didn't register either her name or her job title. She hung a temporary identification badge around my neck and asked me to come with her. We walked along a corridor, the cold stone floor amplifying the sound of our footsteps so that the noise echoed up past the grimy, opaque windows to the ceiling. The walls were decorated to shoulder height with bottle green tiles that must have once been shiny and new but were now dull and chipped, the grouting between them grey and tired. We stopped in front of a lift, and the woman pressed the button.

'Would you like us to call a family member or a friend?' she asked me, her tone solicitous. 'You don't have to do this on your own.'

'No.' I'd already turned down Alec's offer to accompany me, and Ritchie was in Florida with his daughter, Leonie. 'I'll be fine.' Her face was all sympathy and doubt. 'I will,' I said. 'Chances are it isn't my brother.'

The lift took us down to the basement, and we walked a few paces into a sparsely furnished room containing just four chairs and a coffee table, a water cooler, and a pile of plastic cups. There was a window almost filling one whole wall from waist height up to the ceiling. I looked through the glass and into another room where a man in blue scrubs and white clogs stood next to a long table. And on the table, there was a body-shaped bulge lying beneath a white sheet.

'We think his body was in the water for at least twelve hours,' the woman told me. 'There are some injuries to face and neck, most likely where he made contact with a boat or the banks of the river.'

She paused, and I managed a jerky nod of my head to show her I could hear what she was saying. And I could hear what she was saying, but I wasn't listening. I was praying with all my might, making frantic promises to God: I'd never be mean again. I'd give money to charity. Even better, I'd work for a charity. I'd join the church. And I'd never complain, ever again. Just please, please, *please* don't let me see my brother lying under the sheet.

The woman kept talking. The skin colour would be 'mottled'; he was 'dressed in a white gown'.

'I'm ready,' I said, interrupting her. I was beginning to imagine a strange smell in the room: decay, blood, and chemicals, mixed together into an unpleasant cocktail that made me want to vomit.

The woman nodded to the man on the other side of the glass and he lifted the sheet away from the face. He didn't roll it back onto the chest, but held it up in the air, in an attempt to screen the right side of the head and body. The shielding didn't work. I was able to see what he was trying to hide. The man's ear was torn, the side of his face bruised, a four-inch gash on his neck. It took about five seconds for me to register that this bloated and battered corpse belonged to my brother. To you, Dougie.

It was you.

'Is this the body of your brother, Douglas McTeer?' the woman asked.

I nodded, then swayed to one side. The woman caught hold of my shoulders and directed me into one of the chairs.

Over the next hour, I alternated between numbness and sorrow, both intense and disabling, a prelude to the road ahead. The woman took me back upstairs to an administrative office where there was a blur of people and information, but I couldn't retain any of it: faces, words or instructions. One second I was coping, my eyes were open, I could see to read, I could hold a pen, I was nodding and answering as if following what was being said to me. The next second I felt as if I'd been punched hard in the stomach, winded, unable to breathe, curling my spine forward until I was hunched on the chair.

The woman sat down beside me. She gave me a hot mug of tea that grew cold in my hands. I could hear her words of comfort but was unable to respond, until finally, one clear thought emerged. 'I have to tell my dad,' I said. 'He lives in Dundee.'

'Okay.' She nodded. 'And do you have any other family members?'

'My mum's dead. My sister lives in Norway.'

'Was your brother married?'

'Divorced,' I said, from Tania, who still professed to love you, despite the trouble she'd caused.

'Did your brother have any children?'

'No.'

'Do you have a partner who can come to the station and collect you?'

I thought again about Ritchie. 'I have a friend, but he went to Florida yesterday. My ex-husband will come, though. He's a policeman.'

'What's his name?'

'Gavin Coates. He's an inspector. He's stationed at the headquarters in Edinburgh, but I know he's in Glasgow today. Pitt Street, I think.'

She smiled her relief, grateful that at last I had given her something to go on. I watched as she made a phone call, and then an image flashed before my eyes – your battered body lying on a metal table, lifeless as an arctic winter – and a top-to-toe shiver robbed me of breath. I waited until I could breathe again, kept my head up and focussed my attention on the poster on the wall in front of me: a health and safety directive, detailing emergency exits and assembly points.

I was determined not to think about your last moments – how you might have suffered, struggled, called for help. How you could have fallen into the water in the first place – and forced myself to think instead about when I'd last seen you, only three days previously, when you'd come to take Finlay to the football.

'Come on Fin!' I shouted up the stairs. 'Uncle Dougie's waiting.'

'I'll take him for something to eat afterwards,' you said.

'Caitlin's staying over at Gavin's so I thought I'd go and see Ritchie.'

'Love in the afternoon.' You nudged my shoulder. 'All right for some.'

> *I laughed and pushed you away and you fell against*
> *the doorjamb, clutched your arm, feigning an injury.*

You were your usual cheery self, looking forward to spending time with your nephew. There was no mention of a trip to Glasgow. We talked about work, and you told me you were still busy running surveillance for Alec, gathering evidence for the Prendergast insurance fraud. All of it based in Edinburgh.

> *Fin came clattering down the stairs.*
> *'Got your singing voice ready?' you asked.*
> *'Yeah.' He grinned up at you. 'Come on the Hi–bees!'*
> *You laughed and put an arm around his shoulders.*
> *'Say goodbye to your mum, then.'*
> *'Bye Mum!'*
> *'Be good now!'*
> *'We will,' you said. You were halfway through the door, and then you turned back and smiled at me.*
> *'Don't do anything I wouldn't do,' you said.*

Fin and Caitlin were going to be devastated. You were such a large part of their lives. Not having kids yourself had worked in their favour. I didn't know how I was going to break the news of your death to them. The very thought made me want to fall to the ground and weep.

'Your ex-husband's on his way over.' The woman was back beside me. 'He'll only be about twenty minutes.'

'That's great.' I aimed for a smile, but my facial muscles were frozen. 'Thank you.'

'Can I get you another tea?'

'No thanks.'

'Something to eat?'

'No.'

She moved away from me, and I drifted off into memories: you as a child, larger than life and twice as much trouble. You couldn't sit still; you were always up to something. We'd been great friends, me and you, hadn't we? Because Mum was usually busy with Marie, and we were expected to just get on with it. Long school holidays we played together, loading up our rucksacks and setting off on journeys on our bikes. We didn't go far, but we felt like we were intrepid. I always carried the food and the map; you carried the compass and our drinks. We would lie on hills and watch cars go by, recording the licence plates into old school jotters as if the letters and numbers might one day prove to be significant.

Of course, you weren't always nice to me. You gave me Chinese burns, twisting the skin on my wrist around in both directions until I let you have what you wanted – I had to set the table for you, or lend you my pocket money, or lie to Mum and Dad about what you'd been up to after school.

'Isla?'

I glanced up, clocked Gavin's face for a split second before he lifted me off the chair and into his chest, my cheek pressed up against his jacket, which was wet with rain. We hadn't hugged for years and it felt too strange to be comforting. I tried to pull away, but he held me tighter.

'Jesus, Isla! Jesus! This is terrible. So terrible.' He let out a frustrated sigh. 'Why didn't you call me? I could have identified his body for you.'

'Because I was sure it wouldn't be him.' I pulled away again, successfully this time, and stared into Gavin's face. 'Because how could he have drowned? You know what a good a swimmer he was. He's only just swum a mile for Cancer Research. He was fit and healthy and . . .' I threw out my arms. 'Why was he even in Glasgow?'

'There'll be an investigation, Isla.' He took hold of both my hands. 'But for now, we need to tell your dad and Marie.'

'And the kids.'

'And the kids.'

I began to tremble, the enormity of what lay ahead flooding me with fear. I wasn't about to wake up. I couldn't pretend that this was all a mistake, slip back to the office and continue with work as if nothing had happened. I had lost you, Dougie. For good. For ever. And now I was going to have to break the news to the people who loved you the most, and the thought of having to do this proved to be my tipping point. I cried, then. Tears erupted through me, wave after wave, rising from my feet, gathering strength in my middle, and pouring onto my cheeks in an abandonment of hope.

'Isla.' Gavin was hugging me again. 'It's going to be okay.'

'Okay?' Sorrow ricocheted inside me, making my chest heave. 'How, Gavin? How?'

2. This is My Now

The next couple of weeks passed slowly, my emotions swooping and plummeting on a second-by-second basis. My head and my heart were full of missing you, Dougie. I was angry and desolate, but mostly I felt a heart-thumping, dry-mouthed anxiety.

'Grief feels like fear,' Collette told me. 'I remember that from when my dad died.'

As you would have expected, Collette was rallying round. Gavin came over every day to give us an update on the police investigation and, mostly, Collette came too. She brought homeopathic remedies and regular sleeping pills, chamomile tea, and lavender-scented candles, boxes of tissues and bottles of wine. I could have easily thrown most of it back at her, but she shopped and she cooked and she cleaned up after us. She did all the things I had no energy for, and so even though she was the woman who had stolen my husband, I was grateful for her help.

I spent all of my time with Dad and the kids. And while Dad and Fin were mostly quiet, Caitlin stomped around slamming doors, then bursting into sustained bouts of crying that left her exhausted. I spent hours sitting on her bed, stroking her hair while she talked through her pain. It hurt so much to watch her, I can't tell you.

Dad came straight down from Dundee as soon as he heard the news. Gavin collected him from the station, and when I opened the door to them, Dad fell against me, holding me as if he never wanted to let me go. I found it hard to look him in the eye because his expression mirrored my own: both bleak and questioning, the how and the why of your death as yet unknown to us. He spent his time sitting in the corner of the living room on the armchair that belonged to Gran, or walking Myrtle up and down the hills, taking Fin with him. I watched the pair of them crossing the field at the back of the house, Myrtle chasing around at their feet. Dad's arm was on Fin's shoulder, and they leant into each other, holding one another up.

In those early days, it was only Ritchie who brought me comfort. Just six weeks into our relationship and I hadn't expected much from him, but when he called me that first evening the sound of his voice gave my heart the tiniest of lifts. 'We're standing in a queue at Universal Studios,' he said. 'How are things back in Scotland?'

'My brother died,' I blurted out.

'What? *What?*'

'He drowned.'

'Isla, Isla. Sweetheart. This is . . .' He took a breath. 'Listen, I'll come home early. I can easily change our flights—'

'No, no. That's not fair on Leonie. She's been looking forward to her holiday with you.' I closed my eyes and leant up against the doorframe. 'Just talking to you is enough.'

He spoke to me for an hour every day. Or mostly I spoke and he listened. He made me feel as if I wasn't sinking, that I wasn't going mad, and that, while life without you felt impossible, I would find a way through. I would. And he would help me.

You knew about Ritchie, but I hadn't yet mentioned

him to the rest of the family, so I took the calls in my bedroom, always after midnight when everyone was asleep. You thought there was no need for me to keep him a secret, but after the false start a year after Gavin left – my Internet dating disaster – I'd made the decision that I wouldn't introduce a boyfriend to the kids unless I was sure he'd be around for a while. Ritchie was the first man I'd been out with in three whole years. We were just at the point where I was ready to have him meet the family, and then you died.

I wish I'd the chance to introduce him to you, Dougie. You would have liked each other. I'm sure of it.

Three days after your death, Gavin came round with the pathologist's report. Caitlin and Fin were in bed, and Collette was working late. Marie had yet to fly over from Norway because Erik was on the rigs and there was no one to look after the kids. So it was just Dad and me, sitting side by side at the dining table. Gavin passed me the report, but I couldn't read any further than your name at the top of the page. My eyes filled with tears and I held it out to Dad, but he shook his head and shied away from it.

'You'll have to tell us what it says,' I told Gavin.

'This is just the initial report. The full report will be with us early next week and then the procurator fiscal will make a decision as to the cause of death.' He cleared his throat. 'As you know, Dougie's body was taken out of the water close to the Glasgow Science Centre. The marine unit gathered water samples, caught debris and detritus, anything that might help build a picture of how he came to be in the water.'

'And?' Dad's voice was gruff with grief and impatience.

'Nothing of any note,' Gavin said. 'The toxicology report, however, suggests that Dougie had been drinking.'

'Drinking what? Drinking how much?' Dad asked.

'Enough to affect his reflexes,' Gavin said. 'There are no lights on that part of the riverbank. It would be easy for someone who was unfamiliar with the area, and had been drinking, to miss their footing and fall in.'

'But isn't it all lit up around the Science Centre?' I said.

'He didn't fall in there, Isla,' Gavin said.

'How do you know that?'

'Because of the damage caused to his body and the debris that was caught in his clothing, he'd clearly been swept downstream.'

'I need a whisky.' Dad stood up and took a bottle and a glass tumbler from the cabinet. 'I can't listen to this sober, Isla. I'm sorry.' He sat back down again and half-filled the glass. 'I just can't.'

I reached for his free hand and held it. 'Was there water in Dougie's lungs?'

'Yes,' Gavin said. 'He was alive when he entered the river.'

I imagined what that would have felt like – fighting for air, trying to resist the weight of water, holding out against the pull of the tide – and my own breathing stalled. I had several seconds when I couldn't catch my breath, and then I started coughing. Dad thumped me on the back, and Gavin went through to the kitchen to fetch me some water. I drank a couple of sips and then nodded to Gavin to continue.

'Tidal flow allows us to estimate where his body entered the water,' he said. 'In Dougie's case, about half a mile upstream from the Science Centre. Local police have been around the bars and clubs in the area and have discovered he was drinking in a pub called the Lone Star. Several of the regulars said he left the pub alone that night. There was no sign of a scuffle on the riverbank, no reason to suspect anything other than an accident.'

'That's a relief of sorts,' Dad said. 'I was worried about . . . foul play.' He nodded into his whisky. 'Small mercies.'

Neither of us had articulated that particular worry, but it had been at the back of my mind too, crouching there, waiting to rip out what was left of our hearts. You'd been gathering evidence for the case against Ivan Prendergast, and Prendergast was nothing if not a crook. I had been afraid that you might have been targeted by hired thugs. So like Dad said, we were grateful for small mercies.

'He fell in the water because he was drunk?' Dad asked.

'Yes,' Gavin said.

My thoughts switched direction and a fist of anger punched inside me. I stood up and slammed my hand on the table.

'Isla!' Dad's voice was quiet. 'Sit yourself down.'

'He died because he was drunk? That's *it*? *Drunk*?'

'Isla—'

'I've lost my brother because he was drunk and careless and fell in the bloody Clyde?'

'Ssh!' Gavin said. 'You'll wake the kids.'

'Why would he have done that? *Why*?' I walked away from the table and paced up and down in front of the television. 'Why was he even *there* for God's sake? It doesn't make sense!'

'The barman remembers him speaking to people in passing, but no one sat down with him for any length of time,' Gavin said.

'Perhaps he was stood up,' Dad said.

'Maybe by a friend or an ex-marine like himself,' Gavin said. 'That would explain why he didn't take his van with him. He must have known he was going to have a drink.'

'So where is this friend?' I shouted. 'Where is this marine?'

'I understand why you're angry,' Gavin said.

'You know what, Gavin?' I snapped. 'You understand fuck all!'

'Have it your way.' Gavin gave me a hard stare, and stood up. 'I'll leave you both to it.'

'You do that.' I turned my back on him, rage peaking inside me, making my whole body pulse with pent-up aggression. I wanted to smash up the room, tear down the curtains, pull pictures off the walls, up-end all the furniture. But mostly I wanted to take you by the shoulders and shake you. Shake you until your teeth rattled and your jaw dislocated. Because how could you be so stupid, Dougie? *How?*

When I heard the front door close I turned back into the room. 'We still don't know why he was in Glasgow, Dad. I want to speak to the person he was supposed to meet.'

'Isla.' Dad's expression was fatigued. 'I know how you feel, but anger isn't the answer.'

'So we just accept it, Dad? Is that it?'

He gave a weary sigh, and I watched a single tear slide down his cheek as he poured himself another whisky.

The full report came through a week later. The procurator fiscal had considered all the facts, and delivered a verdict of accidental death. You'd been drinking alone.

You left the pub. The riverbank was dark. You fell in the water. Case closed. Your body was released for burial.

Okay – so you liked a drink – I accepted that. But why Glasgow? Why that particular pub? Who were you meeting? And why didn't you tell me about it? I'd seen you just three days before you died, and you never said a word. It could have been last-minute, but still, you'd normally text me. We didn't live in one another's pockets, but we did tend to keep each other informed of our whereabouts.

I couldn't get my head around the sheer unlikeliness of it all, but for the next few days I put my concerns to one side because I needed to arrange your funeral. I paid for an announcement in the *Evening News*; I ordered flowers and cars and a function room for afterwards. I did it all as best I could, but truthfully? I didn't do you justice. I know we'd always joked about going out in style, but that was because we'd imagined we'd both be in our eighties, and death would be a timely end to a life well-lived, an escape from the cruelty of an unhealthy, lingering old age.

You were forty-two. My twin.

It wasn't supposed to be like this.

Marie flew over from Norway, looking thin and tired, but then she had three children under five and now her brother was dead, so it was hardly surprising. She reminded me so much of Mum, with her white-blonde hair and pale blue eyes, cold and piercing when she was angry, but now they were full of tears. The taxi dropped her off at the house just minutes before the cars arrived to take us to your funeral. We stood in the doorway hugging, Dad too, and then we climbed into the cars.

The crematorium was full of your friends, Dougie. People I knew and people I didn't, and it made me proud to see how popular you'd been. Proud and sad, my feelings roller-coasting up and down on an endless loop of hope and despair.

Marie and I walked down the aisle on either side of Dad, holding him under his arms. He seemed to have lost the strength in his legs and kept tipping forward as if he wanted the floor to swallow him up. We sat down in the front row, the wooden benches hard and unforgiving. Along the pew from us, Gavin had his arms around Caitlin and Fin. Caitlin was crying into her hands; Fin's chin dipped down into the Hibs football scarf you'd bought for him, his eyes locked on his shiny black shoes that had been rigorously polished by Collette. I wanted to be with them both, but Dad needed me beside him. His grief came from fathom-deep in his chest and set off a spasm of coughing that doubled him up even more. Marie kept staring at me over his head, her expression an unspoken question mark of worry – we'd just lost Dougie, we weren't about to lose Dad as well, were we?

The last funeral we'd been to was Mum's. Marie was heavily pregnant, and had sat with Erik. You and I were on either side of Dad that time. Mum's death had been swift and cruel, from diagnosis to death in no time.

Two weeks in hospital and already the cancer had stolen her vitality. Her skin was grey, and lines were deepening across her forehead and cheeks. There was no treatment for what she had, and we were all slowly coming around to the fact that we would lose her.

'Now listen, you two.' She held our hands as we sat on the edge of her bed. 'Dad and Marie will take my death hard.'

'Mum, I—'

'Isla.' She silenced me with a steady look. 'I know

*what you're going to say, but you and Dougie have
each other—'*

'But—'

'—and that makes it easier for you.'

I sighed. 'Just let me say it. Please.'

*She glanced at you, and you both smiled. I felt the
briefest tug of jealousy and then she looked back at
me and said, 'Go on then, Isla. Tell me.'*

*'Thank you. Thank you for being the best mother
a girl could ever have. I am going to . . .' I took a big
breath. 'I am going to miss you every day.' My vision
blurred. 'For ever.'*

*She took my head onto her knee and stroked my
hair. It was only a matter of seconds before she swapped
her hand for yours.*

After your funeral, we all gathered in the Swanston Inn
– over a hundred of us – eating and drinking and trying
to make merry, just as you would have wanted us to. I
couldn't pull it off, though. Despair swirled around inside
me like a persistent coastal fog, rendering me cold and
blind to enjoyment.

Lamps, Crofty, and Egg were there, along with several
other men from your unit. I knew that as marines, you'd
go to the ends of the earth for one another, and I found
myself asking the same questions of each of them – When
had they last spoken to you? Had they heard of the Lone
Star pub? Did they know why you were in Glasgow that
evening?

None of them knew anything.

They sat with Dad and Uncle Tam, reminiscing big
time. I was pleased to see Dad smile, but I found it
impossible to join in. They were celebrating you, Dougie,
your achievements, your life, and they were right to do

so, but I just couldn't find a way to be a part of it. Marie had booked herself a taxi to the airport, but I told her I would drive her. I wouldn't see her again for a while, and I wanted to spend more time in her company.

'I hope you know I'd stay with you and Dad longer if I could,' she said. 'But I can't leave the kids for more than a day.'

'I understand.' We were holding hands, awkwardly, across the table in the airport café. I don't need to tell you that Marie and I have never been close, but I really wanted to try to move beyond the friction. It wasn't only the obvious stuff – she likes rom coms; I like thrillers. She can shop for hours; I like to get in and out as quickly as possible. It was more than the sum of all of that. I've always found Marie attention-seeking. She had more of Mum and Dad's time than you and me put together. She was always the one who had to be considered. She played on the fact that we were twins, and Mum and Dad fell for it. She was the cute one, still the baby even when she was thirty. Even when Mum was dying, Marie got the best of her.

Get over it, you told me.

And I tried.

I'm still trying.

'It's okay, Marie,' I said. 'You need to get back home. They'll all be missing you.'

'Erik couldn't get time off the rigs, and the kids are too much for his mother to handle. Especially Martha. She's at that age, talking all the time, into everything.'

'It's fine, Marie. Really it is.'

'Poor Dad. He's so sad. Losing Dougie. And that cough! You need to get him to the doctor.'

'I will. And then he can stay with me for a bit. He doesn't need to go back to Dundee until he's ready.'

'He should move back to Edinburgh to be nearer you.'

'I'll see if I can persuade him.'

'I just can't believe it. I really can't believe it!' She wrestled a tissue out of her pocket. 'Dougie?' Her eyes were brimming with tears. 'He's gone, Isla. How can he be? How can he be gone? Our brother drowned. I don't get it. I really don't get it.'

She rocked back and forth, sobbing into an already soggy tissue. I went to her side of the table to put my arms around her and she clung to me like a child, her speech growing increasingly incoherent '. . . because of . . . it wasn't even . . . I haven't taken . . .'

I wanted to cry too, but I was measuring out my tears into small, ten-second bouts of weeping that merely skimmed the surface of a reservoir of grief, because I was afraid that when I gave in, I would break down completely. Then I'd be no use to anyone.

And I was still angry with you. So fucking angry. Because you'd been careless and you'd left us, and our family was lost without you. I'm not easy-going. I don't have your compassion or your patience. You were the fixer and the comforter and I am a poor substitute. But still I kept my arms around Marie until she'd sobbed herself empty.

'Did you see Tania at the funeral?' she asked, when I had finally sat down again.

'I did, but I didn't speak to her.'

'Crying like she actually cared. Bitch. I never liked her.' She blew her nose. 'Mum didn't like her either, and she was a good judge of character.'

'She was.' (And not just about Tania.)

'Bringing a stranger with her – I mean, who was that guy?'

'I don't know. Tania introduced him to me, but his name went in one ear and out the other.'

'Had he even *met* our brother? Did he even *care*?' Anger was drying her tears. 'Bloody cheek.' She blew her nose again, then rammed the tissue into her jacket pocket. 'God knows what Dougie ever saw in her.'

'Love has its reasons.'

You told me what you saw in Tania. Do you remember? She was funny and smart, you said. She was a survivor. She could turn any situation to her advantage. You admired that about her. And then there was the sex. Epic, you said.

Marie sighed and drank the last of her coffee. 'Are you going to manage to sort through his stuff on your own?'

'Yeah.'

'Don't rush.' Her lips trembled. 'It'll be hard.'

'I'll manage.' I conjured up a reassuring smile. 'I'll make sure to get the house on the market as soon as I can.'

Even as I said it I knew I didn't mean it. Sell your house? Never. You loved it too much.

'What do you think, Isla?' you said, widening your arms to include the damp, dilapidated apology of a house and the acre of land encircling it.

'It's got potential, right enough,' I said. 'It'll be a lot of work, though.'

'I can do most of it myself.' You smiled at me. 'Give me a couple of years. This place'll be a palace.'

'We'd better get you to the gate, Marie.' I stood up. 'Don't want you missing your plane.'

'You need to look after yourself, Isla.' She hugged me as we walked, her head resting on my shoulder. 'And keep me updated about Dad.'

'I will.'

I stood at the departure gate and watched her as she took her place in the moving queue. Every time she turned around to seek me out, I waved, and she waved back. When she was out of sight I went back to my car and sat in the driving seat with my eyes shut. Mum had been on my mind a lot since your death, and while I was glad she wasn't here to suffer your loss, I needed her. I needed her common sense and her steady eye.

'Are you really sure about Gavin, Isla?' Mum asked.

We were in the back garden. I'd come home from town, where Gavin and I had been window-shopping for an engagement ring. You were training in the Far East and it was two months since we'd properly spoken.

'What do you mean?' I replied.

Mum put down the secateurs. 'I'm saying this because I care.'

I braced myself, but I listened, because when Mum spoke we did listen, didn't we?

'Sometimes Gavin seems . . . superficial.'

'Dougie likes him.'

'Does he?'

'He introduced us!'

'Isla.' She took my hands in hers. Her nails were dirty, but it made no difference. She had that Nordic elegance that can't be faked, can't be bought: the way she held herself, the tone of her voice, her quiet confidence. 'Be careful. He's the sort of man who needs to be put first. And that is incompatible with raising children.'

It was years before I understood what she meant.

The next day Dad went to Uncle Tam's. Bronte's litter of puppies was five weeks old, so Caitlin and Fin went too while I kept an appointment with Mr Pirrie. We were both executors of your will, and as your solicitor, Mr Pirrie took charge. There were no surprises; everything was to be divided between myself, Dad and Marie.

'Your brother's house is one storey, with three bedrooms?' Mr Pirrie said to me, regarding me above the line of his reading glasses.

'He had planning permission to expand into the roof space, but he hadn't got round to it.'

'Yes, indeed. And there is an office built onto the side?'

'There is.'

'And will you want to put the house on the market immediately?'

'No,' I said. 'Not straight away.'

We agreed that I would check through your mail, see whether there were any bills or work in progress that needed immediate attention. I left Mr Pirrie's office and drove to your house, my hands gripping the steering wheel. Part of me was afraid that when I went inside your home and sorted through your papers, grief would close in on me, drag me under and hold me there, like a crocodile with an antelope.

But there was another part of me that needed to be close to you. You'd been dead for two weeks. Two whole weeks since I'd heard your voice. And how long was it since that had happened? By my reckoning, almost four years, soon after Gavin left me, and ten months before Mum died. We had twenty years of living in different parts of the country, the frequency of our get-togethers dependent on where you were stationed. But we still managed birthdays and Christmases and plenty of days in between. And then when you left the marines, we were both separated, and we ended up living as neighbours. You set yourself up as a private investigator, and Alec offered you work. It was perfect, Dougie. I saw you most days, the kids loved you; you were just along the road.

If only it could have stayed that way.

I turned off the main road and down the track, my car bouncing its way over the ruts and potholes before I reached your cottage. I parked behind your van and stayed in my car, staring through the windscreen. Steam rose off the earth as the sun warmed the air and chased shadows from the land. At any moment, I expected you to open your own front door and stare up at the Pentlands, rising in a majestic sweep beyond the boundaries of your garden, high enough to give a bird's eye view of Edinburgh. On a day like this, you'd have come to borrow Myrtle to take her for a walk on the hills where sheep grazed. If I'd been free, I'd have gone with you, mad dog Myrtle dodging around the clumps of orange-flowering gorse, ignoring the sheep but growling at the wind, her teeth snapping as she tried to catch the gusts.

I used my key to go inside your house, and once I'd disabled the alarm, I sifted through the mail that had piled up in the porch, most of it company advertising and pizza delivery, offers to fix the guttering or help in the garden. There were a couple of bills 'for information only' because you were already paying by direct debit. This didn't surprise me. You'd always been organised, and your marine training had only encouraged that side of your nature.

I left the post on the breakfast bar and put the kettle on. Your house was eerily still and felt cold and unlived in. I switched on the central heating and made myself a black coffee, careful not to let myself dwell on the fact that you would never walk through your own front door again. I wandered around your living room, lifting photographs off shelves, roaming from one memory to another, from a holiday photo of my own kids, to remembering when you and I were children, camping out on the Isle of Skye, pony trekking, clouds of midges, our first ever ceilidh where we danced the Gay Gordons and the Eightsome Reel and fell in an exhausted heap on our beds afterwards.

Before long, sadness crept in around the edges, and I knew I had to stop. My body ached all the way through to my bone marrow. Even my teeth were aching. I went back into the kitchen to make another coffee, but decided that what I really needed was sleep. I kicked off my shoes and lay down on top of your bed, comforted by the fact that you'd been there.

It was some time later when I was woken by the noise of a key turning in the lock. I sat up and listened, my ears straining for the follow-up sounds. First there was the squeak of the front door as it opened and the rattle of the letterbox as the door was pushed shut, then quick, noisy footsteps, a woman's heels on floorboards, click-clacking their way into the kitchen. I slid off the bed and stood in the shadow of your bedroom door. Daylight was fading, and areas of darkness were opening up in the corners of the room, swirling fact into fiction, turning a chair into a crouching bear, a wardrobe into a doorway to the underworld.

'He's got my Lion, the Witch and the Wardrobe!' I shouted.
'He's only reading it,' Mum said.
'But he always cracks the spines!'

*I tried to grab it from you and you turned away
from me, protecting the book with your body. 'Give it
to me!' I shouted. I kicked your shin. You punched my
thigh. Next thing we were wrestling on the carpet.*

*'I don't want to see you fighting!' Mum hauled us
apart and held us away from each other. 'Now apologise, please.'*

*I cried from the injustice of me having to say sorry
to you. 'It's not fair!'*

*You didn't cry. You said sorry and you gave me
back my book, grinning.*

I thought about who else had one of your house keys
or knew where the spare was hidden – Dad, Fin and
Caitlin, Alec, Tania – only Tania would be wearing heels.

The footsteps had moved to the living room, and I
followed. I was in my socks and I made no sound as
I moved across the carpet. Tania was on her hands and
knees, rummaging through the trunk under the window.
'What are you looking for?'

She gave a scream and whirled around, stumbling to
her feet to face me. 'For fuck's sake, Isla! What a fright!
Why are you creeping around?'

'I'm not creeping around!'

'Bloody hell.' She pulled a packet of cigarettes and a
lighter from the back pocket of her jeans. 'Talk about
giving someone a heart attack.' She lit a cigarette and
caught the look on my face. 'Dougie didn't mind me
smoking inside.'

'Well I do.'

'Fine, then.' She stubbed the cigarette out on the sole
of her shoe, and pushed it back into the packet. 'I didn't
expect anyone to be here.'

'My car's outside.'

'Well, I didn't notice, did I?'

Her hair was sticking up, and there were mascara smudges under her eyes. I could be picky and remind you that her nose was a bit too big, her eyes a bit too small, but she had a lovely smile on the rare occasions that she used it, and even without the smile, she was still beautiful. When you were depressed over your break-up, I asked you whether you still loved her and you said, 'I'll always love her. I know she's difficult, but that doesn't seem to stop me loving her.'

Difficult was one way of putting it. She was all square edges, knocking chips out of everyone else but rarely bruising herself.

'What were you looking for?' I said.

'Money.' She tilted her chin at me. 'Dougie said that I could take it if anything happened to him.'

'I've just come from his solicitor's. It wasn't mentioned in his will.'

'So?' She made a sideways motion with her head – right, left and right again, her neck elongating like a lairy giraffe. 'I'll have you know we were still sleeping with each other.'

'He told me.' I folded my arms. 'He also told me that you'd swapped drink for gambling.'

'Addiction is an *illness*, Isla.'

'If you say so, *Tania*.'

'Whatever.' She turned around and started rummaging in the trunk again, pushing aside photo albums and books before grabbing a Manila envelope. 'This is it.' She held it out to me. 'Two thousand pounds. Count it if you want.'

'Two thousand pounds?' I started back. 'Are you having a laugh?'

'It's not *that* much.'

'It is on the planet the rest of us call earth.'

'God give me strength!' She stared up at the ceiling, sighing loudly.

Did you really want her to have that much money, Dougie? She would only have gambled it away. Surely you would have known that. You'd told me that whenever she had money, she spiralled into self-destructive mode, put herself in danger, lost the money twenty times faster than it took to earn it.

I quickly decided that you didn't, couldn't, have wanted her to have the cash and that she was just chancing her arm. 'I'm sorry, Tania, but this is a considerable sum of money. I know Dougie was still fond of you—'

'He *loved* me, actually.' She bit her lip.

'Yes, I believe he did love you.'

Her eyes strayed off towards the bedroom before she turned them back in my direction. 'Dougie always said you were the brainy one, so think about it. How would I know the money was there if he didn't want me to have it?'

'You were married to him. You know he's always kept cash in the house.'

'Yes, but how would I know it was in the trunk?'

'Because you lived with him for fifteen years!'

'So you're not going to let me have it?'

'Tania.' I sighed. 'Let's be honest, you did well enough out of my brother when you divorced him.'

'Fair enough.' She shrugged her acceptance. 'You and your mum must have rejoiced when we got divorced.'

'My mum didn't judge you, Tania.'

'Not much, she didn't.'

We were in Dalkeith Park. Caitlin and Fin were climbing up the enormous slide. I was standing beside

Mum and Dad not saying much because you'd asked me to keep shtum.

'All that time he's wasted with Tania,' Dad said. 'Now he's finally getting divorced when he should have dumped her years ago and be married to a nice lassie who appreciates him.'

'A marriage can't be ended without heartache, George,' Mum said. 'It takes time to come to those decisions.'

You'd told me what had been the final straw for you and Tania. She'd been dealing cocaine with one of her brothers, despite the fact that she'd promised you she'd never deal again. Heaven knows how you kept her from being prosecuted. I'm sure you ended up owing no end of favours over it.

And I know she was sorry, but still you left her. 'She's toxic,' you said. 'I won't let her drag me down with her.'

'I'll miss Dougie, you know?' Tania said, her expression soft. 'Are you going to be okay?'

This was the way with Tania, wasn't it? One minute she was ready for a fight, and the next, she tuned into the other person's feelings and grew empathetic antennae. It was a counterpoint to her bolshiness, and was what kept you with her for so long.

'It'll be hard.' My eyes stung. I blinked tears away.

'I suppose you're feeling guilty, but I know that Dougie wouldn't want you to.'

'Why would I feel guilty?'

'Well . . . you know. Him being in Glasgow for you.' She gave me a sad smile. 'Although it depends on what you believe. Maybe he was going to die that day anyway. If death isn't a random thing.'

'What?' My heart slowed to a stop. 'What are you talking about?'

'Just that he wouldn't have been in Glasgow if it wasn't for you.'

'I had nothing to do with him being in Glasgow.' My heart stuttered back to life and took off at a run. 'Nothing at all.'

'Why was he there then?'

'I don't know.' I pressed my fingers against my sternum. 'I wish I did.'

'Oh. Well, he said . . .' She trailed off and looked around her. 'Maybe I heard him wrong.'

I stared at the floor, willing myself to stay calm. 'What did he say?'

'The evening he died, I asked him whether I could come round, and he said he'd be in Glasgow. I asked him why, and he said he had something to sort out. For work, I said. And he said no, it's for Isla.'

My eyes flicked up and met hers. 'What did he mean by that?'

'I dunno . . .' She was bored now.

'Tania.' I took hold of her shoulder, and shook her. Not hard. Just enough to make her pay attention. 'What were his *exact* words?'

'I don't rem-*em*-ber,' she said, her eyes challenging. 'But I do know this.' She pulled away. 'If he'd left you to sort out your own life, he'd still be alive.'

I dropped the envelope back in the trunk and jerked the lid shut with my foot. 'Please leave,' I said. 'And before you go, give me back your key.'

'I used the spare. It's on the kitchen counter.' She marched across the carpet and I followed her to the door. When her hand was gripping the handle she turned back to me. 'So he didn't leave me anything in his will?'

'Why would he, Tania?' I crossed my arms. 'Why the hell would he?'

'Fucker.' She wrenched open the door. 'Good luck with the guilt!'

The door slammed shut behind her, and I stood staring at the rattling letterbox, trying not to panic. Tania was many things, but, to my knowledge, she wasn't a liar. So she'd either misheard you or you'd been in Glasgow because of me. I stood there, tense and twitchy, chewing my nails, but I couldn't come up with a reason. There was nothing going on in my life that needed 'sorting'. Nothing at all.

I went into your office and switched on your laptop, scrolling through your online calendar until I arrived at the correct page – Monday, September ninth, the day you'd died. There was nothing recorded for that day, nothing at all. In fact you'd blocked off the whole day as if you had plans for it. I scrolled through the previous month to see whether I could find anything of note, and when I'd finished, I was sure of three things – you were preparing a surveillance report about the Prendergast case for Alec, you were finishing up on a cheating spouse case, and you were still looking for Lucy O'Malley who had disappeared in 2012.

So far, so much I already knew.

The light was flashing on your answering machine – four messages. The first one was from the non-cheating spouse, thanking you for your report. The next two were from me. They were the calls I'd made from the toilet before accompanying the two policemen to the morgue. The sound of my own voice was painful to hear. My tone was panicked but hopeful. I really believed you were alive, and the limbo between hope and despair now seemed like a blissful place to be because the finality of your death was brutal. Utterly.

The final call was from Gordy O'Malley, Lucy's dad, saying he hadn't had any luck with the 'three monkeys' angle'. You'd told me about Gordy. His daughter had been missing for almost two years, and he was convinced that she was still in Scotland somewhere. It was one of those cases that were on a permanent simmer, every so often you'd spend a day following up the slimmest of leads. I suspected that if Gordy paid you anything at all, it would barely cover your petrol, but I knew you had a soft spot for him.

You had a desk diary too, a Christmas present from Fin. I found it underneath a pile of newspapers and opened it to the day you died. And there it was – ISLA – in big blue letters scrawled diagonally across the lower half of the page. I felt a rush of intense, queasy anxiety, the sort that comes from worrying about something important, something vital, that you can't quite put your finger on. I stared at the letters, trying to make sense of them – trying and failing to find an answer. There was no doubt that it was your writing. There was no doubt that the Isla you were referring to was me. Beyond that I couldn't say. It wasn't close to our birthday; you hadn't asked to meet me. I didn't even know anyone who lived in Glasgow.

I closed the diary and sat back in the chair. There was a loud buzzing in my ears, like a bluebottle on the loose. I waited for the sound to pass, and watched the shadows in the room lengthen towards me until they coloured my clothes black.

3. The Trouble With You Two

How often did Mum start sentences that way? The trouble with you two is that you're either as thick as thieves or you're fighting. The trouble with you two is that you never know when to stop. The trouble with you two is that you don't appreciate each other.

We could be annoying. Often we fought. Sometimes we held grudges. But when circumstances were against us, we instinctively knew to back each other up. We defended each other no matter what. We had a visceral co-dependency, a symbiotic bond. You were my everyday. You did my history homework; I did your maths. I got you girlfriends; you got me Gavin. Okay, so that turned out to be something I wouldn't necessarily thank you for, except for the fact that I'd had Caitlin and Fin, of course.

Now here I was facing the aftermath of your death. Mum's death we faced together, and when Gavin left me you were my counsellor, confidant and cheerer-upper all rolled into one. Going it alone felt impossible, Dougie, because we did grow to love and appreciate one another and the absence of you was an acute, persistent ache.

I'd spent an almost sleepless night thinking about my name in your diary, and the more I thought about it, the more it bothered me. I didn't want to be the reason you were on that riverbank. I really and truly didn't, and I was growing increasingly scared that there was something obvious I was missing. Our lives were linked by birth, and I was damned if I was going to let you die on me without me finding out exactly what had happened to you even if the blame somehow ended up being mine.

The first opportunity I had, I brought it up with Gavin and Dad. It was almost ten in the evening, Caitlin and Fin were in bed and Collette was in the kitchen tidying up after our evening meal.

'I saw Tania when I was at Dougie's house yesterday,' I said, pouring myself another glass of wine.

'What was she doing there?' Gavin asked.

'Seeing what she could get for herself, no doubt,' Dad said.

'She said something funny. She said Dougie went to Glasgow because of me.'

'Eh?' Dad was frowning.

'He told her he was sorting something out for me.'

'And was he?' Gavin said.

'No.' I shook my head. 'I mean, I don't know what or why. There's nothing I can think of.'

'She was lying then wasn't she,' Dad said.

'She's not a liar, Dad.'

'She's a right besom. You know that as well as I do.' He gave a perfunctory shake of his head. 'Always has been, always will be.'

'It bothers me that the police never established what Dougie was doing in Glasgow,' I said. 'It couldn't have been for work because there was nothing on his online calendar.'

'We've talked about this already, Isla,' Gavin said.

'I know, but I don't understand why the police didn't take his computer for examination.'

'There was no need,' Gavin said. 'Dougie's death was not suspicious.'

'But he was a private investigator.'

'Yes, but he wasn't working on any cases that would give anyone a motive to kill him.'

'How can you be sure?'

'What are you thinking of? A cheating spouse psychopath who decided to push him in the river?'

'What about Prendergast?'

'Prendergast is being done for fraud.'

'But isn't he linked to other crimes?'

'Leave it, Isla,' Dad said, his tone exasperated. 'You'll have yourself running around in circles and never get anywhere.'

I lifted my bag off the floor and pulled out your diary. 'Look.' I opened it to the day you died and pointed to my name. Dad stared briefly at the page, then slumped back in his seat. Gavin seemed more interested.

'I can see why this bothers you, Isla, but because he already had an online calendar maybe he was using this one as more of a notebook.' He flicked through the diary, stopping at pages that backed up his theory. 'Here's a shopping list: burgers, buns, beer, new football for Fin, something for Caitlin.'

'That was the day before Caitlin's birthday barbecue.'

'"Remember to ask Isla about the hot-water tank."' Another page. '"Take van in for MOT."' And another. '"Ask Dan for season tickets."'

'I get what you're saying, but isn't it a bit of a co-incidence that my name is on September the ninth?'

'He probably wrote down your name to remind himself to ask you something or to call you,' Gavin said, closing your diary. 'If Tania hadn't told you he was in Glasgow because of you, would you give your name a second thought?'

'Yes . . . no. I don't know. It's hard to say.'

'Tania could never be considered a reliable witness.' Gavin had his not-suffering-fools-gladly face on. 'You should discount anything she says.'

'I can't. Dougie's my brother.' I heard myself still using the present tense because I wasn't ready to let you slide into the past and couldn't imagine that I ever would be. 'I need all the gaps filling in. I need to know why he was in that pub and who he was waiting for.' I looked over at Dad. He was drooping on his chair, a tumbler of whisky cupped in his hands. 'Dad? Back me up here.'

No answer. He wasn't listening. His face was grey; his expression was tight. He looked as if he was falling into grief's abyss. 'Dad?'

'Dougie was a private investigator,' Gavin said. 'He would have had all sorts of contacts and meetings he didn't share with you or his calendar.'

'We talked almost every day.'

'People's lives aren't neat and tidy, Isla. There's a good chance we'll never find out why he was there.'

'There speaks the cop,' Dad muttered.

'All I'm saying is that there's no mystery here,' Gavin said. 'We all know that Dougie liked a drink and—'

I pushed Gavin's shoulder and he stared at me, a 'what?' expression on his face. 'You make it sound like it was his own fault!' I said.

He sighed. 'It was unintentional.'

I reached across the table and held Dad's hand. 'What are you thinking, Dad?' I asked.

'My boy is dead.' He tossed back his whisky. 'Dead. Dead. DEAD.' A loud wail erupted from his throat, and he fell forward with force, his forehead hitting the table with a crack.

'Dad!'

'Shit, shit and more shit!' he bawled. 'It should have been me in that coffin!'

'Come on now, George.' Gavin was around at Dad's side of the table in a moment. 'You'll wake the kids up.'

'Forty-two. *Forty-fucking-two.* What age is that to die?' Dad said.

Collette came through from the kitchen, drying her hands on a towel. 'Is everything okay?'

'The whisky's made him sad.' I reached for the box of tissues and passed it to Dad.

'The whisky has *not* made me sad. I was already sad!' Dad shouted. 'It's made me angry is what it's done. Douglas is dead, Isla. *Dead.* And there's not a damn thing any of us can do about it.' He halted a sob in his throat by converting it into a loud, rasping cough. 'I'm just relieved your mother's not here to see her son pass on. It would have broken her heart.' He banged his fists on the table then pushed past Gavin and stumbled out of the room into the downstairs loo.

We stood for a few seconds, shocked in the wake of Dad's outburst, and then, 'Your poor dad,' Collette said, her tone hushed. 'It's all too much to bear.'

'We should get going,' Gavin said, propelling Collette ahead of him. 'I'll pick the kids up from school on Friday, Isla. Unless you want them here with you?'

'No, it's fine. I could do with sleeping for most of the weekend.' I followed them to the front door. 'Thank you for making dinner. And for tidying up afterwards, Collette.'

'You're very welcome.' She hugged me. 'The dishwasher's on and all the leftovers are in containers in the fridge. Gavin and I will keep in close contact with you.'

'We'll be all right.'

She glanced at the toilet door. 'Say goodbye to your dad for me.'

'I will.'

'And Isla.' She took hold of my shoulders. 'We're here for you.'

I nodded, not really listening. 'Thank you.'

Gavin was already out on the step. 'Come on, Collette. I have an early meeting in the morning.' He gave me a hasty hug and then urged Collette into the car.

'Call us any time!' Collette shouted.

I waited until their taillights were out of sight, and then I closed the door and went into the kitchen. By the time I'd settled Myrtle in her bed and turned off the kitchen lights, Dad had come out of the toilet and was pouring another whisky. I was trying not to count, but I knew it had to be his fifth or sixth double.

'Dad drinks too much,' I said. We were sitting on the decking at the side of your house watching the sun go down.

'He lives on his own, Isla. What do you expect?'

'He's not always on his own. I have a feeling he's started going out with Dorothy.'

'Dorothy?'

'She lives next door. She drives the ancient, orange Cortina.'

'Oh yeah.' You put your feet up on another chair and let your head drop back. 'Good on him.'

Dad's hands were shaking, and he was blinking down into the tumbler as if his vision was blurred. I went over to stand beside him, resting my head against his shoulder. 'How's your forehead?'

'It'll be sore in the morning I expect.' His jaw clenched. 'Thank God those two are gone at last. That bloody woman drives me nuts with all her bossing.' He took a drink, holding the whisky in his mouth for a few seconds before swallowing. 'How any man could leave you for her is a mystery to me. Fancy-pantsing around like she owns the place. And bloody Gavin. He's always been an arse.'

'They've both been really helpful since Dougie died.'

'You've forgiven and forgotten then.'

'It has been four years since he left me, Dad.'

'A man cheats on you like that.'

'He's a good father.'

'He's good enough. I'll give him that.' He blinked wet eyelashes before looking straight at me. 'And you're a good girl, Isla. Your mum would be right proud of you.'

'Don't.' Tears gathered behind my eyes. 'You'll have me crying in a minute.'

'Here. Have a slug of this.'

He passed me the whisky and I took a sip, shuddered, and gave the glass back to him. 'It's a bit too strong for me.'

'It's a smoky malt this one.' He downed the remainder in one swift gulp. 'Douglas would've enjoyed it.'

'Talking of Dougie.' I took Dad's hand. 'Dad, I really need to find out why he was in Glasgow.'

'Isla, Isla.' Dad shook his head against the idea. 'I hate to say it, but I think Gavin's right. Whatever took him there we may never know. And Douglas did like his drink. He's not the first drunk who missed his footing, and he won't be the last.' He cleared his throat. 'Now listen, hen. I'm going to get on home tomorrow.'

'Tomorrow?' I couldn't keep the disappointment out of my voice. 'Are you sure? It's only a few days since Dougie was buried.'

'I know. But I should be getting myself back to work.'

'We need to get you to the doctor to sort out your cough.'

'There are doctors in Dundee.'

'I told Marie you'd stay with me for a bit.'

'Well, you'll just have to untell her.' He put the glass down and straightened his shoulders, his posture full of purpose. 'What can't be cured must be endured. The sooner we all get back to what passes for normality the better.'

'But Dad . . .' I reached up and touched his forehead. 'We both still have a long way to go before we'll be able to function normally.'

'I know, hen. I know.' His jaw trembled. 'But I won't be breaking down like that again. It doesn't help either of us.'

We hugged then, and I felt a tremor run through his wiry frame and into mine like an electric current.

'I'm a shaky old bugger.'

'Understandable though Dad, eh?' We drew apart. He looked as if he was about to fall asleep on his feet. 'I'd love you to think about moving back down here.'

He considered my request for second. 'Could do.'

'There's nothing keeping you in Dundee really, is there?'

'I've got my job in the garden centre. Nothing special, I know, but it's company.'

'You could get a part-time job down here.'

He nodded. 'I know. But while I'm able to have my own life I should have my own life.'

'Of course. But you're an Edinburgh man, and you could have your own life closer to us.'

I waited for him to mention Dorothy, but he didn't. He sighed and gave me a speculative look. 'Have you cooked this up with Marie?'

'Aye, maybe.' I smiled. At times like this he made me feel as if I was still fourteen, hot-headed and full of silly ideas. 'Please Dad.'

'I'll worry about you, right enough. Since Gavin left, you've always had your brother along the road, and now you've got nobody close by.'

'I've got friends,' I said. 'I want you to come to live here because I love you, Dad. And Caitlin and Fin love you. We're family.'

'Aye. We are that.' He patted my shoulder, his smile artificially bright. 'I'll be back down here in a year or two, maybe.' I followed him out of the room. 'In the meantime, you look after my grandchildren. And find yourself another man. You're too young to be on your own.'

It was on the tip of my tongue to tell him about Ritchie, but he was already halfway up the stairs.

At breakfast the next day, Dad kept the mood light. He told Fin and Caitlin about the holiday we'd had up near Ullapool, when our cairn terrier, Jinty, fell down that old mine shaft and we lowered you down after her on a rope. (When I think about that story now, I wonder what Mum and Dad were playing at! Sending a ten-year-old down after a dog. Anything could have happened to you.)

Fin was still wearing his Hibs scarf, and Caitlin sat through breakfast with Myrtle on her knee, but the main thing was that they ate their cereal without any tears. I could sense that, after days off for the funeral, they were glad to be getting back to school: they had their teeth cleaned and their bags packed before I had to start nagging them.

Fin followed me out to the car first. 'I don't know what's going to happen about football training, Mum, cos Uncle Dougie usually took me.'

'I'll speak to Stuart's mum. I'm sure she'll be all right about sharing lifts.'

'But you'll be at work. You can't always give us a lift.'

'Between me and your dad and—'

'Dad has to stay at work late! And you can't not turn up on time because Mr Abbott gets really mad!'

'I promise I'll sort it for you.'

'When?'

'Today. When I collect you from school. I'll speak to Stuart's mum and we'll make a plan.'

'Do you really promise?'

I put my hand over my heart and said solemnly, 'I really promise.'

'Okay then. I believe you.' He climbed into the car before adding, 'Thousands wouldn't.' He was watching my face to see how I'd react.

Caitlin had been hanging back, listening but not speaking. 'That was what Uncle Dougie always said.'

'Well, Fin can say it now.' I pulled her in for a hug. 'That's okay, isn't it?'

'I suppose.' She fiddled with the straps on her bag. 'It's a way of keeping him alive, isn't it?'

'It is.' We shared eye contact, the three of us, united in just how much you meant to us and how important it was to keep your memory close.

I'd offered to drive Dad home, but he insisted he would get the train back. 'I enjoy the journey over the bridges,' he said. 'And it's much quicker than going by car.'

I didn't see any reason to argue with him. So first we dropped the kids at school and then I drove him on to Waverley Station. I shouldn't have. I should have insisted on taking him home myself, but I didn't have the benefit of hindsight.

I waved goodbye to him and then drove out of town again, back to your house. I had a plan. When I'd been lying awake overnight, in between nightmares, worrying about why you were in Glasgow, it came to me that I needed to give Gordy a call. Judging by the message he'd left on your answering machine, he hadn't seen your death notice in the paper. But more than that, I was hoping he might be able to tell me why you were in Glasgow. Because no matter what Gavin and Dad said, I knew I wouldn't be able to rest until I understood the how and why of your death.

I parked behind your van again and opened my car door, but found that I couldn't climb out. My legs weren't moving and I didn't have the strength to make them. I pulled the door shut again and sat back in the seat, my eyes staring up at the sky. Rain was imminent. (Isn't it always?) Light reflected off the heather and gorse to stain the clouds a rich, fiery copper. I tried to fix on the view, enjoy the beauty of the hills and the sky, but I couldn't. I was having a moment. One of those moments when I was poleaxed by grief. It was a physical pain that sliced through my middle. I closed my eyes and kept breathing, let the fear and the horror of your death grind through me, and then my mobile rang. It was Ritchie.

'I've just arrived home,' he told me. 'You coming over?'

'Already?' My heart lifted. 'I thought you were flying up from Heathrow this evening?'

'I changed my flight. Leonie's back safely with her mum. There was no need for me to hang around.'

'I'll come now.' I restarted the car's engine. 'I'm only ten minutes away.'

I drove back up to the main road with the heater on full blast. I'd grown cold sitting outside your house, and now I felt as if I needed to stand in front of a roaring fire. Even better – I needed Ritchie. Just hearing his voice had been enough to gently cave in my stomach, making space for sweet, unfathomable lust to bloom inside me.

Ritchie's house was that bit closer to Edinburgh than either you or I could afford. It was a new-build made to look like an old-build, all wooden floors and built-in technology, and with concertina patio doors that opened out onto a south-facing, fairy-tale view. I was greeted by his west highland terrier Rebus, who came running through the dog flap, and then by Ritchie himself. He generated heat like a St Bernard on a Swiss mountainside, and I rushed towards him and wrapped my arms around his waist.

'You're freezing,' he said, rubbing my back.

'I was sitting in the car,' I told him. 'The heater was on but . . .'

'Isla, I'm so sorry about Dougie.' He was stroking my hair, kissing my forehead and my cheeks. His touch felt comforting, made me want to relax into him, and into the grief that was gathering a storm in my chest. 'How are you?'

'I'm okay . . .'

He held my face in his hands. 'Have you found out why he was in Glasgow?'

'No.' I felt a tremor start up around my mouth and tried to smile it away.

'Is there anything I can do to help?'

'I just . . . There is one thing you can do for me.' I kissed his fingers. 'I want to go through to Glasgow and see where he fell into the water.'

'Of course. I'll come with you. When's a good time?'

'I need to pick the kids up from school later, and before that I want to ring Gordy.'

'The man with the missing daughter?'

'Yeah. But maybe over the weekend we could go? The kids will be with Gavin.'

'Okay.' He hugged me again and I took his hand, led him into his bedroom. I wanted to feel better. I persuaded him, and myself, into thinking that sex would do that. He pulled my sweatshirt over my head, undid my trousers and pushed me back on the bed. It was always at this point that I felt as though I shed more than just my clothes. The mother, daughter, sister and once-upon-a-time wife sloughed off her sensible keeping-it-all-together skin and I stepped out as the most stripped back version of me. I was just a woman with a man. That was it. It honestly felt that simple.

I hesitate to describe what we did next, Dougie. You and I were never that explicit about our sex lives when you were alive, were we? You were my brother and it would have felt strange to exchange intimate details with you. But now you've slipped into the shadows, and although I can't see you, I feel your presence like a long-lasting echo, sometimes distant, more often close, but always, always there.

You are my twin, my other half, in childhood a source of laughter and comfort and strife. In adulthood, you were my ally and my friend. And these last few years especially, you were my best friend, a major part of my everyday, a part I am unable to let go of. Death has taken you away but strangely it has also brought you closer. Now you are a voice in my head, the person I talk to. You don't say much, but then you don't need to. I already know most of your answers. I may never have told you this before, but now I can. This is what I know about sex – news flash! – It's complicated.

Or maybe complex is a better word. Sex nourishes me and strengthens me. It makes me feel loved and wanted. Like I belong. Three years without a man in my life was tough. I felt rejected. I felt lonely. When Gavin left me for Collette, he took my self-esteem with him. And you, of all people, saw the mess I was in. Meeting Ritchie was a gift, and while the intricacies of compatibility are beyond me, the proof is in the experience. I was drawn to Ritchie because . . . I just was.

His hands felt as if they belonged on me. His mouth started at my feet and moved upwards, and when he reached the top of my thighs, I felt a rush, a great bobsleigh ride, greased runners, hot friction on cold ice that drove lust into my belly. He pulled me around on top of him and smiled up at me. I felt a surge of joy, a wave of uncomplicated surrender . . . and then I started to cry, because I'd only just buried my brother, and the enjoyment quickly soured. Sorrow washed through me in harsh, pitiless waves while Ritchie held me in his arms and spoke kind words in my ear.

I left Ritchie's a few hours later and arrived back at your cottage to see a man pacing up and down outside the door. I had an idea who he might be and immediately felt guilty that I hadn't called him yet. I climbed out of the car and he rushed towards me. 'I'm Gordon O'Malley.' He held out his hand and I shook it. Your description was spot on. I remembered you saying he had the look of a bloodhound, the flesh on his face drooping to form jowls. His jacket, his trousers, his hair, all dragged downward as if gravity worked harder on him than it did on the rest of us.

'You're Dougie's sister Isla?'

'Yes.' I unlocked your front door and he followed me into the living room. 'I'm so sorry. I should have called—'

'He talked about you,' he interrupted. 'You work in insurance? Bit of an
investigator yourself. That's what Dougie told me.'

'Well, not exactly, but Mr O'Ma—'

'Dougie's been helping me find my daughter, Lucy. I can't get down from Aberdeen as much as I'd like. The wife isn't well.'

'The thing is—'

'Your wee boy's called Finlay. Likes the football? Dougie was saying he's had some interest from the Man U scouts. He's got a footballing brain, your lad.' He tapped his head. 'That's what counts nowadays, you know. It's all about the thinking. My daughter, she was never sporty. More for books and drawing and stuff like that.'

'My brother's—'

'Dougie's been great with payments. And with him having contacts in the police force and everything, it's helped oil the wheels.'

'—dead.'

'Almost two years my daughter's been missing, and your brother's got us further than anyone else. Seems like she was lifted off the face of this earth, but there's never been any evidence to say that she's passed away.' He shook his index finger in my direction. 'There's never been a body. The police have searched, and I've searched. Uncles, cousins, Dougie. We've all been out on the road.'

'Mr O'Malley—'

'She ran off with a boy called Jimmy Pearcy. Puppy love. He was eighteen, in and out of young offenders' – you know the type – and she was fifteen, so he was breaking the law and I dunno . . .' He shrugged, defeated. 'Yer damned if ye do and yer damned if ye don't. We tried to stop her but—'

'Mr O'Malley.' I was growing impatient. 'I—'

'Call me, Gordy.' He held out his hand again and I shook it again, wondering if he'd ever take a breath and I'd be able to get more than a couple of words in. 'Being called Mr O'Malley makes me feel like I've turned into my dad.'

'Gordy—'

'She's got cancer, my wife, you know. She's not long for this world, so it's important we find Lucy. Mother needs to see daughter before she passes on. I'm sure you'd feel the same. We'd all feel the same. Death's so final, that's what—'

'Gordy, please!' I shouted. He stopped, stunned, and stared at me with wide, pleading eyes. I wished I could spare him any more pain. I wished I could give him some good news, because if anyone needed good news it was him. 'Please sit down.'

He sat down at once, as obedient as a well-trained dog.

'Gordy, the thing is . . .'

'Yes?' His expression was wounded. He knew it was bad news. He just wasn't sure how bad.

'The thing is that, sadly, very sadly . . .' I took a breath. 'My brother has died.'

His hands shot up to his face, and he started to cry, huge galloping tears that couldn't be contained within the palms of his hands, and leaked out and down his sleeves. I sat next to him on the sofa and put my arms around his shoulders, which were heaving up and down with his breathing. It was almost unbearable to witness, and it took all my strength not to join in or run away.

When he stopped crying, I made us both a coffee and we sat opposite each other in your living room. The sun was warming the space, light dappling leafy patterns on the walls. It was a perfect backdrop for a read or a chat, but instead I had to tell Gordy how you'd died, about the pub you'd been in and where you'd fallen into the water. I hoped I might see recognition dawn on his face, that he would know the pub and tell me why you'd gone there. But there was nothing.

'Great bloke. Great bloke your brother. Nobody like him in the world. Nobody at all.' He took a handkerchief from his pocket and blew his nose loudly. 'And you were twins? Not identical.' He shook his head. 'No, of course not. With you being a girl and him a boy. That wouldn't work, would it?'

'Gordy?'

'Yeah?' His eyes were bloodshot and puffy from crying, but there remained a residue of hope in his expression.

'Do you know why my brother might have been in Glasgow that evening?' He stared at me blankly. 'I was wondering whether he might have been looking for Lucy.'

'Right, right. Okay, okay.' He was nodding now, leaning forward, his elbows on his knees. 'I've got my thinking cap on.'

I waited, took a sip of my coffee and listened as he talked out his thoughts.

'I last spoke to Dougie on Friday the sixth. I'd told him about a possible sighting in Falkirk. You see, Lucy, my daughter, she hardly took anything with her when she left home, but one of the things she did take was a wee brass ornament of three wise monkeys. See no evil, hear no evil, speak no evil. It's like a paperweight. It was her granny's.'

'I think I've seen one.'

'A while back, I went to an Edinburgh antique fair. Not the posh, high-end stuff, just the bits and bobs, trinkets and the like, you know? And I gave out leaflets with my name and phone number and Lucy's photo on, to all of the traders so that if a girl ever came into their shops looking to sell the monkeys, they could get in touch with me.'

'Good idea.'

'Covering my bases.' He had another blow of his nose. 'So anyway, this dealer called me up and said a girl had come in. I told Dougie, and we agreed I would check it out.'

'You didn't get lucky?' I said, remembering the message he left on your answering machine

'No. I went to Falkirk for the day, but no luck. Never mind.' He rubbed his hands together, then glanced at his watch. 'Keeping the search alive. That's what's important.'

'So there's no reason you can think of why Dougie would be in Glasgow?'

'No. But if I do, I'll give you a bell.' He stared across at me. 'We can stay in touch, can't we?'

'Of course.'

'Sorry I can't be more of a help.' He stood up and pulled some fliers out of his back pocket. 'Can I leave these with you?'

We parted on your doorstep, wishing each other luck. The photo was of his daughter Lucy. She looked barely older than Caitlin's thirteen years. A shy smile, a modest demeanour. Pretty in an ethereal way. Her wispy hair, wan complexion, and eyes the colour of grey sky, making her seem washed out, as if she were fading.

Fading until she disappeared.

I was waiting at the school gates in good time for Fin to come out. I'd only just got there, when Stuart's mum

Julie Corbin

ran up and threw her arms around me. 'How are you doing?'

'Okay.' I shook my head from side to side. '. . . ish.'

'The funeral was wonderful, Isla. You really did him proud.'

'I'm not so sure.'

'You did, you know,' she said, hugging me again. 'You really did.'

Sarah always had a soft spot for you, you know? Once, when we went to the pub after a particularly gruelling parents' evening, she'd said, 'Your brother seems like the perfect man. Kind, handsome, good with kids. He must have his faults, surely?'

'Only that he's attracted to the wrong women,' I'd said. 'His ex-wife is a pain.'

Was that disloyal, Dougie? I thought it was true. You could have had a loving wife who gave you children and built a life with you. Instead you chose Tania, who dropped the no-children bombshell on your fifth wedding anniversary – yes, I remember the details. Enough said.

Sarah and I made arrangements for the football pick-ups, knowing we wouldn't be nearly as much fun for the boys as you had been. Fin was happy that it was sorted, though, and walked back to the car with me, a lightness to his step.

'I thought we could go and have a pizza,' I said.

'On a Thursday?'

'Why not? We'll collect Caitlin from school, then go into town.'

'There'll be an empty chair.' He tucked in his chin and kicked at the kerb. 'It won't feel right.'

'Yeah. Of course. I'm sorry.' I ruffled his hair. 'I didn't think of that.'

'We could get a carry-out, though.' He smiled. 'Uncle Dougie liked the chippie.'

We set off to collect Caitlin from school, and on the journey I got Fin to tell me about the finer points of his football training so that I could hold an informed conversation with his coach when I took him and Stuart along. Caitlin didn't come out of the school building with any of her friends, but was walking by herself, staring at the ground. We were parked in the usual spot and she came towards us on automatic pilot, climbing into the back and closing the door without so much as an upward glance.

'How was school, love?'

She didn't answer, seemed to be too busy yanking her seat belt around her middle. 'We thought we'd go to the chippie.' Still no answer. I turned towards the back seat and reached a hand out to her. 'You okay, love?'

'How can I be okay?' She batted my hand away and glared at me as if I'd suggested the impossible. 'Uncle Dougie's dead! And he's the only person in my life who gets me.'

'Was,' Fin said. 'He *was* the only person.'

'Fuck off!' She leant forward and punched Fin on his ear. 'Twat.'

I don't have to tell you how unlike Caitlin this was. Fin and I sat for a moment, stunned, and then he put his arm up around his face and started to cry slow, hurt tears into his sleeve.

'Caitlin?' I stared back at her, shocked. 'We're all upset about Uncle Dougie. There's no need to take it out on Fin. Please apologise to him.'

'*Please apologise to him,*' she said, mimicking my voice. 'How can you stand it? Uncle Dougie's dead, and you're acting like everything's fine!'

'I'm not, Caitlin.'

'Yes, you are! The chippie? *The chippie?* One minute we're burying Uncle Dougie. The next we're back at the fucking chippie.'

'It's not . . .' I steadied my hands on the steering wheel. 'I understand that you're angry—'

'Don't tell me you understand!' she shouted, so loudly that the car shook.

You were always the first to tell me I was a good mum, Dougie, and I know that most of the time I am. But I couldn't deal with this. I just couldn't.

I drew Fin towards me and kissed his hair, whispering, 'I'm sorry, sweetheart. Just ignore her,' into his ear. Then I started the engine and drove off.

4. Dad

We didn't go to the chippie. I drove straight home and as soon as I'd unlocked the front door, Caitlin bolted upstairs to her room. Fin and I went into the kitchen and he helped me cobble together some pasta with a tomato sauce. When it was ready, I shouted up to Caitlin, but she didn't appear so I climbed the stairs and knocked on her door. 'Tea's ready. Are you coming down?'

She told me to fuck off so I didn't pursue it. Truthfully . . .? Caitlin's temper and tears drained me of the little hope and positive energy I had. I tried to be normal – make the tea, put the washing on, help the kids with their homework – because I knew that you would be the first to say that life goes on, and I was wary of sliding into a state where I saw no reason to get up in the morning. But it was tough, Dougie. So damn tough.

Fin was easier to be with. He was hurting – he was definitely hurting – but he seemed better equipped to handle it. He would disappear to his room for a while and then return to the living room, red-eyed but positive, saying stuff like, 'Uncle Dougie believed in me. He said that if I kept practising I could play for Man U one day.' Or, 'Anyway Mum, for all we know there really *is* a heaven and Uncle Dougie could be up there watching us.'

'Cheering us on,' I said.

'Aye,' he said, smiling.

By eight o'clock, Fin and I were sitting in front of the TV watching Indiana Jones, eating our way through a tub of ice cream and joining in with the bits of dialogue we knew. I didn't hear Caitlin come downstairs and only noticed her when she slid over the back of the couch, wedging herself between me and Fin. She took his hand and said, 'I'm really sorry Fin.'

''S okay,' Fin said solemnly. 'I miss Uncle Dougie too.' He looked across at me. 'And so does Mum.'

Caitlin started crying then and we both hugged her, clinging on to each other like end-of-days survivors. We were a sad threesome, and when later that evening they ended up one on either side of me in my bed, we fell asleep with Indiana Jones in our ears and you in our hearts.

Next day, after I'd dropped the kids off at the school bus stop, I went into work. Alec and I had agreed that I could take another week off, but I needed to have a word with him. Trying to establish why you were in Glasgow was a constant anxiety that squatted at the forefront of my mind. I'd spoken to your friends at the funeral, but none of them knew why you were there. I'd spoken to Gordy; he didn't know. It was a long shot that you were there for an assignment – you didn't have your van with you, you hadn't logged it on your calendar, and currently, as far as I knew, we had no cases that would take you through to Glasgow – but I had to rule it out.

Alec's business could be divided into two halves – the loss adjusting, which landed on my desk, and the more specialist investigations that landed on yours. Alec had been using your freelance services for almost four years, and if your trip to the Lone Star pub was even remotely to do with an assignment then I wanted to know about it.

I arrived at work to find that, as usual, Alec was already there. I joined him in his office and he stood up at once to get me a coffee. 'I didn't expect to see you back so soon.'

'I'm not coming in to work. I'm here because I need to have a word with you.'

'Okay.' He passed me a coffee and nodded to the paper bag on his desk. 'Help yourself to a Danish.'

'I won't, thanks, but cheers for the coffee.' I raised my mug to him and took a sip. 'I'm wondering whether you know why Dougie was in Glasgow?'

'I don't, Isla.' He shook his head. 'You know the police have already asked me this?'

'Nothing work related could have taken him there?'

'Nothing he was running for me.'

I felt my hope deflate.

'Why?'

'Well . . .' I shrugged. 'I don't know why he was there. Nobody knows why he was there! I mean, why would he be? If he wanted to have a drink, he could have had one along the road. Why would he drink in a run-down pub in Glasgow for three hours?'

Alec stared through the window, thinking. 'Sounds like he might have been waiting for someone.'

'Exactly! But who?'

He shook his head. 'Dougie was more than a work colleague, he was a friend, but he said nothing to me.'

'There's something else.' I brought your diary out of my bag. I told Alec what Tania had said and then I showed him my name, written in bold letters, across the page for Monday, September ninth. 'It doesn't make sense to me.'

Alec shook his head. 'Me neither.' He put a hand in his pocket and I heard change tumble through his fingers. 'Are you sure?'

An expression passed across his face, so fleeting that I almost missed it – he was worried – but the worried look was replaced almost instantly with a weary frown. 'Alec?'

'Dougie was too good a man to die so young.' He sat down and gave a heavy sigh. 'God knows there are enough obnoxious fuckers in the world that no one would miss.'

This was a man who normally kept his feelings to himself, but not so today. Alec knew you were dead. It was written all over him, from the ache in his eyes to the slump in his shoulders. I felt myself being drawn in too. My eyes filled and my heart grew heavy. I was grateful when my mobile started ringing and I was pulled back from the brink of tears. I glanced at the number. Not one I recognised. 'Hello?'

'Am I speaking to Isla McTeer?'

'Yes.'

'My name is Margaret Wilshaw. I'm a charge nurse at the Edinburgh Royal Infirmary.'

My heart did a mini-somersault. 'Yes?'

'Don't be alarmed, but we have your father George McTeer here with us.'

'What's happened?' I lurched to one side, spilling coffee over Alec's desk.

'He slipped over late last night and broke his leg.'

I clenched my teeth and swallowed before saying, 'Is it very serious?'

'His injury is not life-threatening, but the fracture is unstable and your father will need to have it operated on today.'

'Why isn't he in hospital in Dundee?' I watched Alec stem the flow of coffee with a wad of tissues.

'I realise your father's home is in Dundee, but he was actually transferred to us from Glasgow. They're short on beds, and when he said his daughter lived just outside Edinburgh the decision was taken to move him here.'

'I see.' I didn't. It was only yesterday that I'd dropped him at the station and he told me he was getting the train home. 'Thank you. Can I come and visit him now?'

'Of course.'

I ended the call and grabbed my bag.

'What's happened?' Alec said, dropping a mulch of coffee-stained tissues into the bin.

'My dad's broken his leg. He's in the infirmary.'

'How?'

'He fell over.' I was halfway to the door. 'I'll speak to you later.'

'Let me know whether I can do anything to help,' he shouted after me.

I waved a goodbye and set off for the hospital. It wasn't until later that I remembered the worried look that had passed across Alec's face.

Dad's bed was beside the window in a six-bedded bay occupied by five other men, all of them slumped and snoozing. His face was ashen, and for the first time he looked older than his sixty-five years, grief and exhaustion accelerating aging. He was tiny in the bed, Dougie. Tiny and vulnerable. I sat down on the chair next to him, carefully avoiding the pulley system that was holding his broken leg still, and waited for him to wake.

I'd been sitting for less than a minute when my mind started to make connections.

Hospitals.
Mum.

*Both of us, standing beside her bed, a drip going into
her arm, urine travelling in a tube from under the
covers into a bag.*

'*Where's Dad?*' *you asked.*

'*He's gone to get a coffee.*'

'*I'll go and join him,*' *you said.*

*Ten minutes later, I found the two of you in the
corridor. It was the first time since we were seven that
I'd seen you cry.*

I stood up and had a look in Dad's locker, took his
clothes out and folded them. Then I refolded them. I
was humming. I couldn't help it. It wasn't a happy tune.
I was simply filling my ears with sound so that I couldn't
hear myself think.

Minutes later, Dad started to groan and his eyes
opened. I moved closer. 'Are you in pain, Dad?'

'Hellish.' He squinted at me. 'You shouldn't have come,
Isla. You've got enough going on.'

'I want to be here!' I kissed his cheek, rough with grey
stubble. 'What happened?'

'Nothing much.'

'Dad, your leg's broken.'

'So they tell me.'

'How did you break it?'

'Dodgy kerb.' He shook his head. 'Useless old git.'

'Don't say that about yourself. Accidents happen.'

His chin collapsed onto his chest. 'It was stupid. And
now . . .' He waved an arm down the bed. 'I've got a
gammy leg to contend with.'

'What were you doing in Glasgow?'

'I just popped down on the train.'

'Why?' I crossed my arms and stared at him.

'You've got your mother's disapproving look on.'

'Have you any idea what a fright that phone call gave me? So soon after Dougie.' I shivered. 'Scared me half to bloody death.'

'I know, hen.' He deflated suddenly, all bluster evaporating. 'I just wanted to see where Dougie'd spent his last moments, that's all.'

'I see.' That made sense. It was what I wanted to do myself, after all. 'I could have come with you.'

'I didn't want you hanging around in a place like that.'

'I'm not twelve, Dad.'

'Prostitutes, druggies, and all sorts.'

'Which begs the question why was Dougie there?' I pulled the chair up close to his bed and sat down. I held his hand in mine, rubbing the bruised knuckles. 'Did you see where he fell into the water?'

'Aye.'

'And the pub he was in, did you go there?'

'I did.'

'George McTeer?' a nurse called from the doorway. We waved her in our direction and she came across, a porter with a trolley following on behind her. 'So, George. Are we ready for the off?' She checked his name bracelet then pulled the curtains around us. 'We'll get that leg sorted out for you.'

'You know my dad has a bit of a cough?' I said.

'The doctor's had a listen to his chest,' she said. 'Shouldn't affect his recovery, but we'll need to keep an eye on it.'

'I'll wait here until you come back from theatre, Dad.'

'You don't have to.'

'I want to.' I kissed his cheek. 'The kids are going with

Gavin straight from school. I'd only be home alone.'

I asked the nurse a few questions about Dad's operation, and then the porter helped her lift Dad onto the
trolley, a carefully executed move that meant minimal
interruption to the traction. I walked with them along
the corridor as far as the lift, all the while holding Dad's
hand and keeping up reassuring chat, as much for me
as for him. As the metal doors closed behind them I had
to stop myself from panicking, remembering the last
time I was in a lift. Going down into the basement to
identify your body. The memory so recent that it shone
with a macabre clarity.

I found the hospital café and bought a coffee before
calling Marie. I was expecting her to give me hell, and she
did. 'How could you have let him go home? You said he
would be staying with you! You let him go to Glasgow by
himself! Grieving over Dougie!' Loud, disappointed sighing.
'Honestly, Isla, I thought I could leave you in charge.'

I was tempted to defend myself, but she was only
expressing what I was already thinking. Why hadn't I
guessed Dad would go to Glasgow? Why hadn't I taken
better care of him? What if he was never able to walk
properly again?

She went on and on. I was 'careless and thoughtless'.
I had no understanding of how difficult it was for her,
so far away, not able to help. And then suddenly her
tone lifted. 'While I've got you on the phone, I was
wondering how quickly Dougie's house will sell?'

The abrupt change in topic took me aback. 'Eh?'

'Two months? Three? More than three?'

'I don't know. I don't—'

'I know I said there was no rush, but now Erik has
the chance to buy a share in his cousin's fishing boat.
It'll save him going on the rigs. Dougie's house must be

worth at least three hundred thousand. So divided between you, me, and Dad, that . . .'

I zoned out from what she was saying because otherwise I felt I might snap her head off. You were barely in your grave, Dougie. This was what I mean about Marie – everything's always about her.

'Isla? Isla? Are you still there?'

'Yes, I'm still here.'

'I know it's maybe the wrong time to talk about this.'

'You think?'

'Don't get all huffy with me, Isla. I wasn't the one who let Dad break his leg.'

'Calls are expensive on my mobile. I'll ring you when I get home.'

I ended the call. Abruptly. Without saying goodbye. Okay, so it was childish of me, and I felt bad for even thinking this, never mind saying it, because Marie is a mother, and her children need her, but shit, Dougie! If I'd had to choose a sibling to lose it wouldn't have been you.

Dad had been gone two hours, and I was back to sitting at the side of his bed, trying to read a magazine but finding my mind chewing on itself – should I have been kinder to Tania? Should I let her have the money? Should I prioritise the sale of your house so Marie can have her share? Is that what you'd want? – when Dad's mobile started to ring. It was in his locker, and I managed to find it just before it stopped. A Glasgow number was showing on the screen.

'George McTeer's phone.'

'Is George there?'

'Not right now. Can I take a message?'

'And who would you be?'

'His daughter.'

'Ask your dad to call me when he can.'

It was a Glasgow number . . . I took a punt. 'My dad told me he spoke to you yesterday.' Silence. 'He said you could leave a message with me.'

'What did he tell you?'

'He told me you'd talked and that you said you'd call him.'

'I didn't say I'd call him.'

The line went dead. I held Dad's mobile on my lap and sat perfectly still while I thought about what the phone call meant. This was what I came up with – Dad went through to Glasgow to see where you died. He was asking questions. The man on the other end of the phone had called to tell Dad something.

That was as far as I could get without reaching or imagining or coming to conclusions that had no basis in fact.

But I knew, Dougie. In my gut I knew that something wasn't right, that something had happened to you, and that Dad knew it too.

I called the number back. It rang four times and then a woman's voice answered. 'Lone Star?'

'Hi.' My heartbeat quickened. The phone call had come from the pub you'd been drinking in. 'I was speaking to someone just now and . . . Sorry, I've forgotten his name.'

'Don McAndrew?'

'That's right. He's the . . .'

'Manager.'

'Yes.'

'You want to talk to him?'

'That won't be necessary. Thank you.'

I ended the call.

*   *   *

Dad was still sleepy when he came back from theatre, which was useful because his guard was down. 'How are you feeling Dad?'

'A' right.'

'Don McAndrew called.'

He forced heavy eyelids open. 'Did he know 'bout Dougie?'

'What was it you asked him?'

'Big 'uns. Lay low.'

'What do you mean, Dad?'

He started to snore, and the nurse appeared at the bedside. 'He'll sleep for a couple of hours.' She tucked Dad's covers around him. 'You're welcome to sit here and wait, but you might want to go down to the café and get yourself something to eat.'

'I will. Thank you.'

I spent the next couple of hours walking the hospital corridors, and when I'd completed several laps I walked around the car park. I didn't feel like eating or drinking. I was strangely excited. After more than two weeks' immersion in grief, I felt like the world was turning again. I called Ritchie, but there was no reply so I left a voicemail. 'It's me. My dad's in hospital; he broke his leg. Awful, but while he was in theatre, the manager of the Lone Star pub called. I think my dad had been there asking questions, and I think the manager has something to tell him. Anyway, I want to go through there sooner rather than later and if you were able to come with me that would be great.'

When I went back up to the ward, I found Dad groggy but awake. He gestured towards the jug of water on top of the locker. I poured him a tumbler and passed it to him. 'Dad—'

'Find me my mobile, Isla, will you?' he said, sipping the water. 'It should be in my locker.'

I didn't have to look hard because it was exactly where I'd left it. I handed it to him and he checked his texts. 'Dorothy's on her way. She's coming down with my stuff. I called her this morning.' He glanced at the clock on the wall. 'She'll be here before long.'

'All the way from Dundee?' I smiled. 'Are you two an item now then?'

He was drinking the water through a straw and his eyes flicked up towards me. 'We look out for each other.'

'That's great, Dad.'

'Everyone needs friends.'

'They do.' I sat on the edge of his bed. 'Dad? Do you remember what we talked about when you came back from theatre?'

He shook his head.

'I told you that a man called Don McAndrew phoned.'

He put the tumbler down on the top of the locker. 'What did he have to say?'

'Dad.' My lips started to tremble. 'What's going on?'

Dad stared at me for several seconds. The whites of his eyes were red with broken veins. 'Nothing.' He sounded dejected. 'I wanted to see where Dougie died and pay my last respects. Ask a few questions.'

I leant in closer. 'What sort of questions?'

'Isla.' He shook his head. 'Our Dougie could take care of himself, but that doesn't mean he was beyond making a mistake. And from what I saw and heard, the police are right. Dougie fell in the river.'

'I still think—'

'Hard to fathom but sometimes the truth is like that.'

'But—'

'Isla.' His tone was stern. 'Promise me you'll let this drop. I don't want you going there. It's no place for a woman on her own.'

'Dad . . .'

He gripped my shoulder. 'Promise me.'

'Okay. I promise.'

His head sank back onto his pillows, satisfied.

Do you remember when we were kids, Dougie, and we'd make a promise to Mum or Dad, but we'd keep our fingers crossed behind our backs and that cancelled out the promise?

Both hands were behind my back, and my fingers were crossed.

I was getting ready to leave when Dorothy arrived. She's small, about five feet, with sharp, beady eyes, and dark hair. As physically unlike Mum as you could get. She seemed genuinely fond of Dad and fussed around him, making him smile.

'Terrible about your brother, Isla,' Dorothy said to me. 'I know how you'll all be suffering. I never met Douglas, but George has told me so many good things about him.'

'He was a great brother,' I said.

'And son,' Dad added.

I looked at my watch. It was already mid-afternoon. 'I'm going to have to love you and leave you.' I kissed Dad's forehead.

'Kids to collect,' he said.

I didn't comment. I turned to Dorothy. 'Hope to see you again soon.'

'Don't you worry about your dad.' She gave me a quick hug. 'I'll look after him.'

I left them together and came out of the hospital, almost running to my car. Before I set off, I called Ritchie, but he still wasn't picking up. Not unusual for Ritchie. He was often called away to problem-solve glitches in the software he designed, and he'd just had two weeks' holiday so I figured he'd be busy with the backlog. I would rather have had his company, but I didn't want to delay any longer. I needed to see where you'd died and I needed to speak to the manager of the Lone Star. It wasn't that I didn't believe Dad. It was simply that I needed to see and hear for myself.

I was on the outskirts of Glasgow when I stopped in a petrol station and bought a bouquet of roses. While I was waiting in the queue to pay, I called the kids. Gavin and Collette had collected them from school and they were on their way to the cinema. I could hear Collette in the background giving them options for places to eat afterwards. I told them about Dad's accident, but kept the worry out of my voice. I said Dad was cheerful and recovering well from his operation. Fin accepted all of this, but Caitlin was more worried.

'Are you sure, Mum?' Caitlin said. 'Are you sure he's okay? Maybe we shouldn't go to the cinema. I could come to the hospital. Are you there?'

I lied. I said I was on my way home. I reassured her as best I could, and then I spoke to Collette. I was past the stage of feeling jealous or left out when the kids spent time with Gavin and Collette, but when it came to comforting and caring for Caitlin and Fin, I wanted that to come through me, so I had a moment's hesitation before telling Collette about Dad's accident and asking her to look out for a reaction from the kids. As usual, she was understanding. She was always eager to be a part of their lives and I could hardly hold that against her.

I wished them all a good time and travelled the last few miles to the Science Centre. As soon as I came to a stop in the car park I had a moment of déjà vu. We'd visited the Centre before – you, me and the kids – last summer during the long school holidays. You'd called in the morning.

'What's on the cards today, then?'

'I'm thinking of taking them through to the Science Centre. They have a special exhibition on.'

'I'm not busy today. Fancy taking their uncle along too?'

'We'd love you to come.' I turned my head away from the receiver and called into the living room. *'Uncle Dougie's coming with us!'*

'Brilliant!' (Caitlin)

'I'll bring the football!' (Fin)

'Did you hear that?' I said. *'You've made everyone's day.'*

I took the roses and walked west, the River Clyde on my right and the Science Centre on my left. Sunlight reflected off the building's giant titanium hull and off the water that flowed steadily beside me. Primary school children were running along the grassy strip between the Centre and the walkway, pushing and shoving one another and falling over with playful abandon. The sky was china blue; the sound of children's laughter was uplifting. Except that it wasn't, because this was where you'd died.

I followed the path around between the Glasgow Tower and the Science Centre to the North Quay where your body had been recovered. I remembered the details Gavin had given me from the police investigation, and I stood at the exact spot where the Marine Unit had pulled your body from the water. I didn't know what I was expecting to see – bloodstains, scrapes on the concrete paving, *something* – some sign that you'd been there, died there, but there was nothing, nothing at all to indicate that your body was recovered from the water.

I stood there and let my broken heart overwhelm me. I had thought I couldn't feel any sadder, any more fearful, any more gutted. But I was wrong, I could.

I threw the flowers into the river and watched them bob and drift on the top of the water before being dragged under. I'd cried at your funeral. I'd cried night after night in my bedroom. But as yet I'd never cried like this. A passing stranger took hold of me when I fell to my knees. He held onto me while I wept. He didn't ask me what was wrong; he didn't try to make me stop. He let me empty myself, and then he helped me stand up again.

'Thank you,' I said.

He nodded, and asked me whether I would be okay. I assured him I would and he walked away.

I felt exhausted. I wanted nothing more than to curl up and sleep, but it felt important for me to know exactly where you'd taken your last breath. You were alive when you fell into the river, but there was half a mile of water between here and the riverbank close to the Lone Star. So how could I ever know? How could I ever be sure what section of the river had taken your life?

I stared into the water, then up at the sky, then all around me. Every thought sparked a feeling: you falling into the water, struggling, suffering, drowning, made my heart splinter; you knowing you were about to die made me feel like I couldn't breathe; you closing your eyes for the last time made me want to scream.

I would have turned myself inside out to save you, Dougie. I swear I would have. I hope you know that.

When my eyes were able to focus, I used the navigation app on my phone to find my way to the Lone Star. I left the Science Centre behind and followed the curve of the river towards the pub. The blue above had darkened to grey, and a light drizzle fell steadily from a murky puddle of sky. Well-fed seagulls swooped and screeched and dive-bombed for discarded sandwich crusts. On one side, the river was steel-grey and troubled, waves rising up to meet the wind. On the other, modern buildings gave way to nineteenth-century brick warehouses lined up in rows, twenty-first-century signs advertising what went on inside: a storage facility, a design studio, a wine warehouse.

The further I walked, the shabbier my surroundings became, and the streets I recognised were soon a long way behind me. I arrived at the Lone Star pub just as the sky darkened to a threatening navy blue and the drizzle became a downpour. The pub had clearly seen better days. Chunks of plaster had fallen away from the brickwork, and the painted sign was cracked and faded. Inside smelt of old carpet, saturated with booze. When I walked towards the bar, heads turned and eyes stared, *Who the fuck are you?* written across their faces. I brazened it out and positioned myself between two hardened drinkers who were propping up the bar, their hands shaky, rheumy eyes almost crossed as they blinked at me.

The barman was about fifteen feet away, at the other end of the bar. He glanced in my direction then continued to stack packets of crisps on a shelf. The two hardened drinkers kept their eyes trained on my face, and as each second ticked by I felt increasingly uncomfortable. When the barman was finished with the crisps he came and stood in front of me.

'What can I get you?'

'Don McAndrew?' I said.

'Who's asking?'

'I'm Isla McTeer. We spoke on the phone earlier.'

'Aye.' He made a point of looking past me. 'So where's your dad then?'

'He's in hospital. He broke his leg.'

'Sorry to hear that.' He had a dishtowel over one shoulder and he whipped it down into his hand to begin vigorously drying the inside of a pint glass.

'About my brother.'

He gave a laborious sigh then jerked his chin towards the quieter end of the bar. I followed him there. A customer was perched precariously on a stool and had fallen asleep, his cheek resting on a beer mat.

'This is not a good place for you,' Don said.

'Why not?'

'Look around you. You're drawing attention to yourself.'

I looked around me. There were about twenty men and one woman in the bar. Four of the men were playing pool – or, at least, they had been playing pool. They had stopped their game and were staring my way, the ends of their cues resting on the tatty carpet. The only woman in the room, apart from me, had a mean expression on a face lined with hard living and too many cigarettes. I was wearing my usual department-store jeans and my old cord jacket – hardly the height of expense or fashion – but still I was too well dressed for here. I held my bag a bit tighter and turned back to the barman. 'Where did my brother sit?'

'Table in the corner there.' He nodded to the far side, and I imagined you sitting there, Dougie, beer glass in front of you, a whisky chaser next to it. You would have had a direct line of sight to the front door, the toilets, and the people playing pool.

'Did you get the feeling my brother was waiting for someone?'

He shrugged, disinterested.

'The police report said he spoke to a couple of the locals. Would you be able to point them out to me?'

'Drunks mostly.' He was still drying the same glass, working away at it with the dishtowel. 'Min Fraser is your best bet.'

'Min Fraser?' I glanced over my shoulders at the mean-looking woman behind me. 'Is that her?'

'No.' He hesitated. 'I take it you're here instead of your dad?'

'Yes.'

He gave another protracted sigh. 'Min Fraser lives in a squat not far from here. I asked her whether she was willing to talk to your dad and she agreed that she was. That's why I called him.'

'She's homeless?'

'She helps out the youngsters, runaways 'n' that.'

My skin prickled. 'Runaways?' I still had the fliers Gordy had given me in the back pocket of my jeans. I pulled one out and held Lucy's photo towards Don. 'Did my brother show you this?'

He didn't even glance at the photo. He leant in towards me, resting his elbows on the bar. 'Look. You seem like a nice enough woman.' His tone was conspiratorial. 'We're well off the tourist route down here, Isla McTeer. You need to sort out your business and get on home.'

While we'd been talking, the sleeping customer had woken up. He rubbed his cheek, sticky with beer, before leaning in to my right ear. 'Get you a drink, darlin'?'

'No thanks.' He smelled of stale alcohol and noxious pee. I couldn't help but draw away.

'Bankers!' His head lolled sideways before his focus

was dragged back into his glass, his fingers claw-like as they clutched the boozy lifeline. 'They piss on us and we call it rain.'

Don was writing on the back of a receipt. When he'd finished he handed it to me. 'Min's address. Now get going before trouble starts.'

I could see what he meant. The mistrustful, who-the-fuck-is-she mood was ramping up a notch. You know that moment just before dogs start fighting, when the air crackles with expectancy? I felt as if a wrong move on my part would suddenly set them off. I was over-staying my welcome. I was an interloper, and I needed to be chased out.

I looked back at Don, as one last question occurred to me. 'Do you remember how much my brother drank?'

'Four pints.'

'Only four pints?' I hadn't read the post mortem report, but Gavin had given me the impression you were well over the limit. 'No spirits?'

'He wouldn't be the first person to slip some vodka into his pint. Supermarket prices undercut us by a mile.'

'He wouldn't do that.'

'Then all he had was four pints of lager.'

The hairs on the back of my neck sprang to life. Two of the pool players had moved across the room to stand behind me. 'Thank you,' I said to Don. 'I appreciate you talking to me.'

I turned away from the bar, and keeping my head down, walked towards the door. The two men followed me. One nudged up against my arm, the other one stepped on the heel of my shoe. I jerked my foot forward, but said nothing. When I got outside the rain had stopped but the street was wet and slippery. I took off at an almost-run, glancing behind me to see whether I was being followed. I wasn't. The two men stood at the door, watching me clear off their patch and as soon as I was out of their sight, I called Gavin. 'Good film?'

'Great fun. We're on our way into Nando's.'

'I won't keep you long.' I leant up against a wall and rubbed my heel with my free hand. 'I'm just wondering how much alcohol Dougie had in his system?'

'He was over the legal driving limit.'

'By how much?'

'The limit's eighty milligrams. His reading was one-twenty.'

'So he was only just over the limit?'

'Almost half as much again.'

'Hardly roaring drunk, though?'

'Why are you asking?'

'I assumed he was properly drunk, but according to the barman he only had four pints in three hours and—'

'According to the barman?'

'I've just left the Lone Star.'

'You're in Glasgow?' There was shock in his voice.

'Yes.'

'Wait a minute.'

I heard him tell Collette and the kids to go inside and that he would join them soon. When he spoke to me again his tone was terse. 'Isla, that's not a safe area.'

'So everyone keeps telling me.'

'Who's everyone?'

'Dad. The barman.' I started talking faster. 'I just wanted to see where Dougie spent his last moments, and the barman told me that Dougie only had four pints, and so I thought I'd check with you, and well, he wasn't that drunk, was he? So how could he have fallen in the Clyde?'

'Even a small amount of alcohol can change the speed of a person's reactions, especially if they're tired.'

'I know. But this is Dougie we're talking about.'

'He was no different from the rest of us, Isla. He missed his footing and fell into the river. It was dark. He'd be disoriented.'

I wasn't buying that, Dougie. You were in the marines for almost twenty years and you'd been a private investigator for four. You knew how to assess a situation. And you knew how to keep yourself safe. If you'd been close to water you'd have taken care. And if you'd fallen into water you'd have swum back to shore, easy peasy.

I didn't say any of this to Gavin because you know what he's like. Whatever I said, he'd have an answer. 'Okay. Thanks Gavin. Give my love to the kids.'

'Are you heading back home now?'

'I'm just on my way to the car park,' I said.

Lying was becoming a habit.

I read the address on the back of the receipt Don had given me. The squat was in another pub called the Ship's Anchor. I entered the street name into the navigation app. The location was less than a mile away – 0.7 miles to be exact. I was hoping it might be back in the direction of my parked car, but it wasn't. It was further along the river away from the Science Centre. I walked quickly because it was close to seven o'clock and the sun was beginning to set. The area was sorely in need of regeneration. Every building I passed was boarded up and appeared to be abandoned. I passed a warehouse that stretched the length of a football pitch and was all smashed windows and broken signage.

I met no one. Not one other living soul. I scanned the streets; I reacted to every small sound – wind rushing through the broken windows and the creaking of wood had me spooked. I was annoyed with myself for not carrying a rape alarm or pepper spray, but anyway, with no one around, I wasn't sure either device would have done me any good.

I steadied my nerves by thinking about Min Fraser, about the fact this was her territory. I imagined what she would be like. I imagined her as a harried, tired-looking woman with an edge of realism, who believed in saving teenagers from the perils of drug addiction and crime. She would never have any money in her pocket, and she would feel like she could never do enough, but she would soldier on anyway because these were her streets.

The Ship's Anchor hadn't survived the recession, and looked fit for demolition. It was larger than the Lone Star and stood back from the river on a sizeable patch of ground. An eight-foot high metal fence had been erected around the whole building but was no longer holding fast. It was weather-beaten and tired, rusted and warped in places, and on the north side, wire cutters had liberated a person-sized hole in the weave. I squeezed through the gap, making sure I didn't catch my clothes on the wire barbs, and walked around the building. Half of the pub exterior was sooty black with fire damage, the windowpanes gone and the wooden surrounds splintered. The other half was boarded up, but looked structurally sound. Vandals had taken spray paint to boards, multiple sets of bubble writing and vulgar drawings vying for attention. At the rear entrance to the pub, a fire exit door had been torn off its hinges and was lying on its side, the push-bar smeared with mud or excrement – it was hard to tell. The smell in the air was an ambiguous mix of river and sewage.

I hesitated before going inside, all my senses on red alert. I knew what you'd be saying to me – *Back off now!*

Don't put yourself in danger for me! – but you know what?
– I was there and I wasn't giving up.

I slipped quietly into the building and waited close to
the exit until my eyes grew accustomed to the gloom.
The concrete-floored corridor was littered with mess:
rags, empty packets, plastic bottles, all manner of detritus
that was an invitation to rats. I could hear a murmur of
voices up ahead and I followed the sound, finding myself
in a large room, about fifty feet by forty feet, a once-
upon-a-time function room at the back of the pub. The
air was stale with the fug of unwashed bodies, and
blocked, grimy windows kept most of the light outside.
Torn, stained mattresses hugged the walls, huddles of
people lying on top of them. Most of the dozen or so
people ignored me, but several eyed me with suspicion,
then a man stood up and came towards me, shoulders
back, chest out. 'You lookin' for someone?' He had the
thin pointed face of a weasel.

'Min Fraser,' I said, standing firm despite the fact that
I was sick with nerves. 'Is she here?'

'Is she expecting you?'

'No. But she might be expecting my father.'

'Name?'

'Isla McTeer.'

'I'll tell her,' he said, adding 'bitch' just in case I
thought I'd won him over. He sloped off – a man on a
mission – through a door at the other end of the room,
closing it behind him.

There was movement on the mattress next to my feet
and I stared down into the face of a teenage girl. She
was pale and underfed. Her head wobbled on her neck;
her hands and forearms were patterned with cuts. She
was propped up against the wall, a sleeping boy draped
across her lap. One of her cut hands rested on the boy's

head, stroking his greasy hair with a steady rhythm. I watched her for a few seconds, wondering whether Gordy's daughter was living like this, wondering whether you'd thought that too and if you'd come here asking about Lucy.

I bent down next to the girl and said, 'Do you know anyone called Lucy O'Malley?'

'What?' Her expression was blank.

'I have a photo of Lucy here.' I pulled the flier Gordy had given me out of my pocket and held it up in front of the girl's face. 'Have you seen this girl?'

She blinked several times, then shook her head.

'You don't remember whether there was a man asking about her, do you? It would have been a couple of weeks ago now.'

'No.'

A dirty trainer kicked at my foot. 'You can go through.' Weasel was back and looking pleased with himself. He pointed towards the doorway and I walked through it, a dozen pairs of eyes watching me. I was in another corridor – shorter and mess-free – with a closed door at the end. I turned the door handle and pushed the door wide. The room on the other side took me by surprise. It was less of a squat and more of a boudoir, putting me in mind of a Victorian brothel. There were close-weaved rugs on the floor, and standard lamps with tasselled shades lit up two cosy seating areas. The room's main feature was the original bar, covered with a brocade bedspread, large velvet floor cushions strewn on the floor in front of it. The mirror behind the bar reflected the light back into the room, and, as I stared into it I saw another door open behind me and a woman of about seventy, maybe even older, came in.

I turned around to face her. She was wearing opaque

tights and ankle boots, and a tweed pinafore dress topped with a soft woollen cardigan in muted shades of purples and greens, expensive fabrics for someone who lived in a squat.

'Hello.' She gestured towards a chair. 'Have a seat.'

I sat down and she sat opposite me, staring at my face, her milky-blue eyes probing. 'So, Isla McTeer, what brings you here?'

'You're Min Fraser?' I was surprised, Dougie: by her age, by the way she was dressed, and by her demeanour, which was still and watchful, and far less harried than I had expected.

'I am. And this is my home.'

'It's very . . . it's unexpected.'

'We have been here for three years,' she said, her accent hard to place. Glaswegian with underlying Croatian or Czech. I couldn't be sure. 'One day the property will be developed, but for now it belongs to us.'

Us? I didn't comment on the obvious hierarchy: stained mattresses, grimy walls and windows next door, and the comparative opulence in here. 'Don, the barman at the Lone Star pub, said you might be willing to talk to me.'

'I thought I was going to be speaking to your father?'

'He broke his leg, so I've come instead.' I held my bag on my knee, clutching it tightly enough to make my fingers ache. 'I think you were one of the last people to speak to my brother.'

She nodded. 'My condolences.' She leant in towards me. Her skin was pale, but had the texture of orange peel. 'You were fond of your brother.'

'Very.'

She kept her attention on my face. I felt the burn of

her stare, saw tiny calculations flare in her eyes. 'Then you must be suffering.'

A droplet of sweat trickled its way down my sternum and into my bra. I wanted to scratch the spot, but I forced myself to sit perfectly still. This woman was not the woman of my imaginings. Nowhere even close. The menace in her glance was palpable.

'He was too young to die.' She gave me a regretful smile. 'But sooner or later it will come to all of us.'

'Had my brother arranged to meet you?' I asked.

'No.'

'So what made you speak to him?'

'I'd never seen him around here and I thought he might be looking for someone.' She plucked at her cardigan, pulling the wool in towards the centre of her chest. 'People do, you know?'

'They come here looking for their runaway teenagers?' I asked.

Her eyes widened. 'They do.'

'And was my brother looking for a runaway?'

'I don't know.' There was a table beside her with a small drawer set into it. She took a bottle of pills from the drawer, her movements slow and deliberate, uncapped the bottle and slipped one pill onto her hand then transferred it under her tongue. 'What do you think your brother was doing in the Lone Star?'

'Well . . .' The room was still enough to hear the proverbial pin drop if it hadn't been for my heart, which was hammering against my ribcage like a trapped rhino. 'My brother was a private investigator, and I think it's possible he was looking for a girl called Lucy O'Malley. I have her photo here.'

I pulled one of the fliers out of my pocket, and Min took it from me. She stared at the photo and said, 'Lucy

O'Malley.' She pursed thin lips and turned her eyes up to the ceiling. 'Lu-cy O'M-all-ey,' lengthening out the syllables. 'I don't recognise her face, and the name isn't sounding any bells.' This time her smile was vacuous, and she spoke, not to me, but to a spot over my shoulder. 'I'm sorry, Isla McTeer. I wish I could help you.'

She was lying. I knew she was lying because she was withholding eye contact. But what was disconcerting was that I sensed she was doing it deliberately. She knew I knew she was lying. It was what she wanted.

'I look after young people seeking shelter.' Her face moved closer. 'Why don't you leave me your mobile number and I'll get in touch with you if I hear anything about Lucy O'Malley?' Her eyes licked greedily around my face. 'Or about your brother.'

Fear was clogging my lungs, affording me the shortest, shallowest of breaths. I had a sense that this woman was more dangerous than all the men in the bar put together. I didn't know how she could be. I didn't know why I felt this. I only knew that I did.

I took a piece of paper from my bag and wrote my mobile number on it. My hands shook and I had to press the paper hard to control the tremor.

'You are anxious, my dear.' She patted my hand. Her touch was cold and dry, like fallen leaves. 'There's no need to be anxious.'

I stood up, felt my knees quake and almost give way. I expected to find someone at the door barring my way, someone like Weasel, but more threatening – a human attack dog – but there was no one to stop me leaving. I made my way past the bodies on the mattresses and back outside. I squeezed through the fence and stood close to the river, staring out over the water, giving my lungs the chance to fill and refill. Min Fraser was nothing like I expected. There was a gulf between the image she sold to the world – nice little old lady who does good for the community's lost children - and what she actually was – a schemer and a manipulator.

Dougie, I wished you were there for me to ask you what you thought. Did you mistrust her too? Or was my imagination running away with me? Was I spooked because I was grieving and overtired? Was I unable to tell the difference between a nice old lady and a criminal?

Because I was convinced that she was like a character from a fairy tale, more closely resembling the old woman who force-fed Hansel and Gretel for the cooking pot than any fairy godmother.

Up ahead, a lone man was coming towards me. Despite the rain and the darkening sky, he was wearing a sleeveless, white vest and jeans. Tattoos patterned his arms like graffiti. When he drew closer I noticed that the side of his face was bruised, an ugly black inkblot staining one whole eye and cheek.

'What you lookin' at?'

'Nothing.' I averted my eyes and walked away from him, dodging the ruptured hillocks where weeds pushed up through the tarmac. I hurried back the way I had come, buildings to one side and the river to the other. I didn't dare look back. I speed-walked fifty yards or more and was just beginning to relax when I felt someone creep up behind me. I turned my head and saw, in that split second, that it was the tattooed man but I wasn't quick enough to stop his right arm snaking around my neck and fastening tightly.

'Your brother promised me my money,' he said.

Two things happened at once. I felt a rush of pure terror that made me struggle against him, kick and scratch and try to bite, and at the same time my head filled with suggestions: I should knee him in the balls, drop to the ground, try to poke him in the eyes. And there was another voice, one that sounded like yours, Dougie. 'It's a Jack Bauer chokehold. You won't die. You'll lose consciousness, that's all.' You and box sets of *24* had got me through my marriage break-up. Endless, impossible situations for Jack Bauer to deal with, and, against all the odds, he always came out on top. We'd laugh at the storyline, you and me, suspending disbelief just long enough to make it through to the next episode.

'Where the fuck is my money?' the man said, his arm tightening.

My lungs were aflame and my cheeks were bursting with blood, and I couldn't have replied even if I'd wanted to because my tongue was a fat, uncoordinated lump of muscle. My hands clawed at his arm, but there was no shifting it. And then my knees softened and buckled, and the world pitched into black.

5. Tell the Truth and Shame the Devil

I was on the ground. Cold water had seeped through my jeans, and my legs felt numb. When I swallowed, my throat burned. I could hear people talking beside me and I slowly opened my eyes. It was the girl who'd been lying on the mattress, the one with cuts all over her hands. And standing beside her was a young man of about eighteen, possibly the one who'd been lying across her knee.

'Tell me the truth, Jimmy,' she said.

'It's nothin'.' His eyes glanced off to the side.

She sighed and took money out of her pocket, passed it to him. 'Here.'

'Ta.' He forced the notes inside the lip of his right ankle boot, which was only a few metres from my face.

'We need to find somewhere else to live,' the girl said, sliding her hands inside his coat and pushing her hipbones into his. 'I don't want to stay there any more.' Her voice was a pouty whine. 'I want to be on my own with you.'

He shook his head. 'No can do.'

'Why not?'

'Winter's coming.'

'Jimmy!' She grabbed hold of his upper arms and gave him a shake. He didn't resist, and the force of her frustration swept through his torso in a wave. 'You know why we have to go.'

He glanced around, fearful, then spotted me raising myself up onto one elbow, and pointed towards me, shouting, 'The woman's awake!'

The girl rushed at me. 'Are you okay?' She bent down and helped me to stand up. 'We were waiting for you to wake up.'

'Is my bag . . .' my voice was rasping.

'Your bag's here.' She reached behind me. 'Were you mugged?'

I rummaged through my bag and found my purse with all my cards and cash still inside. My mobile. My car keys. All the other stuff I normally carry around with me. Nothing had been taken, and that should have made me feel relieved, but it didn't. The fact that I hadn't been robbed made me feel worried. And then I remembered the man, and what he'd said. *Your brother promised me my money.* A light show exploded behind my eyes and I stumbled to one side.

'Be careful,' the girl said, her hand hovering next to my elbow.

'I'm okay.' I waited for my vision to return to normal. 'I got a fright, that's all.'

'You sure?'

'Yeah.'

'I've been mugged before,' Jimmy said, sounding proud. 'Three times.'

'I'm sorry.' I stared along the street and then behind me before turning back to Jimmy and the girl. 'You didn't see who attacked me, did you?'

'No,' Jimmy said. The girl shook her head.

I forgot about my own problems for a minute and focussed on them both. The mother in me wanted to give them advice. They needed clean clothes and a bath. The girl needed to stop cutting herself; Jimmy needed some treatment for his acne. They needed to stop taking drugs. And they needed a future.

'What's your name?' I asked the girl.

'Paula,' she said, her expression verging on suspicious.

'And you're Jimmy?' He nodded. 'Jimmy Pearcy?' I asked. Gordy had told me that Lucy had run away with a lad called Jimmy Pearcy, but Glasgow was full of Jimmies, so what were the chances? At any rate, he didn't answer me. I tried to read his expression, but I couldn't. 'The woman who runs the squat—'

'She's great. She helps us,' Paula said. She took Jimmy's hand and they stood together, defiant.

'You should fuck off,' Jimmy said, his tone striving for a menace that felt more contrived than real, but I wasn't going to push it.

'Okay.' I pointed along the road ahead of me. 'I will. Thank you for your help.'

I wasn't far away when Paula shouted after me, 'You know that girl?' I turned back to face her. 'The one you showed me a photo of.' She was scratching the back of her hand, tearing through the healing skin to make it bleed. 'Are you her mother?'

'No. But I know her dad.'

'We need to go,' Jimmy said. He jerked his head in the direction of the squat. 'Come on Paula.' He tugged on her hand. 'People to see, shit to do.'

'Her dad really needs to find her,' I told Paula. 'He's not angry. He cares about her.'

Paula broke eye contact with me and stared over the water.

'Have you met Lucy?' I asked. 'Do you know where she might be?'

Jimmy started walking backwards, pulling Paula with him. She didn't resist.

The car park was almost deserted when I got back to the Science Centre. I locked myself inside my car and sat for minute, breathing. Just breathing. I was light-headed with panic. My hand kept straying up to my neck because I felt as if there was a huge, invasive lump in my throat.

'Bruising and a bit of swelling, that's all,' I told myself sternly. 'You're okay. Just drive home. Do it.'

Before I drove off, I checked my mobile. I had two missed calls: from Dad and from Ritchie. Only Ritchie had left me a message, and I listened to it at once. 'Isla, I hope you haven't gone to Glasgow on your own? I'm sorry, I was called away to Newcastle. I've been in meet-ings all day and won't be back until much later this evening.'

The sound of Ritchie's voice made me feel less panicky. I listened to the message three times, and then I felt calm enough to call Dad. He was at a low ebb. 'I'm being driven nuts with the noise and the heat,' he said. 'And the surgeon tells me I'll be two months plas-tered like this. I'll be lucky if I'm walking by Christmas.'

It was on the tip of my tongue to tell him about what had just happened to me, but I couldn't burden him with any more worries. I could hear that he felt powerless enough, trapped in a bed, unable to walk, and here I was having broken my promise to him and been attacked into the bargain. He'd told me not to put myself in danger and I had. Now I had to live with the consequences.

'The nurses are coming over,' he said. 'You be sure and have an early night.' He ended the call and I checked the time. It was only nine o'clock. I felt like aeons of time had passed since I'd left Edinburgh. I started the car and drove back home, forcing myself to concentrate on driving. I played loud music, put the windows up and down, kept my eyes on the road, and my mind as far away from what had just happened to me as I could.

Myrtle was giddy with delight to see me, and turned fast, tail-chasing circles on the kitchen floor. She'd been too long on her own and had been running in and out of the dog flap; her face and paws were covered in dirt. I switched on the patio light and saw that she'd been digging up the flowerbeds. Earth and plant roots were scattered across the paving stones. I gave her some food and a cuddle, and then she lay down in her bed.

My neck ached, outside and inside, a beacon of pain, pulsing a reminder of the attack. I remembered the man's arm around my neck, hard as a metal bar. The horror of it. The surge of panic as his muscles tightened over my throat and stopped me breathing.

And thoughts of my panic led to thoughts of your panic. Were you conscious when the water flooded your lungs? Were you aware of everything that was happening to you? Were you, Dougie?

I poured myself a glass of red wine and knocked back several mouthfuls.

Did you fall in, or were you pushed? Had this man attacked you too?

I shivered and poured myself another.

How could you have owed him money? How?

I emptied the glass.

Did you fight? Did he push you into the water? Did you know you were dying?

I wasn't aware of the exact moment I passed out on the sofa. I only knew that I was grateful to feel nothing.

Hurt comes in all shapes and sizes. Sometimes dull and irritating, a tiny stone in my shoe, and other times a barren, relentless Sahara that stretches to the horizon.

Dougie, you were the desert; Collette was the stone. Mostly I was happy that Caitlin and Fin liked her so much, because childhood is short and they deserved to have the smoothest ride possible. But sometimes Collette got on my nerves with her caring and her sharing. And after your death she had the perfect excuse to treat me like I was the third child.

She arrived at the house at around eleven that same evening, used Gavin's emergency key and came right on in. I couldn't have been asleep longer than a few minutes. She shook me awake, the sound of her voice an urgent command in my ear. 'Isla. Isla! We've been calling you. We've been worried!'

'Can't you see I'm asleep?' I kept my face turned into the couch, but Collette was not a primary school teacher for nothing. Reluctance fed her determination. She would get her own way. Oh, yes, she would.

'We called your mobile a couple of times and you didn't reply, so I said to Gavin I'd come over and see how you were.' She straightened the throw on the sofa, pulling the material out from under me, then banged the cushions together so that gusts of air converged above my head, sending strands of my hair flying upwards. 'I said it out of earshot of the kids, of course, because they don't need to be more upset than they already are.'

I pulled my face out of the couch and squinted up at her. 'Are they okay?'

'Caitlin has been really quiet. What with her granddad to worry about as well. You need to sober up and give her a call before she goes to bed.' She moved on from the cushions and held up the two empty wine bottles. 'Really, Isla? Two whole bottles?'

'One was almost empty.' My head was spinning and

my throat ached. 'I'll call the kids.' I looked at my watch. 'Are they not in bed yet?'

'We were playing Monopoly.'

I stood up and swayed on my feet for a second, giving my head time to catch up before I moved. 'I'm just going to the loo.'

'You're drunk, Isla!' she pointed out, as I staggered across to the door.

'I'm knackered,' I told her.

'Come straight back!' she called up the stairs after me. 'I've brought you some Nando's chicken. Fin told me it's your favourite.'

I stayed in the bathroom for as long as I could get away with. I felt like shit. And I felt sad. And worried. And desperate. I looked at myself in the mirror – not a pretty sight – and then noticed that a bruised line was appearing around my throat. It was the first time it crossed my mind that perhaps I should have gone to the police. I'd been attacked. I had the marks to prove it, and while Paula and Jimmy hadn't witnessed the attack, they had found me on the ground. They might even have passed my attacker in the street.

'Isla?'

'Coming.'

I washed my face and cleaned my teeth, then found a jumper with a high neck in my bedroom drawer. I needed to talk to someone I could trust, but I wasn't sober enough to drive, and I couldn't talk to Collette because she'd carry the tale straight to Gavin, and then the kids would find out and they had enough on their plates as it was. I needed to see Collette out of the door and then call a taxi.

Alec. I wanted to go and see Alec again. We hadn't finished our conversation when I was called away to the hospital to see Dad. And there had been something about the look on his face that didn't add up. It wasn't that I didn't trust him because I did, implicitly. How could I not?

I'd been working for Alec for thirteen years when you left the marines.

'What's Dougie going to be doing now then, Isla?' he said to me. He was standing at the door of his office and had waylaid me as I arrived.

'He's not sure. Maybe personal security. A lot of ex-marines do that.'

'Get him to come and see me, will you?'

You went to see him and he told you there was an opening in Edinburgh for a good PI. That he had work from solicitors that he couldn't cover, that you'd be self-employed so could do other jobs too. He had a contact who could set you on the right road.

You went with his advice, and you never looked back.

Feeling better for having made a decision, I returned downstairs. Collette had warmed the chicken in the microwave and set a place at the table. 'This is kind of you, Collette. But I'm going to call Caitlin and Fin, and then I need to go out.'

'You can't drive.'

'I'll get a taxi.' I used my mobile to call the kids, spoke to Fin first and then Caitlin. Fin was cheerful. He was playing table football with Gavin and winning. Caitlin was a bit subdued, but she didn't sound unhappy. I asked her whether she wanted to come home, but she said no. 'I'll see you tomorrow then, sweetheart.' I moved into the hallway so that Collette couldn't hear me. 'You would tell me if you wanted to come home, wouldn't you?'

'I'm okay, Mum. I promise.'

I told her I loved her and ended the call hoping her childhood promises weren't as made-up as ours were, Dougie. I was realising that I didn't know enough about bereavement in children. I was going to have to set aside my own grief and put some thought into helping Caitlin and Fin.

'Isla?'

I went back into the kitchen.

'Here we are,' Collette said. She laid a plate of chicken and salad on the table. 'No excuses.'

'I'll be sick.'

She folded her arms. 'What have you eaten today?'

'Plenty, as it happens.'

'I don't believe you.'

'Please, Collette.' I held a hand up. 'Just back off for a minute.'

She leant towards me frowning. 'What's that mark on your neck?'

'Nothing.' I ducked my chin down into my jumper. So much for thinking it would hide the bruising. 'This looks very nice.' I sat down at the table and picked up my fork.

'Gavin said you were in Glasgow today.'

'I was.'

'We would have gone with you.' She gave a measured sigh. 'First your dad, and now you.'

'Sometimes grief feels private.'

'Isla.' She pulled a chair up alongside me. She was working up to one of her pep talks. 'May I be honest with you?'

I had to head her off at the pass. 'Do you know much about bereavement in children?' I said. 'I want to make sure I do the right thing with Caitlin and Fin.'

'Oh! Okay.' She visibly brightened, and then two seconds

later she was frowning. 'You're trying to distract me.'

'I am. But I'm also serious about helping the kids.'

She stared at me and I stared back. 'Ok-*ay*,' she said. 'I'll give you the benefit of the doubt.' She got her diary out. 'There are charities that organise special days for children who're grieving. I know this because we had a child at our school who lost his father. Why don't I see what I can find out for you?'

'I'd be really grateful if you could.'

She wrote down reminders for herself, and I ate my way through half of the chicken. The other half I sneaked to Myrtle when Collette wasn't looking. I didn't want to behave like a teenager around Collette, but somehow it always happened that way. I persuaded her out through the door at around ten o'clock with promises that I'd go straight to bed, that I wouldn't drink any more, and that I'd call her if I needed anything.

When she started the engine, I called Alec. He answered after a few rings. 'It's me Alec. You weren't asleep, were you?'

'No. We're both still up.'

'I was wondering whether you were free for a chat?'

'Now?'

'Aye.'

'You want to come here?'

'If it's okay with you.'

'Nae bother.'

'I'll be over in twenty.'

When the taxi pulled up outside their house, Alec's wife Jean opened the front door. 'Isla.' She wrapped me in her arms. 'How are you holding up?'

'Okay . . . well, not really okay. It's tough, Jean. Really tough.'

'Alec's been gutted. He was so fond of Dougie. We both were.' She led me through the hallway. 'Can I offer you anything to drink?'

'No thanks. I've had enough for one evening. Hence the taxi. Stop me if I get maudlin and stupid.'

'A strong coffee then?'

'That would be lovely.'

Alec had been standing in the living-room doorway with his hands in his pockets. Jean gave him a pointed look and he stepped aside. 'Come in, Isla. I know it's not even October yet but we've got the fire lit.'

I followed him into the living room. 'Thanks for letting me come round, Alec.'

'No problem. We're late bedders here.'

Alec placed another log on the fire. We both stared into the grate and watched the embers wake up, flames encroaching on the log, heating it up for the burn.

'I don't think Dougie's death was an accident,' I said loudly, no preamble, words straight out into the room.

Alec stiffened beside me. And then he gasped. 'Jesus, Isla!'

The fire crackled, and flames threw more light up onto our faces. Alec's was visibly greying. He dropped down into one of the armchairs next to the fire, and I sat opposite.

'This is why I'm here. I wanted to talk it through with you.' My head was still fuzzy with booze, and I held it very still, focussed on concentrating. 'First of all, when my dad was in theatre having his bone set, the pub land-lord called. His name's Don McAndrew and he wouldn't tell me anything on the phone so I went there today. It turned out Dougie only had four pints in three hours.'

'He wasn't that drunk then,' Alec said, surprised.

'No, he wasn't. And he was a Royal Marines

Commando who could swim long distances with ease. What are the odds of him drowning so close to the shore?'

'I would have thought it a long shot.'

'Exactly. And you know how Dougie's been looking for that girl for a while. Lucy O'Malley?'

Alec nodded.

'I think he was in Glasgow because of her, and I'm not sure how it all connects, but the point is this, Alec. The point is, that what really clinches it . . . the reason I know that Dougie was in trouble is because of this.' I pulled down the neck of my jumper so that Alec could see the bruising. 'A man came up behind me and put his arm around my throat.'

'*What?*' Alec jumped to his feet. 'How? Were you on your own?'

'Yes.'

'What possessed you, lassie?' He was horrified.

'I needed to find out what happened to Dougie.'

'Not on your own!' He banged his fist into the flat of his palm. 'Why didn't you ask for my help?'

'I'm asking now.' Tears were smarting in my eyes. 'I'd be glad of your help.'

'Are you all right?' He sat back down. 'Do you need a doctor?'

'No, no. I just need to talk to you.'

'Isla,' he was frowning, 'this isn't right.'

'Please, Alec.'

'If you were my daughter I'd take you straight to the hospital and then the police station. You know that, don't you?'

'Yes, but . . .' I gave him a pleading look. 'The man who attacked me said, "Your brother promised me my money." Not "Have you got *any* money?" Or "Give me your money." But '"Your brother promised me my money".'

Alec was about to speak and I held up my hand. 'I'm one hundred per cent sure that's what he said and I know he could have mistaken me for someone else, but there was nobody else there. The place was deserted, Alec. Honestly. Apart from the people lying on mattresses in the squat.'

'What squat?'

I told him about Min Fraser, how disturbing she was, and how, as far as I knew, she'd been the last person to speak to you alive. 'Either Min Fraser or someone from the pub could have told the man that I was there. There was nothing taken from my handbag. I had about a hundred pounds in cash and . . .' I caught Alec's expression and trailed off. 'Alec?'

I was confused Dougie, because I expected Alec to tell me I was talking nonsense. I expected to have to persuade him. I anticipated fighting my corner. Alec was a man of opposites, wasn't he? In business he was inscrutable. His skin was coated in a shiny lacquer that deflected any probing. He could broker deals as easily as the rest of us make a sandwich. But anything personal? His skin was porous, and at that moment guilt was leaking out of him like milk through muslin.

Jean came in with a mug of coffee for me, and what looked like Ovaltine for Alec. 'Have you told her yet?' she asked.

Alec took the mug, laid it down on the marble hearth and stared into the fire.

'Told me what?' I cleared my throat. 'Is it something to do with Dougie?'

Alec nodded, and Jean discreetly left the room, closing the door behind her.

'Just spit it out Alec.' I was shaking. Coffee spilt down the side of the mug and onto my jeans.

'I'm sorry, Isla. I should have told you about this before, but I wasn't sure whether it was significant and, well . . . I've been trying to reverse it.' His eyes were heavy with worry and regret. 'You know that I've been thinking about scaling back?' I nodded. 'Well, about two weeks before Dougie died I offered him a share in the business. I would have come to you too, Isla, but . . .'

'It's okay.' I shrugged. 'I don't have any money.'

'Dougie said yes to my offer, and then he transferred the money into my bank account a couple of days later.'

'He didn't tell me.'

'He wanted to surprise you.'

I smiled. That sounded like you, Dougie.

'He planned on telling you on your birthday.'

November the fifth. We always had fireworks on our birthday, didn't we? Mum made sure of it. Sparklers and Catherine wheels and loud, explosive rockets.

'Stand back!' Dad shouted. He had the rockets balanced in a row of empty baked bean tins stuck in the ground, and he walked forward to light them.

'Ten rockets. One for each year,' Mum said. She was standing behind us, Marie balanced on her hip, even though she was almost five, because she wouldn't put her feet on the ground and she refused to watch from the window.

'Count down!' Mum shouted, as Dad ran back to us.

We started counting down from ten, but when we got to zero, none of the rockets had gone off.

'Just wait,' Mum said, her hand on Dad's shoulder. We all waited. I was holding my breath. So, I think,

were you. And then the rockets started firing into the
sky, one after the other. We both cheered and jumped
up and down, and when I turned around to look at
Mum her face was lit up.

'Happy, Isla?' she said.

'Yes!' I jumped up and down some more, clapping
my hands.

'Even when we're old, we'll do this,' you said. 'Even
then.'

Maybe that's why my name was in your diary, because
you were thinking you needed the business for us, for
me. You knew I had been worrying about what might
happen when Alec retired. He made no secret of the
fact that he wanted to spend more time with his grandchildren, and if he'd sold the business to someone we
didn't know they might not have employed us any more.

'Dougie's solicitor didn't tell me he was buying into
the business,' I said.

'Dougie paid me seventy-five grand . . . It's a good
price, Isla.'

'You're a fair man,' I acknowledged.

'I was having the contracts drawn up, and then he
was going to approach his solicitor.' He sighed. 'Two
days before Dougie died, he came and asked me whether
he could change his mind.'

'Why?' I sat forward. 'Did he say?'

'I probed a bit, and he told me he had to take care
of a debt.'

'What debt?'

'It's not come out in his will, has it?'

'No. As far as I can tell Dougie had no outstanding
debts. He only had a mortgage, and that was covered
with an insurance policy.'

'I tried to get him the money back, but I'd already given it to my daughter for a deposit on a house. With the grandbairns and everything.' He rubbed his hands over his face. 'God knows if I'd thought he really needed it back I would have moved heaven and earth.'

'It wasn't your fault, Alec.' I swallowed down some coffee. 'Did he say where the debt came from?'

'He didn't.' Alec stood up and started feeling through the logs in the basket next to the fireplace, sizing up their shape and weight in his hand until he settled for a couple of roughly chopped pieces of timber and stacked them on the fire. 'I can't figure it out, Isla. I thought you might be able to.'

I shook my head. It was beginning to ache again. I thought about last summer when you paid for Dad, me, and the kids to go to Norway with you. We stayed with Marie and Erik.

'Everything's so expensive here,' I said, as we sat down for another meal in another restaurant. The soft drinks bill alone was more than we'd pay in Edinburgh for food and drinks put together. 'We're costing you a fortune.'

'Who else would I spend my money on?' you said.

We saw the Northern Lights and sailed up a fjord. We went back to where Mum was born and where she met Dad. We met some of her relatives, our cousins and their children. It was the holiday of a lifetime.

You had the money to pay for that, though, I know you did because a couple of months later your savings account statement was open on your computer. There was a balance of over eighty thousand pounds in your account. You'd always been a saver. Alec paid you well, and the other PI work you did was the gravy. Unlike me, you didn't have the financial expense of children, and anyway, you could always make money go further than I could.

'I told him I could give him five grand if it helped, an advance on his salary, kind of thing,' Alec said. 'The Prendergast case is set to go on for a while. Dougie was sure to make easily four or five times as much over the next six months, but he said that the debt was more than that.'

'How much more?' I was disbelieving.

'I'm not sure, but I got the impression a lot more. I could see it was troubling him, and I said I could put him in touch with someone I knew who could help with financing, but he said it wasn't as simple as that.'

I swallowed down some coffee and tried to think in a straight line – How had you got yourself into debt, Dougie? How? Could it be something to do with Lucy O'Malley? Or expensive hobbies? . . . You couldn't have had a speed-boat or a racing bike or over-priced wines churning through your cash. You only lived a couple of hundred metres along the road from me. I knew where you were going and what you were doing because we spoke on the phone and saw each other a lot. Gambling? . . . Gambling could have eaten through the money you had – and money you didn't have. But you weren't a gambler.

And then it clicked.

'Tania,' I said. 'I bet it was Tania. I bet that's why he didn't tell me because he knew I don't have any time for her.' I stood up, felt dizzy and sat back down again, my hand on my forehead. 'He must have gone to Glasgow to meet the man who assaulted me.'

'Could be,' Alec said. 'You need to go to the police and tell them what happened. They'll know about the sort of crimes that go on in that area.' He placed a hand on my shoulder. 'Apart from anything else, you were assaulted, Isla. You can't let that go.'

'I bet Tania, was in debt to this man. Probably a loan shark. It couldn't be Dougie. He would never have been that stupid.'

'I agree,' Alec said. 'But I think there's a danger of jumping to conclusions. That's what the police are there for, to separate the fact from . . .' he trailed off.

'The fiction?'

'I'm not trying to—'

'I know. I know what you're trying to say, but did you know that Tania has a police record? That she has four brothers, and three of them have been in prison? She dealt cocaine, not small-time either. That's why Dougie finally left her.'

My hand strayed up to my neck, my fingers tracing along the bruise. I visualised the man's arm around your throat. You were trained in hand-to-hand combat. You would have known how to free yourself. Unless he'd caught you unawares. And with a drink inside you. I shivered, and the shiver was followed by a wave of nausea so intense that I grabbed the coal scuttle, thinking I might vomit.

My mind was muddled with booze, but alert enough to register that your last evening as a living, breathing human being might have ended in a sinister, violent way.

Dougie. Dougie. *What the hell were you involved in?*

I stood up again, more slowly this time. 'Thanks Alec. I'll go to the police tomorrow. I'd better go home now and try to get some sleep. I'll call myself a taxi.'

'No need. I'll drive you.' He swigged back the Ovaltine. 'This is as strong as a drink gets for me these days.'

I said goodbye to Jean and she hugged me again. She

exuded the sort of kindness that felt motherly and warm. 'I'm glad he's told you, Isla.' She looked Alec up and down, her expression both disappointed and forgiving. 'He's a work in progress, this one.'

Alec drove me home, neither of us saying a word. I felt overwhelmed by the turn the evening had taken. I was horrified at what you might have suffered, and more than a little bit hurt. Were you dead because of your loyalty to Tania? Because even though I didn't much like her, couldn't you have told me anyway? I wouldn't have judged you. I'd have been annoyed with you initially, but then I'd have supported your decision. I would have, Dougie.

Alec pulled up outside my door. There was nobody around, and all was quiet apart from the distant screeching of a fox. 'I'm so sorry, Isla,' he said. 'So bloody sorry I didn't step in and help him out.'

'You weren't to know.'

'Dougie never asked me for anything. He was one of the best.'

'He was.'

'When you have time to think things through, let me know whether you want a share in the business, or whether I should look for another partner and get the money back for you.'

I nodded. 'I'll talk to Dad and Marie.'

The fox walked past the front of the car and we both watched it until its bushy tail disappeared behind next-door's garage.

'I wish he'd told me,' I said. 'I wish he'd told me about the debt.'

'He didn't want you to know.'

We'd stopped below a street light, and I could clearly see the expression on Alec's face, his lips pressed together as if he wanted to take the words back. 'How do you know that?'

'It was nothing.'

'What did he say, Alec?'

'Just . . .' He bit his lip. 'He asked me not to tell anyone about it.'

'Anyone being me?'

'I think so, Isla.'

I had a shower and went to bed. I lay there staring at the ceiling, angry with you, Dougie. Angry then hurt then angry again.

You had failed me. I had failed you.

You should have told me! I should have been the sort of sister you could tell.

You wanted to surprise me with the business. But you shouldn't have kept the debt a secret. You shouldn't.

You were wrong. I was wrong. You were more wrong.

I didn't want to talk to you any more.

I did want to talk to you.

I do want to talk to you.

I'll always want to talk to you.

Was I closer to finding out what had happened to you? One moment I thought so. The next moment I thought I was just jumping to conclusions, making leaps that were unfounded.

I gathered together the facts as I knew them.

Fact one: The man who attacked me was under the impression you owed him money. (He had a Glaswegian accent, a black eye, and multiple tattoos.)

Fact two: You'd been drinking, but you weren't drunk.

Fact three: You told Alec you had to take care of a debt.

I chewed over these three facts long into the night, twisting them one way and then another to see whether they would break open and reveal their secrets. And all the while there was an elephant in the room. A vast, grey creature lit up by super trouper lights. The elephant's message was clear: Douglas McTeer was dead, and all this attention to detail would not bring him back.

But detail was all I had, and I would persist until I knew exactly how you'd met your death.

Problem was, Dougie, you'd been successfully keeping two secrets, and now I wondered what else you might be hiding.

6. I Thought I Saw You

The next day I thought I saw you. You were walking ahead of me along the path. I recognised you from behind: curly hair on top, then straighter at the back of your head and down to the nape of your neck, hidden by the collar of your navy jacket. I shouted, 'Dougie! Wait!' and I ran after you. Myrtle jogged alongside me, yapping with excitement. Only seconds later I caught up with you, grabbed hold of your sleeve and turned you around.

It wasn't you.

I hurriedly stepped back, disappointed and embarrassed. 'I'm really sorry,' I said to the man who clearly wasn't you, because although he was six feet tall and of similar build and the backs of your heads were almost identical, his face was nothing like yours. He had brown eyes and no visible cheekbones and a smile that could never be as wide. 'I thought you were my brother,' I said, backing away.

He gave me a non-committal smile and carried on walking.

My mood plummeted. For a moment I had felt a rush of childlike happiness. 'My brother is dead – No he isn't! – He's on the path ahead of me!' Cushioned in denial, I'd run towards my no-longer-lost brother, grinning like a crazy woman. Five seconds of magical thinking and then I was wrenched back to reality.

Tears were never far away and they gathered now. I did some frantic blinking and headed off home again. I needed to keep busy – action being the enemy of thought. I made a mental list: call Dad, call Ritchie, go to the police station, go to your house to check the balance of your savings account, be back for four when Gavin and Collette drop off the kids. Tackle Tania?

When I arrived home I had a quick run around the house gathering up washing for the machine, then I called Dad.

'I've got an infection,' he said.

'In your leg?'

'In my chest.'

'Oh, no.'

'They've put a drip up. The antibiotics go in the bags.' I heard someone talking to him in the background. 'The nurse is coming over to get me sorted.'

'Let me speak to her Dad, will you?' He passed me over to the nurse.

'It was what we thought might happen really, wasn't it?' she said. 'Hopefully the antibiotics will knock the infection on the head. It's making him hot and just a wee bit grumpy isn't it, George?' She gave the phone back to Dad.

'She's got a lot in common with Collette,' he said.

'I know it's frustrating, Dad, but do your best. I'll be in to see you this afternoon. I'll bring you a newspaper and some of those biscuits you like.'

He tried to persuade me to bring him a bottle of whisky as well and I heard the nurse vetoing it. 'So much for patient care,' he said, and hung up.

I stood in the kitchen and drank some water. My stomach was rumbling, but I hadn't eaten any breakfast because my throat felt sore. Every time I swallowed, I was reminded of what had happened the day before. The bruised-cheeked, tattooed Glaswegian who said you'd promised him money had held his arm over my throat until I'd lost consciousness. The memory was fresh in my mind, more real, more tangible than the glass of water in my hand. Avoiding thinking about it was almost impossible, and when I did think about it, panic swarmed through me like a plague.

I had to go to the police.

I had to.

It would mean recalling the memory in detail, talking the police through every stage of the assault. But more importantly, the police needed to know about the debt and about the fact that I now believed your death wasn't an accident.

Ritchie would come with me. I was sure he would. The thought of him beside me as I walked into the police station made me feel instantly lighter. I called his mobile and he answered at once. 'Sorry about yesterday,' he said. 'Unavoidable work stuff.'

'That's okay. Listen, are you home?'

'Yes.'

'I'm just going to stop off at my brother's and then I'll come over, is that okay?'

'Of course. I'll be here.'

I shouted on Myrtle then climbed into my car, deciding it made sense to go to your house on the way to the police station. I could check your savings account and see whether you still had money in there. The more evidence I had to present to the police, the better.

I drove down the potholed track to your cottage and parked outside. The climbing rose at the front was already beginning to look overgrown. I doubted I could cope with both your garden and my own. I'd need to think about calling in a gardener before I put your house up for sale.

I left Myrtle in the car and walked to your front door. As soon as I unlocked it and went inside, I knew that something had changed. The air felt disturbed. There's no other way to describe it. I stood undecided for several seconds, then I took two steps forward and poked my head around the living-room door, gasping at what I saw. Furniture had been thrown around, photos were off the walls, and the stuffing was out of cushions. Books were in tumbled heaps on the floor, curtains torn from hooks. Your two indoor plants had been knocked over, earth scattering across the rug in clumps. The glass coffee table had a huge crack across its centre, and small shards had broken off, spreading around the table like tiny diamonds.

Fear crept up my spine, freezing it into a rigid length of bone. I touched the bruise at my throat, remembering the man's arm on my windpipe, choking the air out of me. My heart was beating so loudly that it filled all the spaces in my ears. I couldn't hear whether there was anyone still in the house. I could only hear the sound of my own panic. My knees were knocking together as I retraced my steps out of the front door and climbed into my car.

I called Gavin. 'It's me. I'm at Dougie's house. It's been broken into.'

'Have you called the police?'

'I called you first.' Myrtle jumped up onto my knee and I held her close.

'I'll call them. Where are you now?'

'In the car with the doors locked.'

'Stay where you are. The police will arrive within ten minutes. I'll be there in twenty.'

Even though I had Myrtle on my knee and the heater on full blast, I couldn't stop shivering. The ten minutes before the police arrived felt like half an hour or more. Half an hour of wondering what I'd do if a man appeared at your front door – not just any man, but *that* man. The one who'd made it clear he could strangle the very life out of me should the mood take him. This could have been a straightforward burglary, unconnected to your last day on this earth, but I didn't think so. While there was no discernible pattern, I knew in my gut that your house being trashed was all part of the whole, a whole that, at that moment, I still couldn't understand.

But I would.

When the two policemen arrived, I walked through your house with them. Whoever had caused all the damage had certainly left their mark. The lock on the conservatory doors had been jemmied with a crowbar. Two sets of footprints were visible on the wooden flooring, moving from the garden into the house. One set of footprints was noticeably larger than the other.

When Gavin arrived, he took charge and I watched the two officers defer to him. 'We might be lucky and lift some fingerprints,' he said to me.

'I think it's all connected,' I said.

'Connected to what?'

'Dougie's death.'

He nodded. 'The house has been empty for over two weeks now. Word gets around.'

'That's not what I meant.' I stepped around the scattered earth and stood in front of him. 'I don't think Dougie's death was accidental.'

'Is this according to the Lone Star barman?'

'No. It's more than that. In fact, I am going to go to the police about it.'

'Bring your kit in here first!' Gavin shouted over my head to an officer who had just arrived. Then he looked back at me. 'Have a gander. See whether you can spot anything missing.' He walked towards the officer. 'Hi Kev. Long time no see.' They shook hands and began to discuss evidence-gathering.

The trunk under the window had been tipped over and emptied out. I bent down to see whether the money was still there. After some rummaging around under photo albums and a smashed mug, I found the envelope and slipped it into my pocket. Then I went into your bedroom. The mess in there wasn't quite so damaging. I couldn't see anything broken, but they'd pulled drawers out and spread the contents across the floor. I knelt on the rug and sorted through your stuff. It took me five minutes to locate the box for your Rolex watch, but not the watch itself. The gold cufflinks you inherited from Granddad and your medal from Iraq were both there. I put them in my pocket and then walked through the kitchen and into your office. It was exactly as I had left it. I thought it odd that the burglars hadn't found their way in here. From the outside of the property, it was obvious that this room was your office. It was a strange sort of burglar who didn't think that a brand-new laptop was worth stealing.

I logged on and went through your bank statements. Just as Alec said, you had transferred seventy-five thousand pounds to him. It left you with near enough twenty-five thousand pounds, which you'd withdrawn on the Monday before your death. And now your savings account was completely empty. *Twenty-five thousand pounds, Dougie!* And no evidence as to where you'd spent it.

I looked in your diary to see whether there were any

obvious connections, and found that the day before you'd
withdrawn the money, you'd gone up to Aberdeen to
meet Gordy. I sat back in the seat and tried to recall
what he'd told me about the last time he'd seen you. I
remembered him saying he'd spoken to you on the phone
the Friday before you died, but I couldn't remember
any more than that. Your mobile phone account told me
who you'd called: dates, times, and phone numbers.
Some of the numbers I recognised – mine, Dad's, Alec's
– most of them I didn't. I printed out the itemised sheet
and put it in the pocket of my jeans.

'Isla?' Gavin said. He'd come into the room without
me noticing.

'Yeah?'

'Do you think anything's been taken?'

'As far as I can tell, only his Rolex watch.' I stood up.
'I have all his passwords and I've been going through
his accounts.' I told Gavin about the money you'd transferred to Alec and then the further twenty-five thousand
you'd withdrawn. 'And there's his mobile account. I can't
see who called him. Only the people he called. Can you
get that information from the phone company?'

'Why?' He was staring at me as if I wasn't making
any sense. 'What's this got to do with the burglary?'

'Everything! The burglary is just a part of it. Look!'
I showed him the mark around my throat. 'I was attacked
when I was in Glasgow.'

'*What? How?*' He turned me around so that light shone
onto my neck. 'For fuck's sake! Someone held you by
the throat?'

'Yes.'

'Are you okay? Did you go to the hospital? The police?'

'If you'd listened when we were in the living room
just now—'

'So you didn't go?'

'I was going to go now!'

'Why, Isla? *Why?*' He threw his arms out. 'Why do you always think you know better?'

'Because in this case I do know better!' I said. 'And it seems that the only way to find out the truth is to do it myself!'

'You are the mother of my children.' He pointed a finger in my face. 'This is not good enough. Collette told me you were up to something, and I was fool enough to defend you.' He took his mobile out of his pocket. 'I'm calling Collette, and then you need to make a statement.'

'A – I'm not up to something and B – What's it got to do with *her?*'

'I'm calling her about the *children*. We were going to the zoo.'

I stood with my arms crossed, staring through the window while Gavin spoke to Collette. Clouds had thrown a veil over the Pentlands, obscuring the hilltop with misty, grey water. I imagined you appearing through the mist, striding down the hill as you often did. I closed my eyes, momentarily convinced that if I wished hard enough I could make you appear. I could—

'Isla?'

I jumped.

'Why didn't you report this attack straight away?'

Gavin was beside me again, and with that look on his face – not-suffering-fools, of which I was clearly one. 'I was shocked. I just wanted to get home and lock the door.'

'But Collette came round in the evening. Why didn't you tell her?'

'Look,' there was a pounding in my temples, 'Collette

is great with the kids,' I tried to breathe, 'but she is *not*, and never will be, someone I would confide in.'

'You need—'

'You're interested in what I need?' I snapped. 'Isn't it a bit late for that?'

'Isla—'

'My brother has been *killed*, my dad is in hospital with a broken leg, I'm almost strangled by some thug in Glasgow, and I'm supposed to unburden myself to Collette? *Collette?*' I grabbed for his shirt and twisted the material around in my fist. 'What I need, Gavin. What I *need* is for you to listen to me or get the fuck out of my way.'

Our eyes held. I was angry enough to knock him through the window.

'How is your dad?' he asked.

I let go of his shirt and took a step back. 'He has a chest infection, but his leg seems to be healing.'

'That's good.' He scanned my face. 'Come through to the living room. You need to give a statement.'

I followed him through, and he called over one of the officers. His name was Archibald Glover, and Gavin sat with us both at your breakfast bar while he took my statement. Glover was keen and exacting. He moved me from one event to the other, teasing out detail. He made the whole process so logical that, for the most part, I managed to stay calm.

'The man who attacked you could be known to the police. Are you able to describe his tattoos?'

I thought back, but could only picture a confusion of ink. 'They were all over his arms, I know that much.'

'Were they in colour?'

'Yes. I remember blues and reds.'

'Good.' He wrote that down. 'Could you make out any of the designs?'

'His arms seemed really busy.' My hand went up to my throat. I tried to swallow but couldn't manage it. Gavin put a glass of water in my hand, and I took a couple of sips. The water sat in my mouth, growing warmer, until it strayed to the back of my throat and I swallowed without thinking.

'Take your time,' PC Glover said.

'He . . . the tattoos took up all of his arms. There wasn't much skin left.'

'Okay.' He paused. 'Were your eyes drawn to any of the designs?'

I took myself back to the moment I first saw him when he was walking towards me. 'I've just remembered – he had a black eye. It was his left one.'

'Great.'

'And then he asked me what I was looking at and I turned away, but not before I noticed the tattoo on his left shoulder.' An image surfaced in my mind. 'It was a dagger with a snake wrapped around it.'

PC Glover was pleased with this. He asked me some more questions and I told him about Paula and Jimmy, about the squat and Min Fraser, about the Lone Star pub and what the barman had told me about Dougie's time there. When he had all the information he needed, one of the technicians photographed my neck and took scrapings from underneath my fingernails. 'You never know,' he said. 'We could be lucky enough to find some skin cells.'

As I was leaving, Gavin walked to the door with me. 'I'll make sure this is dealt with as a matter of priority. We'll have a word with the barman and visit the squat. We'll find the man who did this to you.'

'It might have been Dougie who gave him the black eye.'

'Let's not jump to conclusions.'

'I know someone killed Dougie, Gavin. I can feel it in my bones.' I pressed my fist close to my heart. 'He withdrew twenty-five grand from his savings account the day after he visited Gordon O'Malley. You know Dougie was looking for his daughter?' Gavin nodded. 'I think he took the money to Glasgow with him. You need to check Dougie's mobile account to see who called him.'

He opened his mouth to reply, then seemed to read something in my eyes, closed his mouth tightly and went back into your house.

Ritchie was out the back when I arrived. He was building a low-rise brick wall to separate one area of the garden from another. He put down the brick he was holding and rubbed his hands on his jeans when he saw me coming. We walked towards each other across the grass. He was smiling. I was smiling. It was at moments like this that I knew I was falling in love with him, and the feeling always took me by surprise. I leant into his chest and his arms circled around me. We watched the dogs run off to the bottom of the garden and disappear into the hawthorn hedge. 'Rabbits beware,' he said.

I closed my eyes and relaxed against him.

'You were a while,' he said. He drew back to look down at me. 'What's that mark on your neck?'

'Yesterday.' I hid my face in his shoulder, breathed him in and made a concerted effort not to cry. 'Can we talk?'

We went inside and I sat in silence while he made us coffee. I felt as if I were balanced on the edge of a precipice. My whole life was so badly out of kilter, my heart so sore, my head so full with thoughts and what-ifs and what-nots, hoping that if all the details lined up in some sort of order, your death wouldn't feel like such an awful waste.

Ritchie put the coffee mugs on the table, then said softly, 'What's been happening?' His eyes were serious. 'How did you get that mark on your neck?'

'A Jack Bauer choke hold,' I said.

'*What*? Isla.' He came to my side of the table to kneel down at my feet. His jaw was tight as he reached up and touched my neck, running the back of his hand along the bruising. 'Are you . . . Who did this to you?'

'I'm okay. I knew I wasn't going to die because Dougie and I used to watch episodes of *24*, and when the man . . .' An air bubble of fear rose up in my throat and I coughed it away. 'When he came up behind me . . .' I trailed off again, unable to think about that moment – the rock-hard strength of his arm, the intensity, the terror – and still breathe, so I switched topic. 'I thought I saw Dougie this morning. I chased after some random bloke and swung him around to face me, all ready to shout – Where have you been? But it wasn't Dougie, was it? I mean – of course it wasn't! He's dead!' Despite my intentions to remain calm, my voice was climbing towards hysteria. 'For about five seconds I was really happy. I felt like everything was back to normal.'

'Isla, Isla.' Ritchie stood up, bringing me with him.

'I don't want to cry,' I said against his chest. 'I have to try to concentrate so that I can work it all out.'

It took me a minute or more to pull myself together, and then I talked through the last twenty-four hours, from Dad's accident to meeting the barman and then Min Fraser, being attacked, going to see Alec and finding out about the debt.

'Have you been to the police?' Ritchie said when I was finished.

'Yes. Because this morning, or maybe last night, Dougie's house was burgled. Gavin came with a team of police and I told them about the attack on me too.'

'Did they take skin samples from underneath your fingernails?'

'Yes.' I examined my nails. They were short and ragged, but they looked clean. 'But I'd had a shower in between, and . . . You know about stuff like that?'

'Leonie loves *CSI*. I'm often forced to watch it with her.'

'I probably washed any DNA evidence away.' I sighed. 'And I was married to a policeman too.' I shook my head against my own idiocy. 'It's just . . . I'm finding it really hard to think straight. I'm not sleeping well, and I'm worried about the kids, especially Caitlin.'

'The police have the resources to pursue this, Isla. Let them do their job.'

'Alec said the same.'

'Will Gavin help speed things up?'

'I think so. Maybe. Maybe not. I shouted at him because he was . . .' I rubbed my aching head. 'He was just being Gavin. Trying to steamroller me.'

'How?'

'Just with Collette. I wanted him to listen to me about Dougie. He already knew that Dougie didn't drink much. He'd read the procurator fiscal's report; I hadn't. But still he seems to think Dougie's death was an accident even though the money and my name in the diary and Lucy O'Malley and everything and . . .' I sat back in my seat and bit my lip. 'Do you think that the man who attacked me might be a loan shark?'

'Hard to say. I didn't know Dougie and I don't know Tania. There are ways of borrowing money that don't involve such desperate measures. Is Tania really that type of person?'

I thought about what Tania was capable of. Drug dealing, adultery, and spite sprang to mind. 'She has an addictive personality, and she often makes poor choices.'

'And there's no one else in Dougie's life that you think might have sucked him into their problems?'

'He used to be in the marines, and he would have gone to the ends of the earth for half a dozen of his men, but I saw most of them at his funeral and they were none the wiser than me.' I leant my elbows on the table. 'And then there's Gordy. Dougie always said he was very one-track about finding his daughter. Gordy told me he last spoke to Dougie on the phone on the Friday before he died, but according to Dougie's work diary he went up to Aberdeen on the Sunday, two days later. So either Gordy is lying or Dougie didn't keep the appointment. Maybe Gordy racked up a lot of debt and Dougie felt he should help him out.'

'Is that likely?'

'I wouldn't have thought so, but if Lucy was in some sort of danger . . .'

Ritchie stood up and brought a carton of juice to the table. 'Would you like a glass?'

'Please.'

'Are you going to talk to Tania?' he asked, filling two glasses with juice.

'Yes. Although she's a pain in the arse, she's not a liar.'

Ritchie's phone started ringing. He looked at the screen and I watched his finger hesitate for a second before he pressed the button and answered it. 'Yes?' There was a long pause while he listened. 'Is this really necessary?' Another pause. 'Give me an hour.' He put the phone down on the counter, sighing. 'Isla—'

'You have to go?' I stood up, and drank back the juice.

'That's okay. I need to visit my dad and do lots of other stuff.'

'Sorry.' He kissed me. 'One day I'll have a Monday to Friday job like normal people.'

'I like you as you are.' I kissed him back. 'Thank you for listening.'

'Leave Myrtle here if you want to.'

Both dogs had just come in through the dog flap and were sprawled out together in Rebus's bed.

'It really is a dog's life,' I said. 'I'll come and collect her later.' I thought for a second. 'Do you mind if I bring the kids with me? I'm picking them up at four.'

'No. I'd love to meet them.'

'Okay.' I opened the front door, then stopped, uncertain. 'Shall I tell them we're going out, or play it down a bit?'

'Might be better to say we're friends and take it from there.'

'Will do.'

'And Isla?'

'Yes?' I turned back to him.

'Don't put yourself in danger again.'

'I won't.'

I left his house feeling less stressed than when I'd arrived. Nothing was sorted, but it made me feel better to know that Ritchie cared. The more time I spent with him, the surer I became that he was my future. I just needed to find out what had happened to you Dougie, and then I could move on with my life.

That was my hope.

There were road works on the bypass, so I drove through town to the hospital. I felt better after seeing Ritchie and was managing to think about nothing in particular – I needed to shop for fruit and washing powder . . . arrange something for Fin's birthday next month . . . empty your fridge – when I glanced in my rear-view mirror. Instantly my insides flashed a terror warning. It was him. He was diagonally behind me at the wheel of a Golf. I recognised his bald head, the rough neck and the bruising over his left eye. And the tattoos, creeping over his shoulder and down his arms like a skin disease. I blinked several times, but it made no difference.

I jumped the lights before I even registered I was doing it. Several cars sounded their horns, but I drove on, along Cluny Gardens, past the duck pond and through the Charterhall junction towards the King's Buildings. Just after the turn off to the Observatory there were cars stopped at the lights in front of me and I had to wait behind them. I was humming, a high-pitched whine that increased my sense of alarm. The humming grew louder when the Golf pulled up behind me – and – it wasn't him! It was a perfectly innocuous man with curly hair and Harry Potter specs.

My shoulders slumped from relief, but by the time my heart had returned to an almost normal rhythm, I began to worry again. Would this be the latest thing, then? Along with the nightmares and the persistent grief-ache in my chest, I would start seeing things. First you and then him. A happy, out-of-body high when I thought I saw you and then, when I thought I saw him, a concentrated terror that was slick enough to make me risk my own life and possibly the lives of other drivers.

I drove the rest of the way to the hospital at twenty-five miles an hour, in the inside lane, then sat in the hospital car park with my eyes shut. Five minutes to talk myself out of 'rattled' and into 'calm'. Five minutes to reassure myself that I was alive and my children were safe and everything was okay. You were dead and that was shit. But no one else was going to die. No one.

I spent a couple of hours with Dad sorting out his locker, listening to his gripes, and helping him move from bed to chair. It was a bit of a palaver and he wasn't the best patient. Halfway between bed and chair he had a coughing fit and the nurse came over. We settled him in bed again, and then I had a word with her before I left.

'The chest infection is a setback,' she said. 'And with your brother's recent death he has a lot to cope with.'

'I want to take him back to my house as soon as he's able.'

'That won't be for a week or so yet,' she told me. 'We have to make sure he's able to balance without falling over. And we'll also need to ensure that the chest infection has cleared up.'

'Okay. Thank you.'

I headed out of the hospital fully intending to go straight home, but Tania's flat was between the hospital and home and so it made sense for me to go there. Then I'd know whether or not she had anything to do with the debt. It felt like affirmation from the universe when I spotted a free parking space right outside the main door. (How often did that happen?) I pressed the buzzer for her flat and then after twenty seconds I pressed it again. Second time lucky.

'Yes?'

'Tania, it's Isla.'

I expected to have to persuade her to let me in, but she buzzed me up without question. I climbed to the top floor, bypassing a family of four on their way out. An excited wee boy, aged about seven, was carrying an orange and red box-kite.

'Come on, Dad!' he shouted. 'Before the wind goes away.'

'That's not likely,' his dad said, sharing a smile with his wife.

'Isla, you hold the kite and I'll start running.'
   'It's too heavy!'
   'Just hold it!'
   Off you ran, and within seconds, the kite lifted up, up and away, you hanging on tight to the string. 'Quick Isla! Come and have a shot!'

Small incidents were gateways into memories of you. Would I ever get to the stage where children, restaurants, work, houses, gardens, television programmes, water, pretty much everything didn't remind me of you? I hoped not, because although it hurt, I never wanted to forget that I had a brother.

Tania had left the door ajar, and I walked in, closing it behind me.

'I'm in here!' she shouted, and I followed her voice to the kitchen. She was wearing her strawberry-coloured kimono, her feet were bare, and she was filling the kettle. 'Cup of tea?'

'Great, thanks.'

She put a couple of teabags and some boiling water into two mugs and took the milk from the fridge. 'I'll let you do your own,' she said.

She dunked her own teabag a couple of times, then took the mug over to the window, draping herself on the wide sill. Her face wore a washed-out, exhausted expression.

I sorted my tea, my eyes straying towards a large notice she had up on the kitchen wall: 'Addiction makes you trash your values to meet your needs – don't do it! – call me.' And then, handwritten underneath, was the name 'Simon' and a mobile phone number.

'You must have noticed Simon,' Tania said. 'He came to Dougie's funeral with me.'

'Marie and I wondered who he was.' I dumped my teabag in the bin. 'Known him long?'

'About a month. I might have started drinking again if I hadn't brought him with me. Funerals are exactly the sort of situations where people crack.' She lit a cigarette and blew smoke over her shoulder and through the open window. 'If you don't believe me, go along to a meeting. Talk to people about their stress triggers.'

'I do believe you.'

She gave me a tight smile. 'I take it this isn't a social call.'

'No, it isn't.' I walked across to the window and stood next to her. I wanted to be sure to maintain eye contact. 'Tania, was Dougie helping you pay off a debt?'

'What sort of debt?' She sucked on the cigarette.

'A debt involving a lot of money.'

'No.' She exhaled, and smoke drifted upwards, almost obscuring her face. 'Why are you asking me?'

'Because I know that Dougie often helped you out. And also because you came to Dougie's house looking for money.'

'Only two thousand quid. And it wasn't to pay off a debt. It was to go on holiday.'

'You know nothing about a loan he might have taken out or feel responsible for?'

'No.'

Her eyes were unflinching. She wasn't lying. She was bold, Tania. She had no interest in changing my opinion of her, either through truth or pretence. 'He didn't mention anything to you about helping someone out?'

'No.' She shook her head. 'Dougie was . . .' I watched her eyes fill up. 'Kind.'

I saw my own grief mirrored in her eyes, and it shocked me, Dougie. It shouldn't have, but it did. I'm ashamed to admit that I'd assumed you loved her more than she loved you. But I was wrong. I had no idea how much she cared about you, and in that moment I saw how much. Her pain was acute, jagged as glass. Piercing.

I recoiled from her, stepping backwards, straight into the arms of a warm body. Startled, I whirled around. It was Simon. He was wearing only jeans, his hairless chest pumped up with muscle.

'What are you ladies talking about?' His accent was surprisingly public school. And so was his hair, flopping over his forehead and flicking up in blond waves like a girl's. 'I'm Simon.' He held out his hand. 'And you must be Isla.'

'Yes, I must be,' I said, not taking his hand. My mind was putting two and two together and making six. Simon was half naked; Tania was wearing a silk robe with nothing underneath. I moved very swiftly from feeling that Tania and I were united in grief to thinking that she was suffering from lack of sleep because she'd been up all night having sex with Simon.

'So what can we help you with?' Simon said. He was unsmiling. There was steel behind the posh hair and the manners. He put a proprietorial arm around Tania, and she let him, not encouraging him, but not pulling away either.

'Fuck.' I stared up at the cracked ceiling, then back at the two of them. 'You two deserve each other,' I said, and walked out of the kitchen. It was a poor exit line, but I was hurting on your behalf, Dougie. I wanted to protect you and your memory. I wanted to fight for you.

You and me, aged nine, in the swing park. I'd punched a boy. Blood was spurting from his nose and he was wailing like a banshee. You came running over to see what was going on.

'He kicked Marie!' I said, pointing to our sister who was standing beside me with her thumb in her mouth, her face streaked with dirt and tears, a shoeprint on her skirt.

'We'd better go home,' you said.

You picked Marie up and carried her, half in your arms, half over your shoulder, the mile or so back to our house.

'My hand's killing me,' I said, trying to shake the pain away.

'You need to punch with the front of your hand so your first two knuckles connect with the face,' you told me. 'It was on Bonanza.'

When the boy's mother turned up at our house that evening, you said you'd done it. The boy didn't contradict you because being been beaten by a girl was a double humiliation. Mum smacked you, not hard, but just enough for you to feel it. I spent the rest of the summer giving you my orange juice and crisps.

I was just about to climb into my car, when Tania shouted after me, 'Wait, Isla!'

I waited. She'd thrown on a jumper and some sweat pants, but her feet were still bare. 'You don't think I'm sleeping with Simon, do you?' she said.

'Aren't you?'

'Fuck no!' She screwed up her face as if the very idea was distasteful. 'We were up late. He stayed over. On the couch! I'm not shagging him.' She gave a sharp laugh. 'God, Isla! You really do have a low opinion of me.' She folded her arms across her chest. 'I loved Dougie.'

'I know.' I shook my head. 'But you did—'

'Cheat on him when he was alive?' She held up her index finger. 'Once. Only once, and I know that was bad, but—'

'Your dad had just died?'

'He was a right git, but somehow I still felt sad.' She shivered. 'Weird.'

'I'm sorry,' I said. 'I'm freaked out and tired and . . . fuck. I dunno.'

'It's okay to grieve, Isla.'

I tried to smile.

She sighed and pulled her arms more tightly over her ribcage. 'I've been thinking. I was out of order the other day. I shouldn't have tried to take the money and I shouldn't have said Dougie was in Glasgow because of you. The more I think about it, the more I think I might have heard wrong.'

'No. You heard right. My name was in his diary.'

'Oh.' She frowned. 'Do you know why?'

'No. I'm not sure it means anything, though.' I found myself telling her what had happened so far. I should have kept my mouth shut, but I didn't see the harm in telling her, and she listened, keenly, following the puzzle along with me. And if I'd had any residual suspicion that she was in any way involved, it was dispelled as I spoke. She was genuinely taken aback by the news.

'Fuck's sake! And you think someone killed him?'

'I do. Maybe by accident, maybe deliberately. Think about what a good swimmer he was.'

She walked around in a circle, piecing it all together. 'Could the debt be Marie's? Or your dad's?'

'Dad has his own house and enough money to live on. He'd never climb into bed with loan sharks. And Marie lives in Norway. She has no connections to Glasgow.'

Tania stopped in front of me. 'So what are we going to do?'

'We?' I stepped back. 'Tania, you don't need to get involved in this.'

'I want to get involved.' She leant in towards me so that our faces were only inches from each other. 'I know I brought trouble with me, and I know your mum thought Dougie should have dumped me long before he married me, and I don't blame her.' She shook her head. 'I don't blame any of you. But Dougie stuck by me and I'm going to stick by him.'

I must have looked sceptical.

'Don't shut me out.' Her eyes shone. 'Please.'

I deliberated for a bit, but I couldn't say no. Sincerity radiated off her like heat from a barbecue. 'Okay.' I climbed into my car. Me and Tania as allies? It was a first. 'I'll let you know what the police say.'

'I can go through to Glasgow with you.'

'I don't think that's a good idea. If they have already killed Dougie then what would they do to you and me?'

'Keep me in mind.' She stepped back. 'The offer's there, Isla.'

I drove away feeling as if something inside me was recalibrating. When Tania ruined our fortieth birthday party by having herself arrested for using cocaine in the loos, you were already separated, but still you persisted in standing by her. 'Nobody's just one thing, Isla,' you told me. 'She has a good side.'

It seemed like I was seeing that good side at last. Timing, huh?

7. Dreams Are Made of This

I left Tania's and managed to arrive home just after four. As soon as my car pulled up outside the house, Fin ran out to meet me. 'Have you got Myrtle, Mum? Cos we can't find her. She's not in the garden and she's not in the house.'

'It's okay, love. I left her with a friend of mine.'

'Who?'

'He's called Ritchie.' I climbed out of the car. 'Do you want to come and meet him?'

'Okay.'

'I'll see whether Caitlin wants to come too.'

I went into the house and straight upstairs to my room to stash your money, cufflinks, and medal safely in a bottom drawer behind my winter jumpers. I knew I'd have to yield half the money and either the cufflinks or the medal to Marie, but it would be in my time, not hers.

I found Caitlin and Collette in the kitchen. 'We're making a cake,' Caitlin said. 'To cheer ourselves up because we were looking forward to going to the zoo to see the pandas, but Dad was called to work in the morning.'

'Not to worry,' Collette said, giving me a pointed look. 'We can go next weekend.'

'That's great.' I smiled at Collette who was filling the sink with soapy water. She'd brought her own apron with her; I had to admire her forethought. She was a born mother, and I knew she'd asked Gavin to have his vasectomy reversed, but he was strictly a two-children-and-no-more sort of a guy, and even her persistence wasn't changing that.

'I left Myrtle with a friend of mine,' I said. 'I'm just going to get her. Do you want to come, Caitlin?'

'I'd rather stay and finish this,' she said, pouring the batter into the tin. 'It'll be out of the oven by the time you get home. And then we're going to decorate it.'

'Okay. Fin's coming with me.'

Fin chatted the whole way to Ritchie's. We talked about football and school and then about Ritchie. 'How did you meet him, Mum?'

'Walking Myrtle. He has a Westie called Rebus.'

'Does Myrtle like Rebus?'

'They're kindred spirits. It's all about digging holes and chasing rabbits.' I turned into Ritchie's driveway. 'You'll see.'

'Wow! This is a nice place,' Fin said, taking in the house and acre of land around it. 'His garden's almost big enough to be a football pitch. Does he have any kids?'

'A daughter, but she lives in England with her mum.'

'So he's divorced like you and Dad?'

'I'm not sure he was ever married.'

We climbed out of the car and the dogs came bounding over to meet us. Ritchie was back to working on the wall, and I took Fin over and introduced them to each other. They hit it off straight away. Fin is reliable that way, isn't he? He's always been easy with meeting new people. Soon they were playing football while I sat on the terrace with a mug of tea. I watched them both for a bit, smiled at their friendly banter, then rang the hospital. Dad sounded awful, proper weary, like he needed to sleep for a month. After I'd wished him a good night, I spoke to the nurse in charge. She said the antibiotics weren't working yet, and that they were going to take further sputum samples to send them for analysis. 'He's going to be okay though, isn't he?' I asked.

'Yes, I'm sure he is,' she said. 'But he's got a fair way to go yet.'

I called Marie next and tried to talk to her about Dad and about you, but she was having none of it. 'I can't talk now, Isla. You need to ring me when the kids are in bed. Have you forgotten how exhausting under-fives are?'

That night I dreamt as usual about you and me cycling home, my lungs fit to burst with all the effort I put in. And then there was the horror of your body in the morgue. I tried to wake myself up, but instead I woke into another dream. It was night-time, and I was in Glasgow, running along the banks of the river, running and running, but not moving forward. Min Fraser's face loomed into my vision. She was grinning like a clown. Her teeth were tombstones, and they floated out of her mouth towards me. RIP Douglas McTeer was written across them.

I jerked awake, my hands gripping the duvet, my heart juddering like a truck emergency-braking. I climbed out of bed and went to the bathroom. The air felt thick and dense, and kept me short of breath. I sat on the edge of the bath and stared at myself in the mirror. I was pale and ghostly and I was showcasing a couple of puffy, black half-moons underneath each eye. Mum had been dead for three years. You had been dead less than three weeks. Dad was ill in hospital, and Marie was . . . just being Marie.

Once we'd been a family.

I went downstairs and googled 'twins, non-identical'. If Mum had been pregnant now, she would have come back from her ultrasound scans with photographs of us in the womb. There are loads on the Internet. In the early stages of pregnancy, when there's more room, the babies can be both head up or head down, facing front or back. But as space becomes an issue, they lie top to toe, and heads become familiar with feet. Such a photo would have been on page one of our baby book instead of our christening photo, both of us in long woollen dresses, you much smaller than me because I'd been the greedy twin, pushed my way out first and weighed two pounds more than you. You started your life in an incubator. For over a month Mum carted me back and forth to the baby unit until you were able to come home with us. You'd been the quieter, more cautious toddler. I'd been the one who took risks. Aged three, I'd chipped my front teeth. By the time I was seven I'd broken a wrist and a collarbone. I had my appendix out aged nine. I remembered coming round from the anaesthetic, and there you were Dougie, sitting on a chair beside my bed reading the *Beano*.

At breakfast the next day I was like a half-shut knife.

'I've been thinking about that time just after Dad left us,' Caitlin said, buttering her toast. 'Remember, Mum?' I nodded. 'When you weren't well and Uncle Dougie used to come round and make us meals and all he could make was spaghetti bolognese and he always put too much garlic in it.'

'He was good at cooked breakfasts as well,' Fin said pouring cereal into his bowl. 'Can we go back to Ritchie's again today?'

'Who's Ritchie?' Caitlin asked.

'Mum's boyfriend.'

'*What?*' Caitlin dropped her toast on the plate. 'You have a *boyfriend*?'

'No. I . . .'

'Oh my God, you do!' She shook her head at me, her expression one of exaggerated offence. 'Why didn't *I* get to meet him?'

'You could have come with us yesterday!'

'I thought you meant a woman friend, like Sarah or someone!'

'It's no big deal.'

'I can't believe Fin got to meet him before me! That's so unfair!' She picked up her school bag and flounced to the front door. 'I'm not cleaning my teeth!'

'Sorry, Mum,' Fin said, not looking sorry at all.

On the journey to the bus stop, Caitlin made me promise I would take her to meet Ritchie after school, *immediately* after school, and I had to tell her everything I knew about him. 'I'll need to check that he's going to be there,' I said.

'What does he do for a job?'

'Computer programming.'

'His house is really big,' Fin said. 'And his garden is almost as big as a football pitch.'

'Is he rich, Mum?' Caitlin asked.

'I don't know! We haven't been going out for long.'

'It's about time you got a boyfriend,' Caitlin said. 'Even better if he's rich.'

'Not that you're superficial or anything,' I said.

'It's better being rich. You don't have as much to worry about.'

'Somehow I don't think it's that simple.' I pulled in

at the lay-by close to the bus stop just as the bus was arriving. 'Have a good day.' I gave them both a kiss on their cheeks. 'Work hard.'

I watched them run to the stop. Fin was laden down with football kit and a rucksack almost as big as he was. Halfway to the stop he dropped his kitbag and Caitlin picked it up for him then pushed him ahead of her, roughly, so that he stumbled. Before he landed on the ground, she grabbed the back of his rucksack and held him upright, keeping hold of him until he climbed up the steps.

The bus pulled away and I switched off the car's engine. The sun was streaming in through the side windows, warming the car's interior and making me feel sleepy. Cars and lorries thundered along the road. I found the sound soothing. People going about their business, the stuff of daily living. Since your death I found myself seeking out pockets of time like this, ordinary minutes when I didn't feel any grief or worry for the future, I could simply be, in the moment, just breathing.

I turned my head away from the light, closed my eyes and relaxed into the purple darkness of my eyelids. Sometimes sleep is the most seductive feeling on this earth, isn't it? And I was surrendering, willingly, blissfully. My body melded with the seat. My heart didn't ache. Even the chatter in my head had ceased. I wasn't sure how long I stayed like this, more than a minute, less than five, perhaps. Peaceful . . . until I started to notice a gradual tightening in my solar plexus. The slow creep of ivy, wrapping around my core.

My eyes snapped open and it was suddenly bright again. Movement flashed in my peripheral vision, and I turned around in my seat, but by the time my eyes adjusted to the light I was too late to catch the full view. Whoever had been there was gone, and all that remained was the ghost of an image, like the impression left on your retina after you've been looking at strobe lights. A man's tattooed arm, the ink blurring into a haze of colour. A bare shoulder and a thick fleshy neck.

'You imagined it,' I told myself, speaking out loud. 'You imagined him in the Golf. You imagined him here.'

I started the car's engine and pulled out of the lay-by, humming loudly to myself, drowning out my anxiety until I could think of some words of comfort. Before long I remembered you telling me what happened when you left the marines. Twenty years of service, and you felt lucky to have escaped with your nerves intact. But still you had frightening flashbacks to periods when your life was under threat. 'Post-traumatic stress is natural,' you'd told me. 'You just have to stop it getting out of hand.'

Only two days ago, my life had been under threat. Was it any wonder I was imagining it happening again?

I drove to the hospital on amber alert, watching out for tattooed men driving Golfs, but I didn't see any. Overnight rain had washed the Edinburgh streets clean, and sunlight dried the pavements until they sparkled. I took a detour so I could drive past Arthur's Seat and the crags, spectacular with blue sky as a backdrop.

'Race you to the top!' I shouted, and as usual I gave it my best shot, but you still beat me. Mum, Dad, and Marie were a long way behind and we sat on top of Arthur's Seat playing king of the castle. Edinburgh belonged to us. All we surveyed was ours, and you were the victor so you got to share it out between us. You gave me Princes Street and the West End. You claimed

the Royal Mile and the Castle for yourself, but you'd
let me come inside the Castle if we were being invaded.
'I'll always stand by my family,' you said.

It was a busy Monday morning, and the hospital corridors were teeming with people: porters wheel-chairing
patients from wards to X-ray, doctors moving around
in groups, physios gearing up for the day's exercises. It
wasn't visiting time yet, but I was in early to speak to
the doctor. I went to check on Dad first. He was barely
awake, unshaven and dishevelled, one hand holding an
oxygen mask on his chest, his breakfast untouched on
the tray table next to him. 'Morning Dad.'

He didn't look at me. He stared ahead, seemingly
mesmerised by the blank wall.

'Dad.' I gently shook his shoulder. 'Did you not want
your breakfast?'

He turned his head slowly towards me. 'Isla.' His eyes
were glazed and it made me wonder what drugs they
had him on.

'Are you hungry?'

He shook his head.

'What about this mask, Dad? Are you supposed to
be wearing it?'

'Makes my mouth dry.'

I gave him some water, and he drank it slowly,
savouring each sip.

'I've brought you something from the kids.' I pulled
stuff out of my bag. 'Caitlin wanted me to give you a
slice of the cake she made yesterday, and there's a card
with it.' I moved his breakfast tray onto the windowsill
and placed the cake on the tray table in front of him.
'And Fin printed out the latest blog from that football
pundit you like.'

He nodded, but I could see it was all too much for him. His attention span was fractured, bludgeoned by exhaustion. I waited until he'd finished the water, then helped him with his mask and sat down beside his bed. Almost immediately he closed his eyes and dozed off. I held his hand, warming his cold fingers, worried that he was going to drift away from me, that your death and then breaking his leg had sapped his strength, and now this chest infection was stealing the last of his fight. It was like when Auntie Sheila died, remember? She went into hospital for routine gall bladder surgery, and three months later she was dead. And Mum. She came into hospital for chemotherapy and never left. Seven weeks later, and she was dead.

Dad's doctor was called Dr Brightman. She was a young woman, very professional, but unable to give me much reassurance. When I'd finished speaking to her I wasn't sure I knew any more than I had at the beginning of the conversation. Her message seemed to be a case of 'wait and see'.

I bought a coffee and stood by the vending machine to drink it, then braced myself and called Marie. I told her that Dad seemed much worse to me, and she lost her temper in seconds. 'Is he *really* ill or isn't he?'

'He's weak, Marie. He has a temperature, and his chest is bad.'

'What are the medical staff saying?'

'That they're treating the infection and they hope for improvement soon.'

'So he's fine then?'

'No. He's not fine!'

'Jesus Isla! If you'd taken him to the doctor when I told you.' Protracted, significant sighing. 'Have you got Dougie's house on the market yet?'

'I'm going to the solicitor after I've spoken to you.'

'Well, that's something.'

'His house was broken into.'

'Dougie's? When?'

'Yesterday.' She asked me why the alarm didn't go off. I told her I didn't know. I wasn't about to admit that I must have forgotten to set it even though I was convinced I had set it, because it would give her something else to complain about. 'I'm worried that Dougie's death wasn't an accident,' I told her.

There was a pause and then she shouted something in Norwegian, a dozen words with Martha's name tacked on the end of them.

'Do you need to get back to the kids?' I asked.

'What do you mean, Dougie's death wasn't an accident?'

I gave her a quick summary of events so far, omitting the part where I was attacked because I was sure she would only blame me for going there. I wasn't even sure she could hear me as there was an ever-increasing amount of noise in the background at her end, and then she said, 'You're really doing my head in with all this, Isla.' And she put the phone down on me.

Sisterly support. Marvellous.

When, an hour later, she called me back, I didn't answer. I was already in the car driving to your solicitor's. Then I heard a text message arrive in my phone, and, while I was waiting in a queue at the Kirk Brae lights, I read it. 'I'm stressed, Isla. I'm grieving for Dougie too. You have to take care of Dad. I would join you if I could. I know I'm short-tempered. I'm sorry.'

I didn't reply – okay, so I was deliberately leaving her to stew in her own juices – I went into your solicitor's and waited in the foyer for my appointment. There were details of properties for sale on one of the walls, glossy photographs of houses and flats with huge asking prices. Tiny flats where a noisy neighbour would drive you to distraction, cost more than I had earned in fifteen years. I wondered how Caitlin and Fin would ever get on the property ladder. They'd have to choose careers as bankers or drug dealers. Forget professions like teachers and nurses. Nice guys finished last.

You and I differed on politics, Dougie. You wanted an independent Scotland; I wasn't convinced. You felt we'd better manage our income without Westminster's interference. I worried that an independent Scotland would be bankrupt in five years. I wasn't sure that Alex Salmond and his cronies were really up to the job. And in the real world, David rarely beat Goliath.

I waited my turn and was called into one of the rooms to speak to Bethany Tchuda, one of the solicitors who dealt with conveyancing. She was young and pretty in a healthy, sun-kissed way. 'What can I help you with today?'

'I have a property to register,' I said.

'And what's the address?'

I gave her your address and she typed it into the computer, looking at the screen as she spoke. 'Oh yes! Mr McTeer was in a few weeks ago to discuss a possible sale. It's a lovely farm cottage that one, in a really popular area right now.'

I couldn't speak. I felt like the hole I'd fallen into had just grown twice as deep and I didn't have a long enough ladder to see daylight, never mind climb out. You'd given seventy-five thousand pounds to Alec for part-share in the business, and then you'd emptied your savings account of twenty-five thousand pounds. But that wasn't enough. *You were selling your house?* Your house. The

cottage you'd given body and soul to. Jesus Dougie –
how much *was* the debt?

'Mrs McTeer?'

Bethany's smile was framed with pillar-box red lipstick.
Her skin was flawless. Her eyes were bright as a puppy's.
She looked, in fact, as if her life was a series of happy
walks in the park. If she had a brother, he would never
keep secrets, and he would never drown. Both her parents
would be alive and well, and would live into their nineties.
Her sister would be her best friend.

'Mrs McTeer?' she repeated, her smile holding fast.

'I'm not Mrs McTeer. Douglas McTeer is my brother.'

'Are you joint owners?'

'No. He isn't able to be here.' I scratched my head,
wondering why the right hand didn't seem to know what
the left hand was doing. Only days ago I'd seen one of
the partners for the reading of your will. 'Were you the
person my brother spoke to?'

'Let's see now.' She stared back at the screen. 'Morag
took down the details.'

'Would it be possible to speak to Morag?'

'Yes . . . But I'm sure I can help you with everything.'

'I'm sure you can, but I'd like to know whether she
can remember my brother.'

'Okay.' Her smile held. 'She'll be back from an appointment in about ten minutes.' She typed a little more. 'So
you're here on your brother's behalf?'

'My brother was killed a couple of weeks ago.'

Her smile fell away. Even worse, her lips started to
tremble. I felt mean, as if I had delivered the hot, miserable stench of reality straight onto her lap. 'I'm sorry
for your loss,' she said. 'Very sorry.'

'Thank you.' I stood up. 'I'll wait for Morag, if that's
okay?'

'Of course. I'll let her know.'

I felt sad – again. Sadness had become my default state. Sadness and anxiety, twin companions, set to break me. I went back into the foyer and stood staring at the wall of properties, faking interest in a five-bed detached house in the Grange. Offers over one and a half million. The photographs of the interior were drenched in sunlight. Natural wood gleamed, mirrors sparkled, deep-pile carpets welcomed bare feet. The kitchen was pristine white and steel. Coffee maker, steam oven, five-ring gas hob. And the garden had a stone-built pizza oven and barbecue. It was a happy home for happy people. And it made me want to cry.

Bend but never break, Isla.

You'd said that to me when Gavin left me. You'd helped me more than any other human being on the planet. You'd been a rock, Dougie. An absolute, fucking rock. I never knew who called you. Was it Mum or Dad? Or did you somehow just intuit that your twin was sinking into a depression? I didn't want my children to be brought up without two parents in the house. I missed Gavin as the other half of my couple, but I missed him more as the father of my children. Family life lost all its gloss and ease. The children pined for him and so did I. When I told him that, he said that was the reason he left me. If I'd been less of a mother and more of a wife, he'd never have strayed.

You told me he was a wanker. You bought the cottage close to mine and helped me with the kids. It would be okay, you told me. A long road, a stony road, but I'd get there.

And with your help I had got there.

So why didn't you let me return the support? Over those last few days of your life, you must have wanted to talk to someone, lean on someone, a friend, a parent, a sister?

Not this sister. Not Marie either. Not Dad. Not Tania. Nor Alec. Nor Gordy. No one.

I wanted to believe that you'd written my name on that page of your diary because you were intending to talk to me, tell me what you were going through. I wanted to believe that so badly, Dougie. But I couldn't. Whatever had happened, I felt you'd made the decision to go it alone.

'Miss McTeer?' It was Bethany. I could see that she was already bouncing back. Her smile was almost as wide as before. 'Morag's back from her lunch.' I followed Bethany to another room where an older woman sat, drinking from a mug. She had a severe face – over-plucked eyebrows, hooked nose, and thin lips.

'Hello.' She shook my hand, her manner kindly, belying the severity of her features. 'I'm very sorry about your brother. And about the fact that Miss Tchuda was unaware of his death.' She pointed me towards a chair. 'Our firm has grown so much larger over the years, and it does sometimes mean that wires get crossed.'

'Thank you.' I sat forward in the seat, almost teetering on the edge. Keeping my balance gave me something physical to concentrate on. 'I was wondering whether you could remember what my brother said when he came in to register his property.'

She nodded. 'I do remember your brother. He came in on Monday, the ninth of September, and was very businesslike, in a nice way, but he wasn't really in to chatting. He was keen to know how much his cottage was worth and how quickly it would sell.' She took a sip of coffee. 'He said that if he did put it on the market, he would prefer to sell at a fixed price. I advised him to give it a few weeks with offers over.'

'Did he agree to that?'

'No. He said that he'd be looking for a quick sale.'

'Did he show interest in buying anything else?'

She shook her head. 'I got the feeling he was unsure of exactly how much equity he needed to release. He left by saying that he would come back in when he knew whether he needed to sell or not.'

I thought for a moment. 'Thank you. That's helpful.' I tipped forward and then back on the seat before I said quietly, 'The property can go on the market now.' It hurt to say that, Dougie. I couldn't bear the thought of someone else living in your house, but Marie was on my case, and sooner or later your house was going to have to be sold so it might as well be now.

'I know this is difficult,' Morag said. 'I lost a brother. It'll be ten years ago this month. We still miss him.'

I didn't dare look at her as she said this because her empathy would surely disable me. 'We'll go for offers over,' I said. Then I told her about the burglary, leaving out all the complications. 'I'll need to tidy up before anyone comes to take photographs.'

'No problem.'

She asked me some property questions that I answered to the best of my abilities and then we said our goodbyes. When I went outside, I noticed I'd had a missed call from an Aberdeen number. Gordy? I sat in my car and called the number back.

It was Gordy, and he didn't even bother with a hello, just launched in immediately. 'The police were round here this morning asking me questions about Dougie and whether I knew anything about his trip to Glasgow. It's been upsetting for my wife. Did you know they were coming?'

'I—'

'You might have warned me. It was a shock. I hadn't even told Anne that Dougie was dead. You have to be careful when people have cancer. Being upset like this could send Anne into a relapse.'

'I—'

'I don't know why Dougie went to Glasgow. I told you that already. I never thought you'd send the police round. If I'd known . . .'

I held the phone away from my ear and let him rant. How did you handle him? Was he this insistent with you?

'. . . without making any sense.' He took a breath. 'Are you still there?'

'Yes, I'm here. I'm sorry, Gordy. I should have called you.'

'How could you think I had anything to do with his disappearance? Dougie and I were mates.'

'I know. It's just that the day after he visited you, he emptied his savings account.'

'When? What?'

'It says in his diary that he visited you on the Sunday.'

'He didn't. He didn't visit me on the Sunday.'

I wasn't sure whether to believe that or not. 'There's no trace of the money he withdrew from his account. We think – well, I think – he was meeting someone in Glasgow and giving him cash.'

'For what?'

'I don't know. I did think it might have something to do with Lucy, but if you don't know anything about it?' I expected Gordy to dive in with a long-winded answer, but he didn't. 'The boy Lucy ran off with, what did he look like?'

Silence.

'Gordy?'

'What?'

I repeated my question.

'Jimmy Pearcy? He looked like most of them do. Skinny, brown shoulder-length hair, brown eyes.'

'Did he have acne?' A traffic warden was moving along the line of cars. I checked my ticket and saw that I had ten minutes left.

'A bit, maybe.'

'Do you have a photograph of him that you could email to me?'

'I do. Why?'

'When I was in Glasgow the other day, I met a couple of homeless teenagers. The girl was called Paula, the boy Jimmy. It's a long shot, but you never know. He might be your Jimmy.'

'I'll email you right now. What's your address?'

'Email me at Dougie's; I'm going there in a minute.'

'What took you to Glasgow?'

'I was tracking Dougie's last few hours.' My hand felt up around my throat. 'To see whether I could work out why he was there.'

He started going on again about Anne and how upset she'd been. 'We have a missing daughter, and the police coming to the door is never going to be good news—'

'I'm sorry, Gordy,' I shouted. 'Traffic problems. Have to go.' I cut him off. I was a mother, I had some sympathy for Anne, of course I did, but her feelings were pretty low down on my pecking order of concerns. The traffic warden reached my car and peered at the time on the ticket, then she stared through the window at me. I ignored her and called the police station to see whether I could speak to PC Glover. He wasn't available, so I called Gavin instead. I asked him whether he'd heard anything about the investigation.

'Not yet.'

'Will it be okay if I go to Dougie's and tidy up?'

'Yeah, they'll be finished in there by now.'

'I've just been into the solicitor's. The morning Dougie died, he made enquiries about registering his property for sale. It looks like he needed more cash than the twenty-five thousand he took out of his savings account.' The traffic warden peered at the windscreen again, loitering, ready to pounce the second I went over time. 'I think he took the money to Glasgow with him, that he'd arranged to meet someone there to pay off a debt.'

'Let me follow this up,' Gavin said. 'I'll get back to you tomorrow.'

'Okay.'

The traffic warden rapped on my window and pointed to the ticket on my dashboard. I had about thirty seconds left. I folded my arms and waited as the seconds counted down. I'll go when I'm good and ready, was my message. She wasn't bothered. She'd seen it all before. Just as she went to record my license plate, I started the engine and drove off.

8. Seeing is Believing

Sight is the least reliable of our senses; we're prone to misinterpret images. We see what isn't there and we believe it, because we've 'seen it with our own eyes'. You told me about an experiment in which the participants were 'led'. One half of the group was shown a series of busy photographs, five seconds per image, and was told to press a buzzer every time they spotted a cat. The second half was asked to press a buzzer when they spotted a living creature. There were no creatures in the photographs apart from cats, but still it turned out that the people who were asked to spot a cat were three times more likely to see one than the people who weren't looking out for that particular animal. What's more, several people in the first group buzzed when there were no cats in the picture at all.

On the drive to your house, I thought I saw the Golf again, in my rear-view mirror, briefly. I thought I saw the bald head and the thick neck. This time I didn't accelerate away, I held on to the steering wheel and stared straight ahead, driving a couple of points above the speed limit, no more. Eventually my emergency heartbeat subsided, but still I didn't look back. By the time I turned into your road, I was almost feeling normal. I'd agreed to meet Alec at your house because he needed to collect some files from your office, but really I think he just wanted to reassure himself that I was doing okay.

When I pulled up outside your door, he was sitting in his car, finishing off a sausage roll and listening to the radio.

'Another eejit banging on about the unimportant.' He climbed out of his car. 'It's all a smokescreen, Isla.'

'For what, Alec?'

'Whatever they're going to do us up the arse with next.' He sighed. 'Excuse the language.'

I smiled and unlocked your front door. 'Be prepared for a shock. Yesterday Dougie's house was broken in to.'

'What?' Alec asked. He followed me into the living room, 'Jesus!' He reeled backward. 'They've certainly gone to town.'

We stood surveying the damage, which was even worse than I remembered. I hadn't noticed that the blinds had been torn off the fixings, and there were gouges in the wall next to your TV.

'By the looks of it, they couldn't get the telly off the wall or they would've smashed that too,' Alec said.

'I'm surprised they didn't take a hammer to the screen.'

'Have the police been?'

I nodded. 'Gavin organised it.'

Alec walked across the room, avoiding the splinters of glass scattered over the carpet. 'Did they take anything?'

'Only his Rolex watch, I think.'

'Nothing from his office?'

'No. Strange, isn't it?'

'Aye. And did you tell Gavin about—' He pointed to his own throat and then waved his hand towards mine. 'Assault.'

'I did.' I sat down on the edge of the sofa. 'An investigation is under way. I should know more tomorrow.'

Alec picked half a dozen books up off the floor,

smoothing their pages and realigning the spines. 'You'll need a hand to tidy all this up.' He put the books back on the shelf and got his mobile out. 'I'll give Jean a call. She'll come and help.'

Jean arrived with more than just help. She brought one of her homemade cheese and onion pies and a tomato salad, but we didn't stop for lunch until we'd righted your living room and bedroom. Alec reversed his Range Rover up to the front door so that we could pile the non-salvageable pieces into his boot. There was the smashed coffee table, some broken mugs and glasses, and the remains of your guitar. (They'd snapped off the neck and stamped on the body.) All of that had to be thrown away, but otherwise we put everything back together again. Alec even went into your garage and found tools to repair the blinds and plaster over the holes in the wall next to your TV. Then he found an almost empty pot of the apple-white paint, and painted over the repairs.

I had it in my head to try to separate off some of your personal items – photos, DVDs, and CDs – with a view to giving them away. I found cardboard boxes in your garage and laid them out on the kitchen floor. It felt like the perfect opportunity, bearing in mind I needed to get your house ready to sell. But everything I picked up belonged on the shelf you'd put it on, not in a box. Jean noticed that it was all getting too much for me and took a DVD out of my shaky hand. It was *The Lion King*. It used to be Caitlin's favourite.

'Can we watch it again, Uncle Dougie?'
'Of course. I might fall asleep, though.'
'You won't.' Her expression was wide-eyed and earnest. 'It's really, really good.'

'Let's just put the living room back exactly how it was, Isla,' Jean said. 'You don't need to think about sorting through Dougie's stuff just yet.'

I went along with her, all the while knowing that I was simply delaying the inevitable agony. Because I was going to have to think about packing up your belongings soon, wasn't I? Marie wanted her inheritance and, to be fair, I knew you would have supported Erik's decision to buy a share in a fishing boat. You weren't a sentimental man; you were a practical man, and you would have been the first person to tell me to get on with it.

But by then another thought had stolen into my mind and was beginning to prod away at my temples. The man who'd assaulted me was after money from you. So what had happened to the twenty-five thousand pounds you took out of your savings account? Had you hidden it in your house somewhere? Did you go to Glasgow without the money in the hope that you could talk this man around? Was the burglary his attempt to find the cash? I had told Gavin that nothing was missing apart from your watch, but how could I be sure? Maybe you'd hidden the money here, in your wardrobe, or under your bed, or behind the books on your bookshelves, and that was why the burglars left before going into your office. They hadn't needed to. They'd already got what they came for.

After lunch Alec and Jean went off home, and the first thing I did was to log onto your email. Gordy had left a couple of voicemails on my mobile to say that he'd scanned and emailed me the photograph. I hadn't taken his calls because he was too full-on. I'd have struggled to cope with him at the best of times, and now that I was chest-deep in the worst of times, I was short on strength and patience.

I opened the email and maximised the photo of Jimmy Pearcy. His face was bland. He wasn't attractive or unattractive. His chin wasn't pronounced, nor was it weak. His nose and mouth were average-sized. He had no distinguishing features to speak of, apart from his hairline. He had an off-centre widow's peak, an idiosyncrasy that was difficult to disguise unless the hair was blow-dried forward and forced to take a straighter line. I tried hard, but I couldn't picture Glasgow-Jimmy's hairline. As far as I could remember, his hair was shoulder-length, lank and greasy. The main thing I remembered about Glasgow-Jimmy was that he had full-blown acne. I peered in closer at the screen. Jimmy Pearcy had a few spots, but they fell a long way short of acne. I needed to make a direct comparison, and the only way to do that would be to see Glasgow-Jimmy again – and there was no chance of that. The thought of returning to the squat set off a visceral reaction inside me, blood pumping through my body telling me 'no way!' long before my head told me the same.

I sat back in your chair and swivelled around so that I could look through the window. You'd built your home–office in the perfect spot to take in the view. I put my feet up on the sill and let myself enjoy it. Since your death, September had become October, and it was a corker of a day – no chill, no wind, no water, just a cloudless, turquoise blue sky. The sun flooded the land with light. The grassy hill, sheep-dotted and stripy-patterned with walking trails, had your name written all over it. How many times did you walk up there? Sometimes with Myrtle, sometimes with Fin and Caitlin, sometimes with me.

Whoever bought your home would be lucky, Dougie. Houses bear no allegiance, and yours would soon give itself up to new owners and become someone else's pride and joy. It would be repainted and remodelled. The new owners would most likely complete the en-suite bathroom that you'd never got around to finishing. They could expand into the roof space or build an extension. It depended on how many rooms they needed, how many children they had.

Children.

You dying without children made me think of Tania. Tania and the grenade she exploded at Mum and Dad's wedding anniversary party: their thirtieth and your fifth. (Okay, so I know you won't want to be reminded of that day, but bear with me. This story is your story. And partly my story. And partly Tania's story.)

So. You'd been hoping to start a family, but she'd told you she couldn't conceive, told all of us she couldn't conceive, because back then Tania loved nothing more than an audience, and we were all there. Aunties, uncles, cousins, all gathered for a celebration. Even Uncle Henrik, with his huge hands and blond beard, was visiting from Kirkenes and had brought Mum foodie presents. She had made her lemon baked cod, and rhubarb pudding for afters.

You and Tania had been living in barracks down south and you'd come home on leave. Caitlin was two, and you'd only met her a dozen or so times. She sat on your knee for much of the afternoon, and you stared at her with gentle, indulgent eyes. I was heavily pregnant with Fin, and was girning on about heartburn and fat ankles. The party had been swinging along fine, but then Mum looked at Tania and said, 'Don't let Isla's complaining put you off.'

'Put me off what?' Tania said. She hadn't been

listening. She'd been staring out through the window giving the impression she'd rather be anywhere but there.

'Having children,' Mum said.

'She couldn't put me off,' Tania said. 'I couldn't have children even if I wanted to.' She stared across at Caitlin, who was smearing a blend of chocolate and snot onto your shirtsleeve, before adding, 'Which I don't.'

Your face, Dougie. That was what did it for me and Mum. The hurt and confusion on your face. Tania saw it too, but instead of showing remorse and taking you aside for a private chat, she said, 'I must have told you? I had a coat-hanger abortion when I was sixteen. Bled so much they had to take my womb out. I'm lucky to be here.'

She eyeballed you, daring you to react, brazen as a honeytrap-whore who'd just stolen your wallet and had her brothers beat you to a pulp.

You were too stunned to move or speak. This was the woman you loved, and she was casually describing what sounded like a horrendous experience, the repercussions of which were life-changing. Your hopes of starting a family drained with the blood from your face. Everyone could see that all this was news to you, and she couldn't have chosen a worse time to break it. The atmosphere in the room tightened into a tense, pin-drop silence. Even Caitlin was barely breathing. I didn't need to look at Mum to know that she was shocked rigid. Tania stood up and walked out of the room, cool as you like.

I never knew what you said to her when you joined her outside. I never knew what she said back. All I knew was that something left you that day. An optimism, a faith, a sense of future – I don't know what to call it. It was something indefinable, but tangible nevertheless. You would have been such a good father, Dougie. And if you'd had children, your life would have taken a different course. The debt you'd taken responsibility for might have passed you by.

And you'd still be alive.

I swivelled back around towards the computer screen. Jimmy Pearcy stared at me, a frown dragging his eyes closer. He looked as if he was trying to work out what was going on.

Join the club, Jimmy. Join the fucking club.

I dropped my head onto the desk and had one of those moments of profound hopelessness. I wasn't a detective. I was a loss adjuster for an insurance company. I visited claimants in their homes to decide whether they should be given the full claim amount. I only dealt with the claims between one and five thousand pounds. The really large sums, Alec dealt with himself. And the other branch of the company, the side that dealt with solicitor's referrals for cases of fraud and the like, I had nothing to do with. I had never been part of the skilled surveillance and evidence gathering that was your bread and butter.

I was a mother and an ex-wife. I was daughter to a sick father and I was sister to a dead brother.

I wasn't a detective.

My head started to throb. I wished Gavin would phone and let me know what was going on. It was encouraging to hear that the police had been to see Gordy but, more to the point – had they questioned the barman? Min Fraser? Had they found Paula and Jimmy? Maybe they'd even found my attacker?

Of all the people I encountered that day, Min Fraser was the person I was the most afraid of. When I remembered the way she looked at me, I felt my stomach shrink. Her knowing, penetrating stares. Her faux casual way of talking. Her leading questions.

Why did you talk to her, Dougie? Did you meet her by chance, or was it arranged? Did it have anything to do with Lucy O'Malley? Or was I just being a poor detective?

I asked you these questions aloud, my voice sounding strangely disembodied, as if the words came from the walls, not my mouth. I imagined you standing with your hands in your pockets leaning against the closed door, waiting for me to get it, watching and listening while I went round and round in circles trying to guess what the fuck had gone on.

One of the most annoying things about you when we were kids was the fact that you got a rise out of teasing me – okay, I was a tempting target. I know that now. I should have just ignored you because then you would have stopped, but I didn't, I couldn't, because you were crafty enough to hide exactly what I most wanted. Usually chocolate.

What age would we be? Nine?

It would go something like this:

Me: 'I can't find my Curly Wurly.'

You: (looking up from the *Oor Willie* or the *Beano*) 'What Curly Wurly?'

Me: 'You know what Curly Wurly! The one Dad bought me yesterday. I was saving it.'

You: (nonchalant) 'It must have gone for a walk.'

Me: 'Curly Wurlys can't go for— MUM!' (wailing)

You: (grinning) 'She's taken Marie to the play on the chute.'

Me: (slapping you on the head) 'Give it back to me. Or ELSE!'

You: (dodging my hand) 'Or else what?'

This would go on for a while, until I grew frustrated and just wanted it over with, no matter how much humiliation was involved. I agreed to play the game. I had to hunt for what was mine while you sat on a chair supposedly giving me clues. I looked behind the couch and the curtains, unzipped cushion covers, rummaged in drawers, cupboards, Mum's ironing pile, in plant pots, under tables.

You: 'You're cold, cold. You're getting warm . . . warmer . . . warmer . . . hot, hot, hot, freezing.

Me: 'How can you go from hot to freezing?' (wailing again)

Then we'd argue about the rules, and usually I'd start crying, and then you'd give me my chocolate. Once you'd climbed on a table and a chair to tuck a Milky Bar into the lampshade. Another time you were sitting on my Eclairs.

As I looked around your office, I felt like that nine-year-old again. I didn't know whether I was close or not. Hot, cold, lukewarm? I had no idea. *Nada.* Was the answer staring me in the face and I was too stupid to recognise it? Or would I have to search between layers and layers of confusing contradictions before I discovered what had happened to you?

I didn't know. And I was exhausted from trying to work it out.

'Stop staring at people!' Caitlin hissed at Fin. 'Mum, tell him. He's being really rude.'

We were walking along the hospital corridor and several trolleys had come past us from A & E. The patients lying on them looked seriously injured. They had masks on their faces and lines going into their arms, and each trolley was accompanied by a nurse and a doctor with busy, concerned expressions on their faces. Fin wasn't so much staring at them as being sucked towards them like debris towards a vortex. I took his arm and brought him back in step with Caitlin and me. 'I know all this is fascinating, Fin, but try to keep walking with us.'

'Do we know any doctors?' he said. 'Cos we've got careers day coming up.'

'No, I don't think we do. How about asking Dad?'

'He's got the most boring police job in the whole world of police jobs.'

'Uncle Dougie was always great for careers day,' Caitlin said. 'Being a private detective is cool.'

'Mind the lady with the wheelchair.' We stood aside to let an elderly lady and her even more elderly husband shuffle past, and then carried on walking until we got to the ward. 'This might be a bit upsetting for you. Granddad has been feeling very tired with all the medicine he's on. But we won't stay long. I just want to make sure he's okay and then we'll go to Ritchie's.'

We found Dad in his usual position, slumped in the bed, half-asleep. There was a huge bunch of mixed flowers, mostly roses and irises, in a vase on his locker. I read the card. 'Get well soon, Dad. Thinking of you. Lots of love from Marie, Erik, Danny, Jess and Martha xxx'.

'Granddad!' Fin said, going close to his ear. 'We've come to visit.'

Dad woke up with a coughing fit that sounded as if his lungs were full of phlegm. I gave him a tissue and sat him forward, supporting him until the coughing subsided. His back felt hot and sweaty. 'You're really boiling, Dad.'

'It's this place.' He reached out to Caitlin and Fin, who didn't look as upset as I thought they might. Caitlin's expression was wary but pleased to see him; Fin had spotted Dad's plastered leg, which was poking out from underneath the covers.

'Can we write on your plaster, Granddad?'

'Aye, go on then. There's a pen in my locker.' He knocked on the plaster cast with his fist. 'In my day we called it a stookie.'

'Is it itchy inside?' Caitlin said.

'A wee bit.'

'Mum's got a boyfriend,' Fin said, finding the pen.

'Does she now?' Dad said, grinning at me. 'She's been keeping that quiet.'

Caitlin and Fin sat on Dad's bed and took turns drawing on his stookie while I went to speak to the nurses. I was given the same 'wait and see' story. He wasn't any worse, but he wasn't any better either. The antibiotics hadn't kicked in yet. His leg seemed to be healing, though. That was good news. (I wasn't sure I believed that – how could they tell what was going on inside the plaster cast? – I needed you beside me, Dougie. I was sure they'd have been more forthcoming with you.)

By the time I returned to Dad's bed he was wilting. He was still making a valiant, upbeat effort to project cheerfulness, but his hands were shaking and he kept determinedly blinking to keep himself awake.

'Right you two. We should leave Granddad to have a rest.'

'Aye, I'll need all my energy for tomorrow right enough,' Dad said. 'They're sending me on a rocket to the moon. I've got some experiments to do up there.' He winked at Caitlin and Fin. 'I say these things for your mum's benefit. She thinks I'm heading for dementia.'

'I do nothing of the sort!' I kissed his cheek. 'Don't be giving the nurses any trouble. I'll be back in tomorrow.'

Ritchie had made an effort. He'd set up the table tennis table and bought enough soft drinks and sweets for half a dozen children. We'd collected Myrtle from the house and she ran to Rebus straight away, then they were off down the garden barking in unison. 'They really like each other!' Caitlin said.

'It was how we met,' Ritchie said. 'Didn't your mum tell you?'

'No.' Caitlin looked across at me. 'She's been keeping you a secret.'

'I haven't,' I laughed. 'Well, I have . . . but not for *that* long.' I caught Ritchie's eye but had to look away because I wanted to kiss him, and I thought that might be a bit too much for the kids at this stage. (Over-protective mother . . . I can hear you saying it . . .) 'We met when we were walking the dogs. On the hill behind Uncle Dougie's house.'

'You met our Uncle Dougie?' Fin said to Ritchie

'No. Unfortunately, I didn't.'

'He was really nice,' Caitlin said. 'He was the best uncle in the world.'

'He loved you too, Caitlin.' I gave her a hug. 'Even when you were being annoying.'

She screwed up her face at me and we both laughed.

'So!' Ritchie clapped his hands together. 'What I thought we could do is order in some pizza and then play a game of table tennis while we're waiting for it to arrive.' He handed Fin and Caitlin a menu each. 'Cast your eyes over that.'

'Can we have a whole pizza each?' Fin asked.

'Of course.'

'We're not usually allowed.'

'Uncle Dougie used to let us,' Caitlin said.

'He earned more than Mum,' Fin said.

'Much more,' Caitlin said. 'Mum's always on a budget.'

'Would you two stop with the candour!' I said.

'What's candour?' Fin asked.

'Too much information!'

Ritchie laughed. 'We'll get your mum out of the room and then you can tell me all her secrets.'

'She doesn't have any apart from you,' Fin said with complete authority. 'But she hates chrysanthemums. So if ever you want to buy her flowers, roses are her favourite.'

'I'll keep that in mind,' Ritchie said, all serious.

We ordered our pizzas, then played doubles at table tennis. Ritchie had to play with his left hand because he was so much better than the rest of us. Every so often he caught my eye and we smiled at one another. And when the kids were busy feeding Rebus and Myrtle, Ritchie and I had five minutes alone. I could have spent all of that time kissing him, but we had the day to catch up on. I told him that I'd discovered you'd made enquiries about selling your house and that the police had been to see Gordy. 'I still don't know how any of it is connected,' I said. 'But we have to be getting closer.'

When the pizzas arrived we gathered around the table and the kids told him about school and about their Granddad's leg, and they told him about you, Dougie.

'Uncle Dougie was good at football.'

'He was good at everything.'

'Especially swimming.'

'That's why it's so weird he drowned,' Caitlin said. I watched tears spring into her eyes. 'I don't believe he's gone, really. I don't.'

'It's hard, love,' I took her hand. 'We'll never forget him, but it will get easier.'

'Can we play a game of football?' Fin asked.

'In the dark?' I said.

'Oh, yeah.' He stared out through the window. 'The time's gone really quickly.'

'Next time, though,' Ritchie said.

'And could we watch a film?' Caitlin said.

'Definitely.'

'Let's help Ritchie clear up.' I looked at my watch. 'Then we'd better be getting home. You're already way past your bedtimes. And you have school tomorrow.'

'Don't worry. I'll do the clearing up.' Ritchie took the plates out of my hands. 'There's not much.'

We said our thank yous and goodbyes and set off home. The kids were full of their evening. 'He's sooo nice, Mum!' Caitlin said. 'Imagine having a cinema room! I wish we had that.'

'Not that I'll ever forget Uncle Dougie, Mum, but Ritchie said that he can get season tickets and can take me to some of the big matches,' Fin said. 'He could even take Stuart as well.'

'I might want to come,' Caitlin said. 'Have you met his daughter, Mum? Is she nice?'

'I haven't met her.'

'What's her name?'

'Leonie.'

'Leonie what?'

'Ritchie's surname is McFadden, so his daughter's probably will be too, unless she has her mother's surname.'

'I'm going to look her up on Facebook.' She started typing into her phone. 'Oxford, yeah?' I nodded. 'We might be related one day. I'd like to have a sister.'

'You're really getting ahead of yourself there!'

'I'd rather have a brother,' Fin said from the back seat.

'Found her!' Caitlin said. 'She's really pretty, Mum, look.'

'Not while I'm driving.'

'She likes *The Princess Diary* and *Valentine's Day,* and her favourite band is *One Direction.*' She rested her mobile on her knee and said in a dreamy voice, 'We'd really get on. When is she coming to visit?'

I called Ritchie when the kids were in bed. 'You were a runaway success,' I said. 'You've charmed both my children completely.'

'They're good kids.' He laughed. 'And I found out a lot about you. I'll be calling the florist's in the morning.'

'Ha!' I laughed. 'Caitlin can't wait to meet Leonie. She's checked her out on Facebook and has decided they would be best friends.'

'She's coming up here over the October half-term. We can set something up for them.'

'Okay.'

'Isla?'

'Yeah?'

'You know I love you, don't you?'

I didn't actually. He'd never really said it, except in the throes of sex, when we were lost in each other and we couldn't be held to account for anything we said because the cold light of day was far, far away. 'Say it then.'

There was half a second of a pause. 'I love you, Isla.'

I let his words soak into me, permeate muscle and bone, and I used the sensation to make me feel less sad, more capable. For the first time that day, I felt as if I

could see a way through the quagmire that had become
my life. I was still chest deep in grief and shit and
confusion, but I could see dry land on the horizon. I
just had to keep moving forward, find out what had
happened to you, look after Dad, arrange the sale of
your house, placate Marie, and at the end of it all, Ritchie
would be there and – touch wood, fingers crossed, God
willing – I'd live a decent future. Caitlin and Fin would
grow up happy and strong and I'd maybe even be a
granny one day.

I didn't want a future without you, Dougie, but I knew
I needed one, and having Ritchie in my life made that
feel a whole lot easier.

Thirty minutes later when I went to bed I still had a
smile on my face. Love does that, doesn't it? It makes
us feel as if anything is possible. I'd just turned off the
light when my phone buzzed with the arrival of a text.
I reached onto my bedside table and read the message:
Are you there?

I sat up and switched on the light, checked to see
where the message had come from. It was an 0787 mobile
number, with double fours and triple sixes. I knew I'd
seen the number before. I climbed out of bed and found
my jeans in the wash basket. The printout of your mobile
phone call history was folded up in the front pocket. I
unfolded the paper and scanned the numbers. There it
was. You'd called the number twice: once on the day
before you died, the second time at six o'clock on the
evening of your death.

A second text arrived: **I've left something for you.
Proof**

My mouth was dry. I hit the reply button and texted
back: **Who are you?**

Almost immediately the answer came back: **Paula**

Paula. Homeless Paula who had helped me to my feet after the assault. Why would you have called her, Dougie? And how had she got my phone number?

I had a frantic walk around the bedroom, two steps one way and I butted up against the wardrobe, two steps the other and I was out into the hallway. I texted her back: **What do you mean by proof?**

I put it through your letter box

I stood at the top of the stairs, my pulse jumping in my throat. I was afraid of what I might find when I went downstairs. People videoed events on their mobiles nowadays. What if Paula had done that? Recorded the moment you ended up in the water?

I clutched at my stomach and sat down on the top step. I couldn't watch that, Dougie. I couldn't. Like Caitlin had said earlier, I didn't really believe you were dead. Even though I'd identified your body. Even though I'd been to your funeral. I still didn't truly believe you were gone. I felt as if I was living inside a crack in time. Real life had been suspended. We were running on the back-up generator, and, until the power came back on, I had to try to live in this world, act in this world, make sense of a world without my brother, and bide my time until normal service resumed.

I took two breaths and ran downstairs. There was an envelope on the mat, a mucky white envelope that had been Sellotaped at the edges. I tore it open, and inside was a small brass ornament – the three wise monkeys: hear no evil, see no evil and speak no evil. I turned the brass over in my hand, thinking about runaway Lucy O'Malley and Jimmy Pearcy, and about you in the Lone Star pub.

I slipped the ornament into my pyjama trouser pocket and made my way back to bed knowing sleep wouldn't come for a while.

9. Shadows and Lies

We were cycling, the chains on our bikes rattling as we rode over the bumps. I was breathing fast and quick, cold air chilling my lungs. Then time slipped and I was in the lift. Dread pulsed in my temples. The lift doors opened straight into the room, with the trolley and your body. Don't look. *Don't look!* I looked. I looked into your empty, dead eyes and woke with a start, a scream in my throat.

The first thing I saw was the brass of the three wise monkeys waiting on my bedside table. The monkeys were sitting in a row, their large hands obscuring either their eyes, ears or mouth. The brass itself was dull and covered in minute scrapes. I picked it up and held it for a good minute or more, then got out of bed.

No more texts had arrived and I hadn't replied to the last one Paula had sent because I didn't want to be pulled in any deeper. I wasn't going to think about what the texts or the brass ornament meant. I'd spent the days since your death worrying myself into sore, complicated knots that I couldn't undo. I was going to present the brass monkeys and the white envelope (fingerprints?) to Gavin, and let the trained bobbies come up with answers. I was all answered out.

I got the kids out of bed and off to school, and then, as I was sitting at the bus stop watching the bus drive away, Gavin called. 'I'll be working from Fettes today.

Are you able to come in for a chat? Archie Glover will fill you in on the investigation thus far.'

I agreed to meet him at eleven, which left me time to take Myrtle for a walk. I'd been avoiding the places that reminded me of you – what places didn't? – but I had an urge to walk off the previous night's pizza, feel the wind on my back and the salty tang of sea air on my face. I collected Myrtle and drove to Crammond, parking at the top of the hill parallel to the shoreline. As soon as I opened the boot of the car Myrtle went off at a run, across the grass and down to the beach.

By the time I caught up with her she had left the pavement and was scampering around on the beach, digging holes. Sand, seaweed and broken shells were flying up behind her tunnelling paws. I stood and waited, staring out over the water, the wind casting a shiver on its surface. My eyes followed Crammond Causeway and out to the island beyond, where, as kids, we'd often picnicked. Egg sandwiches and bottles of lemonade. Paddling in the water. Marie niggling on at Mum and Dad because she couldn't keep up with us. The one time we went without you (you were off on a football trip) I ended up in trouble. Marie had followed me over the rocks and fallen down between two of them, scraping the backs of her legs. She told Mum and Dad that I'd pushed her – I really hadn't – I hadn't even noticed she was there – but I had done the sisterly thing and helped her up.

'I did not push her! It's not my fault she always falls in!'

'You need to look after your sister, Isla,' Dad said.
'I do! God!'
Mum wasn't herself. She hadn't smiled all day and

had been ignoring Dad since we left the house. Me
misbehaving was the excuse she needed to let rip. She
grabbed for a stick and slapped the back of my legs
with it. 'You're a nasty little girl sometimes, Isla McTeer.
Why can't you be more like Douglas?'

I sat on my own and ate my sandwiches and watched
Marie get all the Jammie Dodgers. Or so I thought.
Dad saved one in his pocket and he slipped it to me
on the walk back to the car when Mum wasn't looking.

I arrived at Fettes Police Headquarters in plenty of time.
The officer behind the desk telephoned Gavin, and I sat
in the waiting area until he came downstairs to meet
me. I felt calm. I even felt a wee bit optimistic. I had
the brass ornament in my pocket, and every so often
my hand gravitated towards it, found meaning in its
tangibility.

Gavin took me to his room on the top floor where
PC Glover was waiting. I sat with my back to the door
and a view of Fettes College through the window. Its
imposing main building with the steeple at the centre,
rising high into the sky, looked suitably sombre. PC
Glover launched into the details of the police work so
far. He told me they'd been following up on the two
separate investigations: the burglary and the assault. They
were doing all the usual things. The evidence was being
processed. They hadn't as yet been able to isolate any
DNA from the scrapings taken from underneath my
fingernails, but the lab wasn't finished running tests yet.
He was confident that something would turn up, if not
from DNA then from the description I gave of my
attacker. 'We have photographs of known Glasgow crim-
inals who fit your attacker's description for you to look
through.'

'Great.' I nodded. I didn't relish having to look at his face again, but if it helped the investigation then I would do it.

'Gordon O'Malley is being questioned in connection with the burglary.'

'Is he?' I didn't expect that. 'How come?'

'He lied about his whereabouts. We have CCTV footage that places him close to your brother's house.'

'Gordy?' I couldn't hide my surprise. 'Why would he burgle Dougie's place?'

'We won't have an answer to that until we've finished questioning him.' He shuffled the papers on the desk into a neat pile. 'I'm sorry we're not further forward, but I want you to be reassured that we are pursuing both crimes.'

'I'm not so bothered about the attack on me or the burglary for that matter. It's my brother's death that really bothers me.'

PC Glover looked across at Gavin. 'That's not part of my investigation at the moment.'

'Why don't I take it from here?' Gavin said, sounding all 'big-boss'.

PC Glover seemed relieved. We all shook hands and I agreed to come and go through some mug shots with him after I'd spoken to Gavin.

Then the fun really started. Can you guess what's coming next, Dougie? Because I couldn't. I wasn't exactly blissful in my ignorance, but I was quietly sure of my ground. I already knew that you could keep secrets. I also knew there might be shocks ahead. What I didn't know was quite the extent of those shocks.

But first Gavin had to explain to me why he didn't think there was reason enough for an investigation into your death. 'The nature of policing is that we have to ascertain whether a crime has been committed. Usually a crime is reported by a member of the public. We are called to the scene, we find evidence and we investigate on behalf of the person who has been burgled, assaulted, or murdered. Whatever the crime may be. In the first instance, we have to make an assessment based on what is reported to us, and in the second instance *what we find.*'

'Are you telling me you don't believe Dougie's death is suspicious?'

'That's right. I don't.' He lowered the volume of his voice. 'I liked Dougie, Isla. He was a genuine man. He was great with our kids, and I know he was a good brother to you.'

'But?'

'But . . . you'd be amazed how many members of the public are convinced that their loved one couldn't have died the way they did. The stages of grief are well documented, and one of those stages is denial.'

'I'm not . . .'

'I get it, I really do. But the truth is that accidents happen to the unlikeliest of people. Hard to accept, I know.' He sighed. 'I wish I could help, but there's no evidence to suggest that Dougie's death was anything other than accidental. Believe me, if there was any evidence, I would be the first to pursue it.'

The fact that Gavin was being so reasonable made me feel suspicious. And then I realised that he was using his work persona on me. Nothing could be too much trouble. I was a member of the public who needed reassurance.

And time.

I needed time to process the truth. I had to climb aboard the hamster wheel of grief and run through the stages from anger to bargaining, denial and depression, round and round, until I finally landed on acceptance and stayed there.

'Did the police find the squat?' I said.

'Yes.'

'Did they speak to Min Fraser?'

'They did, and she had nothing to add to the enquiry. Either about the man who attacked you or about Dougie's death.'

'Maybe she doesn't know the man who attacked me, but she definitely spoke to Dougie that night.'

'She admitted speaking to him. The officer who questioned her said she was very forthcoming.'

'I bet she was.' I sat back heavily in my seat. 'If you met her Gavin, you'd see that she's creepy and manipulative and could be hiding something.'

'Thinking someone's strange isn't evidence of wrongdoing.'

I gave Min Fraser my mobile number. That's what I suddenly remembered as I sat there. I gave Min Fraser my mobile number. She could have given it to Paula. 'But I didn't give her my address,' I said, out loud.

'Isla, look at me.'

I didn't look. I stared through the window at the college spire. I was thinking back to the squat. I remembered my shaky fingers gripping the pen as I wrote my mobile number on a piece of paper and handed it to her. I definitely didn't give her my address.

'There is no evidence that anything happened to Dougie. I'm not saying there aren't unanswered questions. But there is no evidence of wrongdoing.'

He almost had me, Dougie. I was so tired. My neck was aching from sleeping on it badly. My stomach was churned up, burning with acid. I wanted your death to have an easy solution. I could have walked away. Listened to Gavin, and walked away. But you were my brother. If I didn't pursue this, then who would?

'This is what I know, Gavin.' I shut my eyes and took a breath before opening them again. 'My brother was an ex-marine. He drowned in the Clyde despite the fact that he was an excellent swimmer. He told Alec that he had a debt to pay off. He took twenty-five thousand pounds out of his account. We don't know where the money is. We don't know who he owed it to.' I brought the envelope and the monkeys out of my pocket. 'This envelope was pushed through my letter box last night. The brass monkeys were inside it.' I held the envelopes and the brass out to him. 'When Gordy O'Malley's daughter Lucy went missing she took this with her.'

'This exact brass?' He sounded exasperated. 'How do you know that?'

'I don't, but Gordy could probably tell us one way or the other.' I showed him the text messages and watched as he read the conversation I'd had the previous evening with Paula. 'The phone number is the same one Dougie called the night before he died and the day of his death. Paula is the homeless girl I met. She helped me up after I'd been attacked.'

Gavin was just staring at me now, his foot tapping on the floor.

'Dougie might have been in Glasgow because he was looking for Lucy O'Malley. I asked Paula and her friend Jimmy about Lucy. I think they know who, and maybe where, she is. I think that Dougie's death must be linked to Lucy's disappearance.'

He was no longer staring; now he was glaring. 'How could it be linked?' he said flatly.

'I don't know. Perhaps he was having to pay someone

to get Lucy back? I was hoping the police might be able to find out.'

'Sounds unlikely,' Gavin said. 'Extremely unlikely.' He held up the monkeys. 'And this isn't the only brass ornament in Scotland. They're on mantelpieces everywhere.'

'Yes, but Lucy was really fond of it. It was her granny's. It had a special significance for her.'

He sighed and dropped his head in his hands.

'What?' I said.

'So if this Paula did ring Dougie and he did meet her, then how could it have led to his death?'

'I don't know.'

'You met her.' He shrugged. 'Do you think she was capable of killing Dougie? And if she was, then what could possibly be her motive?'

'I don't know.'

'Dougie wasn't robbed.'

'I know, but—'

'It makes no sense.'

'Not yet, it doesn't, because we haven't worked out the connections.'

'Isla,' he said sharply, 'no man tells his sister everything.'

'What do you mean?'

'Perhaps he was having a relationship with this girl, and her intention is to get some money out of you?'

'*What?*' I wasn't buying it. 'That's ridiculous! She can't be more than eighteen!'

'Dougie will have had his secrets from you.'

'I know that! But, now he's dead and you're a policeman, and if nothing else, you must surely wonder where the money's gone? Twenty-five thousand pounds can't just disappear into thin air!'

'Dougie had his own life, his own friends, his own

plans,' Gavin said. 'Perhaps he'd decided to buy a holiday property abroad and was saving it as a surprise for the family.'

'Without telling anyone? Tania? Dad? Marie? Alec? *Me?*' I shook my head. 'He wouldn't have done that. He'd just bought into Alec's business. That was the surprise.'

'We have two definite crimes here, Isla. Number one, you were attacked, and number two, Dougie's house was burgled.'

'Couldn't you ask the police in Glasgow to look into Dougie's death as a favour to you?'

'I already have. There's no compelling evidence of a crime scene, or a crime for that matter. *None at all*,' he stressed.

'But I know something isn't right, Gavin. I can feel it. I swear I can. I wouldn't be pushing like this if I wasn't so sure.'

He stood up. 'I wish I could help you, Isla, but we simply don't have the budget to investigate crimes on the basis of a hunch.'

'Just stop for a minute and think about it. Please.'

He watched me, hands on hips, his expression tight.

'This is Dougie we're talking about,' I said, standing in front of him. 'Dougie, who was trained in combat techniques.'

'Do you think I'm obstructing a possible investigation? Because if you do, I can give you the number of the police officer in Glasgow who investigated the circum-stances surrounding Dougie's death.'

'No! Of course I don't. I just wish you would trust that I'm right about this. I can feel it in my bones.'

'Okay. Okay.' He held up his hands. 'I don't think—' he stopped. I could see he was choosing his words carefully. 'I don't think we . . . you . . . are always the best judge of what is and isn't right.'

'What's that supposed to mean?'

And then came the sucker punch. 'Richard McFadden.'

We both let the name hang in the air until it grew heavy with a significance I didn't yet understand.

'Ritchie?'

Gavin nodded.

'What about him?'

'Do you trust him?'

'Yes.'

'You haven't felt anything in your bones as far as he's concerned, then?'

'What's that supposed to mean?'

'Well . . . for example . . .' Gavin rubbed his hands on his trousers. 'How does he make his living?'

'He works for a computer software company.'

'Doing what?'

'Writing programmes, I think.'

'You think?'

'I don't know the ins and outs of what he does because . . .' I shook my head. 'Why are you asking me this?'

'I didn't want to say anything to you. I was going to let your relationship with him run its course.'

I stared out of the window and willed myself not to react.

'We've been watching him. And while we were watching him, we saw you visiting.' He paused. 'And staying the night.'

'Who's been watching him?' I asked quietly.

'Serious and Organised Crimes.'

'Why?'

He pulled a file out of his briefcase, took half a dozen pages from it and slid them across the table. 'I shouldn't be showing you this, but I know you won't believe me otherwise.'

He left me alone in the room. I started reading. Within thirty seconds my stomach turned over. Within a minute my heart was aching and my head was calling me a fool. I read the first two pages and skimmed the rest. When Gavin came back I was standing by the window. The Fettes College students had come out for a break and were moving around, the younger ones running and playing, the older ones talking in groups.

'I'm sorry you had to read that, Isla.'

He sounded sympathetic and kind, which only made me feel worse. I faced into the room and heard myself say, 'Do you think there's any way Ritchie might have had something to do with Dougie's death?'

'No. But while SOC had him in for questioning, I asked him about Dougie.'

'What did he say?' I felt detached. I wasn't talking about Ritchie, not my Ritchie. I was talking about some other guy. A man who meant nothing to me.

'He said that he'd met your brother once, over a month ago.'

What? That was a blow. You'd met each other – when? why? – and how come neither you nor Ritchie had thought to tell me?

'They were both in the marines,' I said, staring down at the papers on the desk.

'McFadden was in four-two commando,' Gavin said. 'Dougie was in forty. But McFadden said they didn't meet back in the marines. They were in separate units, and those units were never deployed to the same country at the same time.'

'Do you think that's true?'

'I do.'

I circled the desk. 'Why didn't you tell me about Ritchie sooner?'

'I didn't want to interfere in your life.'

'You're kidding aren't you?' I circled the desk for a second time. 'I took Caitlin and Fin to his house.'

'They told me.'

'They thought he was great.'

'I know.'

'You enjoy seeing me humiliated, is that it?'

'Of course not.' He moved towards me.

'Don't touch me,' I warned. 'It's a long time since you could be of any comfort to me.' I continued my journey around the desk. 'I bet you weren't pleased when they told you – Sorry sir but your ex-wife's been shagging one of our suspects.'

'Isla . . .'

'I know how you think, Gavin. I was your wife for long enough.' Misery and embarrassment and sheer all-consuming hurt spilled through me, filling every small space. I wanted to cry, right there, right then, but I'd already spent the last couple of months making a spectacle of myself, giving Serious Crimes something to tell Gavin about over a beer. I imagined their long lens cameras taking photos – were the blinds always closed? – and Ritchie's bedroom bugged so that every sound we made was transmitted to an undercover van and recorded for all to hear.

'So your logic would have it that because I misread Ritchie, I'm misreading the evidence around Dougie's death?' I asked.

'There is no evidence, Isla. That's my point.'

'I have no credibility? I can see that.' I nodded. 'And it's not the first time I've been deceived, is it? You were having an affair with Collette for how long before you told me? Oh, I remember now! Eight months. About two hundred and forty days. And you did have to tell me – I didn't guess – because, pardon me for being a gullible fool, but when I'm in a relationship, I do actually trust the other person.' I stopped in front of him and narrowed my eyes at his. 'That doesn't mean I'm wrong about Dougie.'

'Isla—'

'Fuck you, Gavin,' I said with a controlled rage that had me trembling. 'Fuck you.'

I walked out. I walked through the station with my head up. I was supposed to find PC Glover and look at mug shots, but I didn't. I had to get out of there before I broke down. When I opened my car door, Myrtle jumped up onto the passenger seat to welcome me. Her eyes grew worried when my hand didn't reach out to stroke her. She watched me start the engine and drive out of the car park. I stopped a few hundred yards away in a parking space outside the entrance to the Botanical Gardens. Myrtle gave up seeking my attention and curled up on the passenger seat beside me.

Ritchie didn't design software. He was working for Ivan Prendergast, who was being prosecuted for tax evasion and insurance fraud. Prendergast was thought to be guilty of more than that – drug dealing and people trafficking had been mentioned – but couldn't be proven. How involved Ritchie was in any of that was difficult to say because, according to the file, despite questioning him on several occasions, they couldn't pin anything on him.

But what about your part in all of this, Dougie?

You met Ritchie and Ritchie met you.

You didn't tell me.

If you'd told me that you'd come across Ritchie when

you were gathering evidence for the Prendergast case, I would have stopped going out with him – or at the very least I'd have paused for thought, forewarned is fore-armed. And I certainly wouldn't have introduced him to the kids.

Did you think you were protecting me?

Maybe you thought I'd go off Ritchie soon enough so there wasn't any point in you saying anything. You could see I was happy, and I might have shot the messenger. I could just about believe you had my best interests at heart. Just about, Dougie.

Just a-fucking-bout.

I was gullible. That's the way it looked to the police. I was a woman who'd been going out with a liar and a criminal and was stupidly ignorant of the fact. Me, who'd been married to a police officer and had a private inves-tigator for a brother, couldn't tell an honest man from a fake.

Alec had sent me on a couple of courses to suss out the average liar because it made the work of a loss adjustor easier. Telltale signs: a shift in gaze, looking up to the right, shielding their face with their hair etc. Bog standard behaviour that most of us succumb to when attempting to lie convincingly. I'd met several petty crim-inals who'd tried to outwit the system by filing a false insurance claim. They usually gave themselves away. Careful questioning, especially if it involved them repeating their story several times, invariably tripped them up.

I hadn't sussed Ritchie. I'd never had a moment's doubt about him. Not a millisecond. I started going back over our relationship, poring over it as if it were a treasure map. Except that instead of treasure, I was looking for the details that had clouded my vision. He was five years younger than me. He was fit and handsome. He could have anyone, but he chose me, a forty-two-year-old woman who'd pushed out two kids. I couldn't afford expensive clothes or face creams that made my skin eternally youthful, or salon treatments that gave me shiny, TV hair. I'm not bad looking, but I wouldn't turn a lot of heads. So why did I turn his?

We'd met on the hillside when we were walking our dogs. Rebus and Myrtle hit it off before we did. They ran off together, and while we were waiting for them to come back, Ritchie and I got talking. Nothing out of the ordinary, just small talk about weather and dogs and how wonderful it was having the Pentlands on the door-step. A week later I'd bumped into him in the petrol station. He told me he'd been looking for the reservoir and hadn't been able to find it. I told him I could show him where it was and we arranged to meet.

Within three weeks we were sleeping together. He told me I was beautiful. He told me he'd never met a woman who made him feel the way I did.

I'd been sucked right in because he'd told me what I wanted to hear. He desired me and I was flattered.

Sad, or what?

I sat in my car. And I sat. And I sat some more. Expressions like 'dark night of the soul' and 'rock bottom' popped into my head like handy little road signs to anchor me to the landscape. I remembered something Mum used to say to me. 'There are no flies on you, Isla.' She always told me I was quick on the uptake. That was our family myth, wasn't it? I was the clever one. You were the sporty one. Marie was the creative one.

I felt far from clever. I felt abandoned, betrayed, and right royally fooled. I cried from frustration and embar-rassment and heartache. I'd started to love him, for God's sake! After almost four fallow years on my own, I'd fallen in love with Ritchie. And he'd lied to me.

I closed my eyes and let myself slide into despair.

I must have fallen asleep because the next thing I knew my phone was ringing. The call was from Fin's mobile.

'Mum where are you?'

'What?' The sun had moved around the sky. It was already late afternoon.

'I knew you would forget. I knew it!'

Football . . . I hung my head. 'I'm coming, Fin. I'm coming right now.' I fumbled for the ignition key. 'I'm really sorry.'

'Stuart called his mum. She's going to take us.'

'I'll collect you afterwards, then. I'm sorry,' I repeated. 'I fell asleep.'

'You promised you'd be as good as Uncle Dougie was.' He made a loud sniffing noise, and I realised he was crying. 'You promised.'

'I'm sorry, Fin. I—'

He cut me off. 'Fuck.' I bit my lip and stared at the phone, misery enveloping me like a rolling fog. I'd let Fin down. And Stuart and Sarah. I'd let you down. And Dad. Everything in my life was going to shit.

Everything.

I indulged in a moment of profound self-pity. More than a moment, five minutes to be exact. I colluded with the most depressed and fearful part of me, and saw a bleak future. You were dead, Dad was on a slippery, slidy slope to a sickly old age, and I'd fallen in love with a liar. I wasn't coping with any of this, and so the kids would begin to tire of me, hate me even. They'd ask to live with Gavin and Collette because Collette was a far better parent than I could ever be. She listened, she made cakes, she was never late. I'd lose my house because I would be too sad to go to work and so I wouldn't be able to pay my mortgage. I'd soon be whiling away my days in the soup kitchen in the Grassmarket with all the other men and women who'd lost their way and spent their nights slumped on the pavement with a beaten expression on their faces and a bottle of cheap vodka under their coats.

After five minutes of thinking like this, shame crept in around the edges of my self-pity. I was wallowing. And I had no right to. You were dead – there was no getting away from that – but in time Dad would recover. And I was fortunate enough to have two vibrant, healthy children. I'd move heaven and earth to be their mum. They were everything that was good about me.

I thought about whether, God forbid, when Fin and Caitlin were grown up like us, something happened to Fin, and Caitlin found out that the circumstances were suspicious, what would she do? They weren't twins, like you and me, but that was irrelevant. They had a blood bond that ran as deep as it got. I knew what Caitlin would do. She'd forget all the times her brother got on her nerves, lied to her or kept secrets. She'd do everything she could to find out what had happened to him.

So enough with the self-pity and the trusting other people when I should be trusting myself. My own instincts were sound – yes, I'd fucked up with my love life – again – but that aside, I had to listen to my own intuition. I sat up straighter, blew my nose, and wiped my face. Myrtle wagged her tail beside me, pleased to see I was coming back to the present. If the police needed evidence, then I'd get it for them. I couldn't just sit on my hands, because every day that went by took you further away from me and washed the evidence away too.

I was going to find out what had happened to you. I was.

I opened the car door and took Myrtle into Inverleith Park for a run around. She sprinted off across the grass and joined in a game of football with several lads in their late teens while I walked along the path. Mothers with pushchairs were out in their droves, most of them single buggies, but there was one set that looked like twins, boy and girl, just like us. It was all I could manage not to run up to the mother and pour out my story.

Halfway along the path, my phone registered the arrival of a text. It was Paula.

Will you meet me?

Rather than faff about with texting, I called her. The phone went straight to voicemail. 'I will meet you, Paula. I can come through to Glasgow tomorrow. Let me know.'

I was about to put my phone back in my pocket when I noticed that Tania had left me three voicemails over the course of twenty-four hours. I pressed the button and listened to them. The first – 'What's happening with the police. Call me back.' The second – 'What the fuck, Isla? You said you'd keep me posted. Get in touch.' And the third – 'Am I going to have to take a taxi out to the sticks? Because God knows what it will cost me. And I don't have any cash so I'll be asking you for the money.'

I looked up at the sky, down at the grass, and up at the sky again. I deliberated. I formulated a plan. I tried to work it through. It was rudimentary; it was full of holes.

But it was something.

Something I couldn't do on my own – not because I wasn't brave enough, but because it required two people.

I'm telling you this, Dougie, because I want you to know that I didn't take the decision to involve Tania lightly. I didn't. I promise.

I called Tania. 'Your offer of help. Are you still willing?'

'Of course.'

'It could be dangerous.'

'So?'

I told her what I wanted to do.

'I'm in,' she said.

10. Small Mercies

I collected Fin and Stuart from football. I apologised to them. I apologised to Mr Abbott and to Sarah. Luckily Fin couldn't hold a grudge for long, and by the time we arrived home he'd forgiven me. I spent the evening being a mum. I made their favourite tea and we ate it in front of the TV. We played Wii tennis. (I got resoundingly beaten – you would have loved it.) I allowed Fin to go on the PlayStation for as long as he wanted while I sat at the table helping Caitlin with her design project. We were cutting photos out of magazines and turning them into a storyboard of sorts. Schoolwork was never this much fun back in the day.

Okay, so I did have an ulterior motive.

'Would you mind staying with Dad and Collette for the next day or so?' I asked.

Fin shook his head, his eyes on the screen. He was playing FIFA 2013, his quick fingers driving the ball up the field.

'Why?' Caitlin asked.

'Tania and I are going to spend some time together.'

'I thought you didn't get on with Tania?'

'No. Well, yes. Not normally. But I've realised she really loved Uncle Dougie.'

'Not as much as we did,' Fin said,

'It's not a competition,' Caitlin said.

'So you two don't mind?'

Caitlin shrugged. 'No.'

'And then I thought us three could do something special over the weekend.'

'Like what?' Fin asked.

'What do you fancy?'

'What about Granddad?' Caitlin said. 'Who's going to visit him?'

'I thought maybe Dad or Collette would take you in. I'll be on the end of a phone.'

'Alton Towers,' Fin said. 'I saw an advert for it. They've got a new rollercoaster. It's called the Smiler. We could go with Ritchie and Leonie.'

'Yeah, Mum,' Caitlin said, brightening. 'We could save our money for then.'

'Good idea.' I disappeared under the table to pick up a dropped glue stick. I couldn't tell them about Ritchie and his lies, not yet. 'I'll arrange it when Tania and I get back.'

Caitlin sat back in her seat and regarded me almost warily. 'Where are you and Tania going?'

'To a few places that meant something to her and Dougie. A pilgrimage of sorts, I suppose.'

'Won't that be really sad?'

'Yes . . . but it will also be uplifting, I think, I hope.'

She asked me some more questions – the specifics of time and place. I couldn't remember ever lying to the kids before. I'd told a couple of white lies around Father Christmas and the tooth fairy, and of course they knew very little about the reasons Gavin left – although I'm sure they gleaned plenty – but apart from that I'd always been truthful. Lying through my teeth didn't feel good, but I knew I had no option.

I was worried about leaving Dad without one of his children visiting him, and when the kids were in bed I called Marie on the off chance she could drop everything and fly over.

'The flowers you sent Dad are lovely,' I said.

'That's good.' Her tone was flat. 'You never know when you order these things online.'

'I was thinking, Marie. I know you'd love to see Dad, and Dougie had cash in his house and—'

'Isla . . .'

'Let me finish. You could use the money to come to Scotland. You could bring Martha with you and then Erik's mum would only have to look after Danny and Jess.'

'I can't.'

'I know it's hard leaving your kids when they're small, but time with Martha on her own would only be good for her. It would make her feel special.'

She sighed. 'You don't get it, Isla.'

'Then help me to get it.'

There was a pause. I could hear her breathing. It sounded ragged, as if she was about to start crying, and then she blurted out, 'I'm pregnant and I don't want to be. I'm drowning in children. Morning, noon and bloody night. And winter's coming again and it's dark. It's pitch black and freezing, but Erik won't move because he loves it here.'

'Marie, I'm—'

'*Don't*, Isla. Don't say anything.'

'I was only going to say that I understand.'

'Do you? Do you *really*? You've only got two children! Are you saying you've been in my position? Considering an abortion because you were worried about your own *sanity*?'

'No, but—'

'And I know what Mum would say. I know what she

would *think*. I'm being weak and selfish. A baby is a gift, and here I am putting myself first like I always do. I know how disappointed she'd be in me.'

'How can you say that?' I was flabbergasted. 'Mum would have been on your side! I'm one hundred per cent sure of that.'

'No, she wouldn't! God Isla! You know how impatient she got with me. How proud she was of you. I could never compete.'

'*What?*' I honestly didn't know where that came from. The Mum I knew championed Marie at every turn.

'But Dougie was her favourite, wasn't he? The boy. The prince. I was like a consolation prize because you two had each other. Why do you think I came to live in Norway? So she'd be proud of me. She'd have a reason to come here. She could have visited all the places and people she knew and spent time with me. She would have been a fantastic granny, but she goes and dies, and Dougie dies, and—'

The phone went dead. I stared at the receiver and then I reeled back against the wall. What the hell? Even for Marie that was quite an outburst. I wasn't sure whether I should be worried about her or not. I thought about what you would do, Dougie. You'd have called her back. You'd have flown over there if necessary. But it probably wouldn't have been necessary because she wouldn't have got so mad with you in the first place. She wouldn't have put the phone down on you. She would have poured her heart out and you would have come up with a solution.

I left it ten minutes, then I called her back. There was no reply so I left a message. 'Marie, please call me. I want to help, please.'

Would you have called Erik? I wasn't sure about

doing that. I didn't want to make things any worse for Marie. I decided to let her cool off and call her in the morning.

Just before I went to bed, Paula sent me a text message to say that she could meet me at the Lone Star pub at eight o'clock the next day. I texted back that I'd see her there. I'd stopped thinking I could avoid going back to Glasgow. That was where the answers lay. So that was where I had to go. No more delaying the inevitable.

Collette agreed to look after Caitlin and Fin for a couple of days. I told her I was going away with Tania, and she said much the same as Caitlin, 'I thought you two couldn't stand the sight of each other?'

'I know, but she's grieving too. So if you don't mind . . .'

'Of course we don't mind.' She gave a meaningful cough. 'Gavin said . . . Well, he said that . . .'

'I made a fool of myself over a man?'

'No, no. Not really.'

'It's okay, Collette. I've been strung along with lies. I'll get over it. It pales into insignificance when compared to losing Dougie.'

Sad to say that wasn't entirely true. I'd begun to see Ritchie as my present and my future. It hurt like hell when Gavin told me he wasn't who I thought he was. It wasn't as traumatic or as disorientating or as painful as losing you, Dougie. But it hurt. It really did.

The next morning I hugged Caitlin and Fin tightly before we got into the car.

'You will be all right, Mum, won't you?' Caitlin asked.

'Of course!' I forced a smile. 'I expect Tania and I will bicker every now and then, but we'll be fine.'

'Call me every day,' Fin said.

'I'm only going to be gone a day or two.'

'I know, but call us.'

'I will.'

When they climbed out at the bus stop my eyes followed them greedily, savouring every last second before they got on the bus. I would see them again. Of course I would. I'd placated the part of myself that told me I'd be out of my depth in Glasgow, with my inclusion of a safety net. Tania. Tania would mind my back. She would know where I was at all times. If the situation got out of hand she would call the police. That was what would keep me safe.

But before I went to Tania's I had to see Ritchie. He'd called me twice since Gavin had shown me the police file, but I hadn't replied and he didn't leave a voicemail. When the bus departed with Caitlin and Fin on board I drove to his house. I wanted him to explain himself. I felt calm. I did. But anger was floating on the surface, like crude oil spilled across the sea, just waiting for a spark to set it alight.

His car was parked outside – a six-month-old BMW 5 series – why hadn't I at least wondered where all his money came from?

Ritchie opened the door, took one look at my face, and stepped away from me. I walked past him into his hallway and he followed me. When I was in the kitchen I swung back around to face him. 'Don't bother with I'm sorry and I wanted to tell you and I never wanted to hurt you and all that shit, because I won't believe you and you'll just be wasting our time.'

His eyes were worried and I could see the tension in his stance as he stared at the floor, at the gunmetal grey slate tiles that stretched across the five metres of kitchen to the triple-glazed, concertina doors framing a view of the Pentland hills in all their glory.

'This place is straight out of *Ideal Homes*,' I said. 'And here was I believing you earned it from software designing. What was it you told me? Customer specific software for RBS and the other big banks.' I shrugged. 'I suppose software engineers do make the sort of money that buys a place like this, but you don't do that for a living, Ritchie, do you?'

He took a breath and looked at me. 'No.'

'Why did you lie?'

'I always have a cover story.'

I laughed. 'Go on then! Tell me you're actually an undercover cop whose cover is so deep that even Serious and Organised Crimes don't know about it. You're involved in bringing Prendergast to his knees, is that it?'

'No.'

'You're not the good guy then?'

He hesitated. 'No, I'm not.'

My heart squeezed, sending ripples of disappointment all the way to my fingertips. I suppose I'd been hanging onto a slim thread of hope that the whole thing was a bit *Spooks* or Jason Bourne. That maybe there was an explanation for Ritchie's behaviour that would absolve him of any blame and prove that he did genuinely love me after all. That's right. I was like a bleating lamb to the slaughter, refusing to believe I was standing in an abattoir until I saw the blade for myself.

I tried to hide my feelings, but you know what I'm like – everything shows on my face. Ritchie saw how upset and disappointed I was. 'Isla . . .' His mouth twisted. 'I'm not the bad guy either.'

'I told you – don't bother defending yourself.' I felt resigned – not a helpful feeling – not if I was to get some answers. I focussed my attention on his lying face and clenched my fists. 'I'm going to ask you some questions. Will you do me the courtesy of answering honestly?'

'Yes.'

'Did you meet me by chance or was it planned?'

'Chance, of course.' He raised his eyebrows. 'What else would it be?'

I examined his body language for signs of lying, but couldn't see any. (Not that I considered myself the best judge of that. Not any more.) Mileburn was halfway between our houses and was the obvious place to dog walk. Not many people regularly walked their dogs there – a couple of dozen maybe? Myrtle was dismissive of most dogs, but Rebus had attracted her attention and that was what started Ritchie and I talking. But still it seemed a bit of a coincidence that I had a cop for an ex-husband, a private investigator for a brother, and Ritchie worked for an Edinburgh criminal.

'Why me?'

'I liked you from the start. I'd seen you a couple of times before we spoke. The way you looked up at the sky, smiled at Myrtle. I remember you—'

'Don't,' I warned. I wasn't about to be charmed. I'd already decided that if he hadn't targeted me for my brother/ex-husband connections then he'd started something with me because he could see I was lonely. And desperate. And attention from a man like him would dazzle me. I wouldn't ask him any questions. I would believe everything he said because being wanted and desired would render me trusting.

'You're an ex-marine?'

He nodded.

'And how do you earn your money?'

'By being useful to men who have a lot of it.'

'Is it legal?'

'Just about.'

'Does it involve drugs, or people trafficking?'

'No.'

'Not directly?'

'Not at all.'

'How can you say that when you're working for Prendergast?'

'It's the truth.'

I drew breath. 'I saw part of your police file. Until recently you were employed by a private military company.'

'I was never a gun for hire if that's what you're thinking. Most of the work I did, and still do, is security detail. It's not uncommon for ex-marines to move on to this type of work.'

'What exactly do you do for Prendergast?'

'Personal security for his wife and children.'

'So why are the police watching you?'

'They're watching everyone who has anything to do with Prendergast. They're gathering evidence to prosecute him.' He shrugged, unconcerned. 'It's what the police do.'

'It's no big deal?'

'It's no big deal,' he affirmed.

'You're not afraid of being taken down with him?'

'No.' He shook his head. 'I tread a careful line. I rarely break any laws.'

'Why not just tell me you were in personal security? Why a cover story?'

'It protects the client. I've always preferred to say as little as possible about the job.'

I almost laughed, not because what he said was funny, but because it was familiar. You know who he sounded like, Dougie? He sounded like you. Was that something you were taught in the marines? Keep your own council. Don't be telling the girlfriend or the wife stuff she didn't need to know.

'Would you ever have told me the truth?'

'Of course.'

'When Ritchie? *When*?'

'When we got more serious. When I could see our relationship was going to be long term.'

'I don't believe you.'

'Isla . . .' He took hold of my shoulders. 'Don't do this. Don't—'

'*Me*?' I pushed him off. 'I'm not doing anything! You were the one who spoiled this. Not me.'

There was a commotion behind us. Rebus came running through the dog flap and launched himself halfway up my leg. 'Hello, boy.' I stroked his head and he bobbed up and down, knocking his wet nose against my knee. Then he did a quick turn around the kitchen looking for Myrtle and came back to stare at me when he couldn't find her. 'She's not here,' I told him. He cocked his head to one side, hearing sounds I couldn't, and ran off outside again. I watched him through the window as he hurtled off down the garden, barking at the hills.

'Isla—'

'Did you have anything to do with Dougie's death?' I said loudly.

'Of course not.' He frowned. 'What do you take me for?'

'Why did he come and speak to you?'

'You'd told him you were going out with me. He remembered my name from the marines, and he looked me up.'

'That's all?'

'He'd also found out that the police were investigating me. I already knew that, but I appreciated him telling me.'

'So you knew each other in the marines?'

'Not really. But I knew of him. As he knew of me.'

'Boys stick together?'

'He was giving me a heads up. I'd have done the same for him.'

'My children asked you whether you'd met Dougie and you said no.'

'I shouldn't have done that.'

'No, you shouldn't.' I folded my arms. 'What did Dougie think about you lying to me?'

'Isla.' He sighed. 'When I lied to you about what I did for a living we'd known each other five minutes. I didn't think we'd last. After a couple of weeks I knew we were going somewhere, but I hadn't yet found the right moment to bring it up.'

'But what did my brother think?'

'He told me to tell you the truth. He said you'd understand.' He looked up at the ceiling and sighed again. 'And he told me not to hurt you.'

'Too bad you didn't take his advice.' My voice was quiet. I was shaking. I clenched my fists again. Anger felt so much better than misery. 'I think you didn't tell me because this is the game you play. This is you. You shag a woman for a month or three and then you move on to another. You don't want questions. You don't want promises. You don't actually want intimacy or togetherness. You just want to get your end away.'

His shook his head.

'You want control. You want convenience. You choose a woman who already has kids and has been let down in the past, because then she'll be grateful. She won't talk marriage. She won't force commitment. She'll be happy with a relationship that feels young and uncomplicated. One that you can drop on its head as soon as another woman appears on your radar.'

'You've got it all worked out,' he said, his tone flat.

'Yeah, I have.' I stepped closer to him. 'You see the trouble with deceit and lying is that it sets a precedent. Now I know you can lie. I know you can lie convincingly. So how the fuck can I trust you?'

'Just . . . take some time to think about it. Please.'

'I have. Last man on earth?' I looked him up and down. 'I still wouldn't want you.'

I was on the way out of the door when he stopped me. 'Wait.' He laid a hand on my arm and I stared at the hand until he removed it. 'After you spoke to me the other day, I got in touch with a contact of mine in Glasgow. I think I might know who attacked you. I'll get the photos.' He backed away from me. 'Don't leave. Wait a second.'

I kept my hand on the door handle, torn. I was annoyed I couldn't make my exit, but curious to see if he'd found the tattooed man. Ritchie returned before I'd made my mind up whether I should stay or go. He had sheets of paper in his hand and he laid them on the hall table. 'Come and see,' he said. I gave him a dirty look then walked across to stand beside him. There were three photographs on the table. He pointed to one of them. 'Is this the man?'

I stared at the photo and instantly recoiled backwards.

'His name is Brian Laidlaw,' Ritchie said.

It was him, Dougie, minus the black eye. He wasn't looking at the camera. He was smoking a cigarette and staring at someone or something to the left of the photographer. I forced myself to pick up the photo and hold it in my hands. I stared at him, willing my heartbeat to settle down. I needed to accustom myself to the sight of him, and then I'd be more in control if I had to clap eyes on him again for real.

'He's a career criminal, and he has a brother called Gerry who's similar.' Ritchie pointed to another photograph. 'This is Gerry.'

Gerry looked like a less tattooed, less meaty version of his brother, but they had a mean, don't-fuck-with-me expression in common.

'Min Fraser is their aunt.' She was the person in the third photograph, looking all sweet-lady in her cuddly cardigan and ankle boots.

'That makes sense.' It was a relief to hear this. I had a hunch that Min and the man who attacked me had to know one another, otherwise there would be breaks in the chain of connection. You were searching for Lucy O'Malley, Lucy knew Paula, Paula stayed in the squat with Min Fraser, Min Fraser was Brian Laidlaw's aunt. When Brian Laidlaw attacked me he said you'd promised him money. We were back to you again. The circle was complete.

'Can I have these photos?' I said, hating to ask Ritchie for anything, but they would be useful to show to Tania.

'Of course.' He gathered the sheets together and handed them to me, then he stepped away from the table so that he was standing in front of the door. 'These people are not to be messed with.'

'I wasn't planning on messing with them. I'm going to give these photos to the police.'

He nodded. 'Good.'

'Could you move away from the door, please?'

He didn't move. 'I have a mortgage on this house and my car is leased.'

I gave a deliberately laboured sigh. 'And you're telling me this because?'

'I'm not a player. I don't mess women around. I'm more likely to be the one who's on the end of the messing. My ex-wife took the time to set up a whole new life for herself before she left me. She ended up with the house, she emptied the joint bank account, she took Leonie.'

'You could have fought for your daughter.'

'I did. It took me six months and ten grand to get joint custody.' He squashed his hands into his pockets. 'I don't talk about my feelings, Isla. I don't talk about anything serious if I can help it, but that doesn't mean I don't love you and I wouldn't go to the ends of the earth for you.'

'I don't need a man to go to the ends of the earth for me. I need him to be in my life, day to day, *telling the truth*.' I faltered and drew back because being this close to him made me want to kiss him, bed him, forget about the lies. But I wasn't twenty any more, and I wasn't about to compromise on honesty, not for any man. 'Move aside.'

'Isla . . .'

'Never contact me again.'

He moved aside and I walked away. I don't know how I made it to my car because my heart was screaming 'turn around!' while my head forced one foot in front of the other. I could have made him grovel a bit more, make promises, tell me how much he loved me, and then I'd feel wanted again and I'd have someone who was on my side, who would investigate your death with me. I could have asked him to come with me instead of involving Tania.

I should have done that.

* * *

Tania was ready and waiting for me when I arrived at her flat. She was dressed top to toe in black, including a peaked cap that covered half her forehead. Her red hair was plaited, and she was wearing very little make-up. 'I used to dress like this when I chummed Dougie on surveillance.' She bent her right leg up backwards at the knee and caught her foot in her hand. 'These trainers are great for running in.'

'You're not going to be running, Tania. You're going to be in the van.'

'About that . . .' She registered my closed expression and held up her hand. 'Hear me out.'

'Okay.' I leant against the wall. 'But I'm not changing my mind.'

'Have you thought the plan through?'

'As far as I can. I don't want to overthink it because then I'd see everything that could go wrong and back out.'

'Okay.' She walked up and down, her hands moving through the air as she spoke. 'So we meet this girl Paula today, and she takes you to Lucy or tells you where Lucy is?'

I nodded.

'And then what?'

'I find out why Dougie was there. And I'll record the conversation. The money and Lucy seem to be linked. Her dad Gordon was questioned yesterday about the burglary.'

'Did he rob Dougie's place?'

'I don't know.'

'We need to find out.'

'I could call PC Glover.'

'Go on then.'

Tania sat on the arm of the sofa while I made the

call. PC Glover answered his phone with the words, 'I'm pleased you called, Miss McTeer. You left yesterday without looking at the mug shots.'

'Yes, I did. I'm sorry about that. How did your questioning of Gordon O'Malley go?'

'He was in the vicinity of your brother's house because he was visiting a young adult who had been on the streets and was now living back home.'

'I see.'

'He denied all knowledge of the robbery, and as far as we know, he doesn't have a motive for breaking into your brother's house.'

'And did you find out whether my brother went to Gordy's house the Sunday before he died?'

'Your brother did go there, but at the request of O'Malley's wife. O'Malley wasn't home. Apparently his wife wanted to thank your brother for everything he'd been doing.'

'Okay.' That made sense. 'Thank you.'

'Are you able to make it in today to look at the photographs?'

'I don't need to. I've found out the man's name. He's called Brian Laidlaw.'

'He's known to us,' PC Glover said, sounding pleased. 'Might I ask you how you came by his name?'

'A friend told me.'

'And this friend, would he have anything else to share with the police?'

'Not that I know of.' Tania was making faces at me. I put my hand over the mouthpiece to address her. 'What?'

'Don't do their job for them,' she said.

'I'm having a couple of days away,' I told PC Glover. 'But I'll have my mobile with me if you have any news.'

When I hung up, Tania was looking thoughtful. 'What if you get to speak to Lucy and she can't tell you anything?'

'Then I'll sit in the Lone Star pub until Brian Laidlaw comes to find me.'

'And if he doesn't?'

'He will. He wants his money, remember?'

'But suppose he robbed Dougie's place and found the money, he won't come to talk to you, will he?'

'Then I'll go to the squat. Min Fraser is Brian Laidlaw's aunt.'

'And all this time I'm sitting in the van?'

'Yes.'

She nodded. 'This is a good plan.'

I smiled.

'If you want to get yourself half-strangled again.'

'Oh come on!' I stood up. 'It's not that bad.'

'You have no element of surprise! They'll know you're recording the conversation! They're not criminals for nothing. You have to outsmart them.'

'All I want, Tania, is for one of these people, hopefully Paula, to tell me what happened to my brother that night. Not even the whole story, just enough for the police to begin an investigation. Paula may give us that. I had the feeling when I saw her in Glasgow that she wanted to tell me something, but her boyfriend Jimmy pulled her away. And he might even be the same Jimmy that Lucy ran off with.'

'You're not seeing the wood for the trees,' Tania said. 'They're not going to talk to you, because they know you're Dougie's sister! It makes sense for me to be the one who goes in, and I'll tell you why.' She shrugged as if it were obvious. 'They don't know me. I could pretend to be looking for a homeless girl, and infiltrate them that way.'

'We don't have time to infiltrate them. We have to keep this simple. We're not trained in undercover work.'

'What makes you the boss?' It was a flash of the petulant Tania, and she caught herself immediately. 'Okay.' She held up her hand. 'But I want to make it clear that this job fits my skills set much more closely than it does yours.'

'How?'

'Have you ever tried to stop a man from beating you? Raping you?'

'Of course not! But I don't expect to be in that much danger. I'm not going to try to bring these people down. I'm not an idiot!' I laughed. 'And we're not in *Charlie's Angels*.'

'I was thinking more *Thelma and Louise*.'

'They both died in the end.'

'Sex with Brad Pitt would have made death worth it, though.'

I laughed again. 'Maybe, but I have children. I have to stay alive.'

'I know.' She took my hands and held me still. I could see that underneath the sudden burst of humour she was deadly serious. 'I know what this is, Isla. I know what these men will be like.' A muscle jerked in her cheek. 'I was brought up, delete that, dragged up, delete that . . .' She shook her head and stared up at the ceiling. 'I dragged myself up in a house where my brothers and father treated me like a pet animal to kick or spoil depending what mood they were in.'

'Tania—'

'I'm not looking for sympathy. I made Dougie suffer for all the shit men who abused me, and now this is my chance to use my smarts against these people. For Dougie. And if anyone can do it, I can.'

'Tania . . .' I trailed off. I didn't want to hurt her feelings, but there was no way I was going to let her put herself in danger. 'I admire your strength. I do. I absolutely do. And I admire your ingenuity.'

'I've been on surveillance with Dougie. I know the score.'

'But we have to work as a team.'

She smacked her lips together. 'I'm a team player when I need to be.'

'I know.' I kissed her cheek. 'And listen, when I was lying in my bed last night I remembered the last thing Dougie said to me. He'd come to pick Fin up for the football, and as he was going out the door he looked back at me and said – don't do anything I wouldn't do.'

She smiled. 'Then we've got all the permission we need.' She grabbed my hand. 'Let's go.'

11. No Matter What

'Before we pick up Dougie's van we should go and see Sandy Farmer,' Tania said.

We were driving from her flat up past the Western General. I'd stopped at the pedestrian crossing to let a clutch of primary school children cross the road. They were wearing high-vis jackets, and there was an adult at the front and back of the line shooing them on like chicks.

'Why?' I said.

'Dougie bought his equipment from him. I've been there a couple of times.'

'But everything we need is in Dougie's van, isn't it?'

'Did you ever go on surveillance with Dougie?'

'I wish I had, but I never got around to it.'

(Why hadn't I Dougie? Why did I miss out on spending time with you? You'd asked me to come with you on a 'stake out'. You made it sound like fun: a cross between an all-night party and a whodunit. Gavin and Collette had taken the kids to the Lake District so I was free to leave the house, but I was busy feeling sorry for myself. I was in a mood for sleeping and wallowing and eating too much ice cream in front of the telly.)

'How were you planning to record your conversation with Paula or Lucy or whoever you end up talking to?' Tania said with forced casualness. I could tell that she was itching to take over.

'Well . . . I know my phone would be too obvious. I'm thinking Dougie must surely have something I can use.'

'He has a recording device that's built into a key fob. It looks like your car key and you'd get away with it with Paula or Lucy, but don't expect it to work with Brian Laidlaw. He'll suss it in seconds.' I could feel her staring at me. 'I'm just saying,' she added.

'So what do you suggest?'

'Sandy Farmer will have something that you can attach to your clothing.'

'Does Dougie not have anything like that?'

'I don't think so. He shot mostly video, and took photographs.'

'That's true,' I acknowledged.

'Sandy will sell us something. He operates from his ground-floor flat in Marchmont.'

'I'll turn around at the roundabout.' I drove on a couple of hundred yards, birled all the way around, and headed back into town. 'When I went into the squat last week, it struck me I should have had pepper spray and a rape alarm with me.'

'Could do,' Tania said. 'Pepper spray's pretty useless, though, unless you go around with your finger on the trigger. By the time you've got it out of your pocket your attacker will have you on the ground.'

'But the rape alarm would go a long way to alerting you if I was in trouble, wouldn't it?'

'Depends how far away I am.' She was looking at the three photographs Ritchie had given me: the Laidlaw brothers and their aunt, Min Fraser. 'These brothers look like mean fuckers. And I wouldn't want to meet their Aunty Min on a dark night either.'

'She's proper weird,' I said. 'She dresses like

everybody's granny, but gives off Hannibal Lecter vibes.'

'And yet you want to meet her again?'

'No, I don't!' I gave a short laugh. 'Not if I can help it.'

'I wouldn't mind going a couple of rounds with her,' Tania said, all hopeful.

'Tania,' I glanced across at her, 'you've agreed to be the back-up.'

'Absolutely.' She put the photographs on the back seat and settled her hands in her lap, demure as a debutante. 'I'm going to do exactly as I'm told.'

I remembered you telling me about Sandy Farmer. He'd been a mercenary soldier in Biafra and Angola in his twenties and thirties, and had untold horror clogging him up. He'd had a breakdown in his forties, got back on track in his fifties, and ran his business on a word-of-mouth basis. We had trouble getting through the front door until I showed him ID that proved I was your sister, and then he reluctantly allowed us over the threshold, holding the door just wide enough for us to pass through, and sighing as if we were annoying little kids who'd kicked our ball into his garden.

'We're looking to buy a recording device,' Tania said.

Farmer was wearing highly polished shoes, a well-pressed shirt, trousers with perfect creases down the centre of each leg, and a completely blank expression on his face.

'I think my brother might have been murdered,' I said.

'We're looking to find some evidence,' Tania added.

'To present to the police,' I continued. 'So they'll conduct an official enquiry.'

'We're going to Glasgow,' Tania said. 'We think—'

Farmer held up his hand. 'No details. And before you ask, I don't give advice.'

He turned away, and we followed him deep into his lair. You'd told me he was a neat freak, and you weren't kidding. The flat smelled of furniture polish and bleach and the sharp tang of alcohol, the sort used to clean and sterilise equipment. We passed an open door, and I glanced inside. The room was furnished with two easy chairs, a coffee table, and an enormous television. There were no magazines lying around or mugs to be returned to the kitchen. No family photos or any personal items to give me a sense of who he was. This was a functioning space without frivolity or weakness. There was a place for everything and everything was very firmly and exactly in that place, although I imagined that not much was allowed to enter the flat to begin with.

At the end of the hallway, Farmer stopped in front of a double locked and bolted door. He opened it with keys from his pocket and switched on the light. It was a windowless box room with equipment stored on purpose-built metal shelving. My eyes roamed the shelves, taking it all in. There was everything a spy would need, from night-vision goggles to lock-picking tools, a desk calculator that doubled as a voice recorder, and sunglasses with a built-in camera. Fin would have loved to be let loose in there. Even Caitlin would have enjoyed it. Farmer showed us a tiny video and audio recording device that resembled a button.

'I wasn't really looking for video, but it won't do any harm to have both,' I said.

'The microphone is good for several metres. It will help if you keep your body facing the source of the sound, especially if there's background noise,' Farmer said. 'Recording time is two hours.'

I held the button in my hand, marvelling at the compact nature of such a sophisticated device. A small memory card slotted into the back of it. Playback was on a separate two-inch screen that resembled a mini television, and could be plugged into the back of the button via a connecting wire.

'It's similar to the button on your jeans,' Tania said.

'You're right. I'll take my button off and fix this one on in its place.'

'When you're sitting down at a table in the pub, it'll be hard to catch the sound,' Tania said. 'And there'll definitely be no picture. Why don't we take the watch as well?' She picked up a watch fitted with a video and recording device. 'It's good to have two devices, in case one of them malfunctions.'

'Belts and braces?' I said.

'Why not?' She shrugged. 'We only have one shot at this.'

I looked at Farmer to ascertain whether he had an opinion to share, but his face remained blank. 'How much do they cost?' I asked.

'The button cam and recorder retail at one nine, nine. The watch is one twenty.'

'We'll take them both,' I said. I also chose a rape alarm key fob, and an aerosol of pepper spray, then Farmer double locked the box-room door and took us into an adjacent room where he had an office with a large window facing onto the back green, vertical bars on the outside. I gave him cash, and he used a different set of keys to hide the money away in a safe that was built into the wall. I thought he might wish us luck or express regrets at your death, but he didn't. Transaction complete he saw us to the door and closed it behind us without even so much as goodbye eye contact.

Out in the street the wind was whipping up and I automatically glanced up at the sky. Clouds, clouds and more clouds.

'He was a bit disconcerting,' I said as we climbed into my car. 'I thought he would at least mention Dougie. Show some feeling.'

'What you see is what you get with him,' Tania said. 'In a way it's refreshing. No bullshit, no trying to be nice.'

'I suppose.' I started the engine and pulled out into Marchmont Road. 'Okay, so . . . we'll get Dougie's van . . .'

'Sew on the button cam.'

'Sew on the button cam and head off to Glasgow.'

Tania fiddled with the lever next to her until she'd angled the seat back to forty-five degrees. Then she lay back, closing her eyes. 'Wake me up when we get to Dougie's.'

I laughed. 'We'll be there in twenty-five minutes.'

'I usually only go to his place after dark. All that emptiness. Grass and sheep. I like shops and people.'

'Dirt, noise and the endless hum of traffic?'

'Reminds me I'm alive.' She pulled her cap down over her face and lifted her feet up onto the dashboard, her legs crossing at the knees. 'I accused Dougie of moving to the country to get rid of me once and for all, but really it was to be close to you.'

'He helped me through my break-up with Gavin.' The ache in my throat doubled in size. 'He was great.'

'My brothers would see me dead before they'd help me.'

'Opposites attract,' Mum said. 'Tania had a tough upbringing. Not like you and Dougie.'

Mum was sitting at the kitchen table smoking a rare cigarette. We were surrounded by the aftermath of the wedding anniversary party. Dad had disappeared into his shed, and everyone else had gone home apart from me and my pregnant belly. Used plates and cups were balanced on tables and windowsills, but Mum and I had yet to begin tidying up. I was still shell-shocked, feeling sad for you and angry at Tania's spoiling of your hopes and dreams, telling you she couldn't get pregnant in front of over twenty members of the family. Who does that?

Mum was in a reflective mood. 'Dougie's easy to love, but Tania?' she said, talking as much to the room as to me. 'That girl's a challenge.' She flicked ash onto a plate. 'He has his work cut out for him. Does he just.'

I drove along Charterhall Road, braking beside the duck pond to allow a car to reverse into a parking space. Parents and children were moving towards the gates, brothers and sisters with bags of breadcrumbs and smiles on their faces racing on ahead. I remembered the time when the old man sat next to Mum on the bench. Do you remember, Dougie? Dad had dropped us off at the entrance, then gone off in his van to deliver a bureau to a house in Lasswade. (It was when he was trying his hand at selling antiques.) We were both keen to climb the Blackford Hill before we visited the pond, but Marie was in the buggy so we had to stay on the flat. We must have been about seven because we'd both recently lost our front teeth, and I remembered standing next to the pond feeling for the gaps along my gum with my tongue. We each had a bag of crusts that we'd spent the car journey tearing into small pieces for the ducks. Mum sat on a bench facing the pond, while we stood at the edge scattering bread in small handfuls and running sideways to avoid the two swans who followed us along the path, pecking in our direction.

Marie fell asleep almost at once, and so Mum was able to relax, smiling as we elbowed each other at the water's edge. There was no deep water for us to fall into; the grassy bank was a gentle slope leading down to the edges of the shallow, stony-bottomed pond. We had competitions to see who could throw the bread the furthest, and we made Mum the judge. She was diplomatic in her replies, never one to encourage our competitiveness.

An old man was walking towards us, taking for ever to negotiate the curved path, his walking stick feeling the ground ahead of each of his feet before he was willing to commit to taking a step. He was wearing a heavy, tweed coat even though it wasn't cold, and his face was more lined than any face I'd ever seen before. Mum told me off for staring, but the old man smiled and held a shaky hand out to me. 'You are having fun, I see.'

He wasn't Scottish. His accent was thick with extra sounds that lengthened the consonants and distorted the shape of the vowels. He sat down on the bench next to Mum and admired Marie, who was all pink-cheeked and cherubic. And then he asked about us. She told him we were twins and that we played well together but that we also 'had our moments'.

'Because they are children,' he said, nodding at the rightness of that.

'The biggest difference between them,' Mum said, 'apart from the obvious fact that one's a boy and the other's a girl, is that Isla's more practical. Dougie sets his cap for lost causes. He wants the world to be a good and a right place. Isla is more accepting.'

We were playing hide-and-seek by then, and I was

crouched in the bushes behind them, listening but not really understanding. I was fascinated by the way the man was looking at Mum. Like she was the sun and he was a worshipper. He was enchanted with her. She was gorgeous, wasn't she? With her white-blonde halo of hair and her warm blue eyes that had us running towards her for a cuddle, unless we were misbehaving, and then her eyes would narrow and freeze, and we'd stay out of her way until she defrosted.

'Ice cool,' Dad used to say. 'My Princess Grace.'

I'd been thinking about Mum a lot since you died. What it must have been like for her to leave her home at eighteen and come to live in Scotland. Marie had done it in reverse, with her Norwegian Erik, and beautiful blond children. Like Mum, she had an aptitude for languages. Mum's Scottish accent was near perfect. We never appreciated that about her, and when I remember her now I think about all the things she never got any credit for.

But the thing about Mum was that she knew us so well, didn't she? Perhaps the only thing she didn't know was how much I wished I was more like you.

I swapped the button on my jeans for the recording device, while Tania rummaged around in your freezer. She found a couple of frozen meals to put in the microwave, banging and crashing around as if she was making a three-course meal in a hurry. She was a forceful personality in a small, neat frame. One of those people who is larger than the body they inhabit. When the meals were cooked she brought them to the breakfast bar and we sat there on stools, your belongings all around us.

'Are you not going to finish yours?' she said, watching

me poke my fork around in the veggie pasta looking for nibs of corn.

'The pasta's a bit claggy.'

She reached over and speared a lasagne sheet with her own fork. 'Waste not want not.'

I sat back. 'Be my guest.'

'Need to fuel up for what lies ahead.' She stuffed the pasta into her mouth, wiping dribbled cheese sauce off her chin with the back of her hand. 'I've always loved my grub. Most alcoholics can take it or leave it, but not me.'

'I don't know how you stay so thin.'

'Me neither.' She jumped off the stool and went to the kettle. 'Cup of tea?'

'Go on then.'

'We can smash this, you know?' she said when she came back to the breakfast bar with two mugs of tea. 'It's all about staying in the moment. Don't panic. Don't let them scare you.'

'Them?'

'The old woman and her attack dogs.'

'You think Paula's working for them?'

'Why not? Do you really think she's doing this out of the goodness of her heart?'

'I guess not.'

'But don't worry,' Tania said. 'I'll be right beside you.'

Dougie, if this is sounding like solidarity, then that's because it was. We were getting on well. Genuinely. When I took time to think about it I was gobsmacked. If only it hadn't taken your death to unite us in a common purpose.

'Junction twenty-four,' Tania said. 'Turn right off the slip road.'

It was a measure of just how friendly we were that I didn't tell her I already knew that, after all it was only days since I'd been there. 'There's a cheap hotel not far away from the Science Centre,' I said. 'I phoned ahead and booked us a room. The van's not comfortable enough for us to spend the night in it.'

I paid the desk clerk in cash, counting out enough for one night. I was steadily working through the two thousand pounds you had left in the trunk in your living room, but if using your money to find out how you died wasn't a good way of spending it, then I didn't know what was.

The hotel room had a damp, mouldy feel to it, as if too many bare feet had walked across the carpet and too many skin cells and dust mites had mingled with the fibres. Tania threw herself onto one of the twin beds, wriggling around to test the mattress for comfort. 'Not bad, considering.' She kicked her shoes across the room, then seconds later was back on her feet raiding the minibar. 'I'm only going to eat the chocolate,' she said, pushing aside the miniature bottles of spirits. 'Do you want any?'

'No thanks.' I marvelled at her ability to keep stuffing her face. My stomach had shrunk to the size of a baby's fist. I was increasingly nervous. Sweaty palms, racing heartbeat. I'd have thrown up if it wasn't for the fact that the little pasta and veg I'd eaten had already passed through my stomach.

'Why are you pacing?' Tania asked. She'd switched on the TV and arranged two pillows behind her head as if she didn't have a care in the world. 'You're jittery as fuck!'

'We're not here on holiday, Tania, are we?'

'You don't need to be anxious about tonight.' She

snapped off a chocolate triangle from a bar of Toblerone. 'It won't kick off yet.'

'How do you know that?' I let out a nervous laugh. 'Paula could be luring me into a trap.'

'She is luring you into a trap. The Laidlaws will be close by, but they won't hurt you in a pub, no matter how run-down it is.' She pressed a button on the remote control and the TV went mute. 'It's simple.' She shrugged. 'What do they want? They want their money. How can they get it? By putting the frighteners on you. They know you'll be shitting yourself. They know you'll have a plan, but they'll also know that this isn't your life, so your plan won't be up to much.' She munched on another triangle of chocolate. 'I expect they'll want to drag it out over a couple of nights until you're a nervous wreck.'

I didn't want to believe that. I wanted to believe that I could catch them unawares, and that it would all be done and dusted this evening. I wanted to believe I was in control. 'They might already have their money,' I said. 'They might have found it when they burgled Dougie's house.'

She shook her head, certain. 'You wouldn't be meeting Paula if they had.'

'Paula could simply be helping me find Lucy. I mean, she could, couldn't she? Perhaps we're overcomplicating this.'

'From the way you described her, I'd say Paula is a serious addict. And addicts will do anything, meet anyone, have sex, steal, lie, and cheat, whatever it takes to get their next fix. I speak as one who knows.' She turned on the volume again. 'Now can I watch this? I love the way the houses turn out.'

While Tania was gripped by *Grand Designs*, I went into the bathroom and called the hospital. Dad sounded

less breathless and more cheerful. 'Dorothy's been down
to see me again. Don't worry about your old dad. You
have a couple of days off. I'm doing fine.'

'Brilliant, Dad.'

(Thank God something was going right.)

After Marie's pregnancy revelation the day before, I
wanted to be sure she was coping. I called her mobile
and Erik answered.

'It's me, Erik. Isla.'

'Yes. I saw your number. Marie is not here, I am
afraid. She is out.'

'Is she okay?' After her outburst about the unplanned
pregnancy, I had visions of her going through an abortion on her own. 'She sounded a wee bit . . . fraught,
yesterday.'

'She is fine.'

'Right. Only you would tell me, wouldn't you? I mean
with Dougie dying and everything, I know Marie's
grieving. I'd hate to not be there for her.'

'Of course. She knows that you support her.'

I waited for him to say more, but he didn't elaborate.
Marie had once told me that the English language had
ten times as many words as Norwegian. They used their
words sparingly and with exactitude.

'And Erik. About the fishing boat. Dougie's house
should sell fairly quickly.'

'What boat?'

'The share in the boat that—' *you wanted to buy.*

'What boat? I don't think I understand.'

'Nothing. I'm sorry. I'm tired.' I shook my head,
inwardly cursing Marie. 'I always talk rubbish when I'm
tired.' I asked Erik to pass on my good wishes to everyone,
and hung up. Honestly, our sister! Would she ever be
straightforward? She'd always had a tendency to lie,

hadn't she? I remember Mum sitting her down at the kitchen table when she was about ten and explaining to her the difference between fantasy and reality. Marie liked to lie about where she'd been and what she'd done, pretending to her friends that she was leading a far more exciting life than she was. But saying Erik wanted to buy a share in a boat – what was that all about? And was she even pregnant?

I pushed her out of my mind and called Fin and Caitlin. Collette had collected them from school and cooked their favourite Mexican meal with refried beans, tortillas, and dips. I wasn't being missed at all except perhaps by Myrtle who'd dug up another flowerbed.

Family dealt with, I sat down on the lid of the toilet seat and leant back against the cistern. I shut my eyes and let myself think about Ritchie. I was missing the sight of him. His smile. His hands. Touching him. Kissing him.

I need you like a heart needs to beat.

I'd said that to him. We were lying in bed and I was post-orgasmic tipsy. I'd gone all poetic on myself and said it with feeling, knowing that I really meant it, that the words absolutely articulated what I felt. There's nothing quite like making love is there? The physical, emotional and intellectual all combining into one almighty firework.

I was aching for him. Aching and wishing and wondering.

'Are you okay?' Tania's fist rapped on the bathroom door.

'It's not locked.'

The door opened and she stared inside. 'Why are you sitting there looking so miserable!' She grabbed my hands. 'Come and lie down.'

She led me through and pushed me onto one of the beds. 'A horizontal hour will do you the power of good.' She swung my feet around onto the psychedelically-patterned bedspread. She even arranged pillows under my head. 'How does that feel?'

'Good. Thanks.'

She sat down on the bed beside me. 'So, tell me what you're thinking.'

'I can't . . . nothing. Really.'

She stared at me for a couple of seconds, then licked her lips. 'Christ, I need a fag.'

'Don't let me stop you.'

'Will you be okay here on your own for five minutes?'

'Of course.'

'Good.' She grabbed her bag. 'I'll be back in a tick.'

The door closed behind her and I lay there with my eyes open, my thoughts flitting around, landing on one topic and then another. Brian Laidlaw with his tattoos and his muscles and his mean, hardman face. Fin and his football. I had to do better. Be a better mother. When I went home, I'd dedicate all my time to them both. You were dead. Drowned. Your ashes were waiting to be collected from the undertakers. And we still didn't know whose debt you'd died for.

Marie. Marie and her lies. Erik knew nothing about a boat. Why would she say that? Did she desperately, secretly, need the money?

I let myself wonder whether her lies could have had anything to do with your death. I held the thought at the front of my mind to see whether it would take root and start to grow.

Could she? Could she have amassed a debt that she couldn't service and so she'd got in touch with you? Is that why she was so keen to see the completion of your house sale? When she came to Scotland for your funeral I didn't doubt that she was grieving for you, but had she managed to separate the part she played in your death from her grief?

I didn't know the answer to any of these questions, and short of flying over to Norway I didn't see myself getting an answer any time soon unless Brian Laidlaw volunteered the information. He might. I simply had to get myself into a position where I could ask him. Face to face.

A sharp, urgent tremor started up in my hands and began to spread up my arms.

'Fuck this,' I announced to the embossed wallpaper. I stood up and got my mobile from the bathroom. I still had the print-out of the numbers you'd called during the month before you died. You hadn't called Marie, and unless you'd deleted her messages, she hadn't emailed you, nor you her. We had our once-a-week Skyping session, Mondays at seven, when you came over to mine, and we Skyped Marie and the kids, and we all chatted to each other, cousin to cousin, brother to sister, sister to sister. But otherwise, neither you nor I were in the habit of calling her.

The door opened and Tania came back in. She looked flushed from being outside. 'What are you doing?' she asked.

'Calling Alec.' As she passed me I caught a whiff of tobacco and stale food. She must have been standing next to a kitchen vent. 'I need him to do something for me.'

'Don't tell him where we are.'

I shook my head at her. 'Of course not.'

He answered his mobile with my name. 'Isla?'

'Alec, I know this is strictly speaking not exactly legal

and I wouldn't ask you if I had another option, but could you find out who called Dougie's mobile in the month before he died?'

'It's downright illegal is what it is.'

'I know. And, as I said I wouldn't ask you if I didn't really need to.'

'Gavin won't help?'

'No. And I know you know people . . .'

'Where are you?'

'I'm with Tania. We're visiting places that meant something to Dougie, to feel closer to him.'

'Where's that, then?'

'We're up . . . Loch Lomond way. You know he liked to swim in the loch.'

'What's the weather like?'

'Raining and then stopping for a bit. The usual.'

'Uh huh?'

He knew I was lying. I could feel his liar-baiting skills coming at me through the airwaves. 'Will you find out about the calls? I know it'll cost. I have money.'

'Don't insult me, lassie. I'd do anything for you or your brother. You know that. Any numbers in particular you're looking for?'

'Marie's.'

'Marie's,' he repeated. 'Why's that then?'

'She's been lying to me. And while you're at it, maybe you could check his house phone as well.'

'Will do. And Isla?'

'Yeah?'

'You know your limits, don't you?'

'Aye. Cheers, Alec. Love to Jean.'

Tania was lying on her bed again. 'What's going on?'

I told her about Marie and the boat-buying lie. 'I thought she had no connection to Glasgow but then I remembered she came over here about a year ago for a hen night. One of her friends from university, she said, but maybe she came to borrow money.'

Tania wasn't convinced. 'Marie's a pain in the arse on so many levels, but I don't think she's got the balls to borrow from a loan shark, not unless her kids' lives were at stake or something, and you'd know about that surely?'

I didn't reply because my mind was moving on. 'I wonder whether Paula will bring her Jimmy with her?' I took Jimmy Pearcy's photo, the one that Gordy had emailed me, out of my bag. 'I'm hoping they're one and the same Jimmy. It would be a bonus to find Lucy, wouldn't it? Dougie spent God knows how many man hours looking for her.'

'She might turn up right enough,' Tania said, looking at her watch. 'It's 7.15. Are you ready for the off?'

'I think so.'

'Do you know how to switch the recorder on?'

'Yes.'

'Show me.'

I'd been practising switching it on and off without looking down at my waistband, so my fingers found their own way there and settled for a second on the button, pulling the jeans away from my waist as if adjusting the fit.

'Try not to make it so obvious,' Tania said.

'I thought I wasn't being obvious.'

'You are a bit.' Her tone was kind, but she gave me a look that told me I was an amateur. And she was right, of course. I was an amateur.

'I'll hold on to the van keys, but I've moved your house keys onto a separate ring and added the fob rape alarm.' She handed it to me. 'You should wear the watch too.' She undid my watchstrap and swapped my watch for the one we'd bought from Sandy Farmer. 'Deep breaths.' She pulled my jacket sleeves straight and ran her hands down my arms as if she were a mother fixing her child's school uniform. 'How are you feeling?'

'Honestly? I'm shitting bricks.' The thought of going back into the pub was scary enough, but the thought of bumping into Brian Laidlaw made me want to run a hundred miles.

'Don't worry. I'm your wingman, remember?' She kissed my cheek. 'You'll be fine while you're in the pub. And when you come out, keep your trigger finger on the rape alarm. I'll be in the van, close enough to get to you if you need me.'

I know what you're thinking, Dougie. You're thinking of all the things that could go wrong, and I was too – not least the fact that Paula might not even be there. Brian Laidlaw might be there instead. He could bundle me into a car and drive off before Tania had time to start the van, never mind follow him. I could be gone, taken to anywhere in Glasgow, any abandoned warehouse or lonely patch of waste ground.

I knew the risks, but I was going to do it anyway.

'You're like a dog with a bone. Stubborn as!' Dad shouted at me. 'Douglas!' he bawled up the stairs. 'Come down here and talk some sense into your sister!'

'If I don't do it now, I'll never do it!' I shouted back.

'It's all very well having a yen for adventure but, as sure as not, you'll end up in trouble.'

You came down the stairs to see what all the ruckus was about. We were nineteen. You were in the marines by then and you were home on leave. 'What's going on?'

'*Your sister's planning a trip to Russia. It's a
nonsense!*'

'*Come on.*' *You angled your head towards the front
door.* '*Let's go to the pub.*'

You listened to me. That's one of the things you were
good at, by the way. Listening. Not everyone can listen.
People aren't deaf. They can hear, but they don't listen.
You did. And then you talked to me. You talked common
sense, so I scaled down my plans. I didn't take the train
from Moscow to Vladivostok. I went around Scandinavia
instead. 'One day we'll take that train journey together,'
you told me. But we never did.

So much in life comes too late.

Paula was waiting for me. She was sitting in the Lone
Star pub in the exact same seat you had sat in. I walked
towards her, looking neither right nor left, but I could
feel the what-the-fuck-is-she-doing-back-here stares
from the men playing pool. Paula was wearing a top
with spaghetti straps that showed off her collarbones.
There wasn't an ounce of spare flesh to cover her skel-
eton. My eyes followed the ridges on her sternum, ribs
arcing out on either side. Her breasts were smaller than
plums. Her arms were like a map I once saw of boats
in the English Channel. Crowded. Crowded with cuts
and needle marks and bruises and sores. Self-abuse on
a grand scale. I knew I couldn't trust her, not someone
who did this to herself.

And then her eyes stared up into mine. Open as a
two-year-old's. Honest as a sunflower. Huge chocolate-
brown eyes that promised me. Just. Exactly. What. I.
Wanted.

I remembered Tania's warning about addicts.

Chameleons who will do whatever, and be whoever, you want. I wondered how many boys and men had ignored the emaciated frame and the torn-up arms so that they could fall into those eyes.

I pulled back. 'What can I get you to drink?'

'Vodka and Coke.'

I walked across to the bar to where Don McAndrew stood with his face trippin' him, not bothering to hide the fact that he wasn't glad to see me. 'You again,' he said. 'Did we not scare you enough the last time?'

'I arranged to meet with the girl over there. She's called Paula. She's one of the homeless kids who lives with Min Fraser in the squat.'

'Her money's as good as yours.' He rested the flats of his palms on the bar. 'Are you staying for a drink?' His tone was accusing.

'If you don't mind.' I kept my voice light. 'A vodka and Coke, and an orange juice, please.' The two drunks on either side of me raised their heads to peer in my direction. I'd already decided I wouldn't make eye contact with anyone except Paula and McAndrew unless I absolutely had to. 'Do you have any food?'

'Crisps, peanuts, or pork scratchings.'

'Nothing hot?'

'Piss off. This isn't one of your trendy wine bars.'

'I'll have a packet of each.' I took some money out of my purse. 'Can you tell me, did you ever see Paula with my brother?'

'I've told you enough already.' He leant right in to my face, his teeth gritted against me. 'And now I'm telling you to fuck right off.'

'Thank you for your advice,' I said evenly. 'But I'm staying for just now.'

'You've been warned.'

He went off to get my order and I counted to twenty in my head. The drunks on either side of me had slid their pint glasses along the bar towards me and shuffled their stools closer. One was staring at the side of my face, his alcohol breath condensing on my cheek, willing me to turn towards him. The other one was arranging beer mats in front of him, singing softly to himself. It sounded like 'Oh Danny Boy' . . . (It really did) I wasn't intimidated by either of them. The men at the pool table bothered me more, but as long as I didn't look at them I felt I might be able to stay in their radar's safe zone.

When McAndrew returned with the drinks and snacks, he made a point of staring beyond me, as if I'd written myself off with my foolishness and he was playing no part in my downfall. I paid him, and walked back across to Paula. 'Here you go.' I passed her her drink and nudged the three snack bags into the middle of the table. 'I thought you might be hungry, but there's not much in the way of food in here.'

I sat down opposite her, but immediately thought better of it. I didn't want the pool players at my back, so I shifted onto the long, padded bench-seat next to her. Paula watched me do this, then lifted her glass and moved into the single seat I'd just vacated. 'Musical chairs.' She smiled. Her teeth were surprisingly white and even, proof of another life. 'It's easier to talk if we're across from each other,' she said, and then she shivered, rubbed her hands up her arms.

'You're in the draught there,' I said. 'Are you warm enough? I have a scarf in my bag. It'll cover your shoulders.'

'I'm okay.' She shook her head. 'I bet you're a really nice mum.'

'How do you know I'm a mum?' I remembered I

hadn't switched on either of the recording devices. Fiddling with the watch would have felt too obvious, so I placed my bag between my feet and as my hands came up from the floor, the fingers of my right hand made a swift detour to my belt.

'You look like one.' She took a mouthful of vodka and Coke. 'My mum was really nice. She was a nurse. In a hospice.'

'What happened to her?'

'She died.' Her eyes filled. Then she blinked and a lone tear travelled slowly down her cheek. 'Ended up in the hospice herself.' She took several more mouthfuls of vodka. 'It was weird. One day she was working there; the next day she was dying there.'

'I'm sorry.'

She glanced up at me through lowered lashes, checking she was garnering my sympathy. 'It was all downhill from there.'

'What about your dad?'

'I never knew him. Mum got herself pregnant at eighteen.'

'There was no one who could look after you?'

'Social services sent me to a foster family, but I didn't do well there.' She shrugged her skinny shoulders. 'They weren't paedos or anything, I just didn't get on with them.'

'What age were you?'

'Twelve.'

'That's rough.'

'Shit happens.' She swirled the liquid around in her glass. 'I like it when they give you a slice of lemon in the Coke.'

'You could suggest it to Don McAndrew,' I said. 'But you might get a mouthful of abuse in return.'

'He's not as bad as some of them in here,' she said, and began to tell me a story about one of the other barmen who'd thrown her and Jimmy out on the street for not spending enough money.

'You didn't bring Jimmy with you?' I asked, resting both my hands together on the table.

'I finished with him. I want to get myself cleaned up and out of this life. Lucy does too.'

'Was Jimmy Lucy's boyfriend?'

'What do you mean?'

'I know that Lucy ran off with a boy called Jimmy.'

'No, no.' She laughed. 'Lucy wouldn't spend time with a loser like him.'

'Must have been another Jimmy then.'

'Must have.' Her eyes widened. 'I mean, yeah. I knew him and everything, but he disappeared a while back.'

'Disappeared where?'

'London. That's where everyone goes.'

'I can't wait to meet Lucy.' I sipped my orange juice. 'Her mum and dad will be so pleased to get her home.'

'She's worried she might be in trouble.'

'She's not in any trouble. Her parents just want her home where she belongs.'

'She's living in a different squat. Not the one I was in. It's a bit further away from here. We can go there tomorrow.'

'Why not now?'

'I don't know. She said tomorrow.'

There was loud shouting over by the pool tables. Four-letter words fractured the air, and then the pushing and shoving started. 'Take it outside!' McAndrew bellowed across the room, and one man hauled another two through the door. Cold air rushed in and Paula shivered again.

'Pricks,' she said. 'It's always the same in this pub.'

'Why did you ask to meet me here, then? It's a fair distance from the squat.'

'Believe it or not, it's the safest place to meet if you're a stranger. Like you.' She drained her glass. 'Apart from the soup kitchen, that is. Three evenings a week they set one up under the bridge along there.' She waved her arm to the left. 'You get soup and sandwiches and sometimes there's people to chat to. That's where I met Lucy.' She started to tell me about her and Lucy, about how at first they were wary of each other but then they hit it off. How they talked and talked for hours, sharing all their secrets. How they'd known each other for a year now, and would do anything for each other. When she was fully engaged in her tale I threw in a comment.

'Lucy's sister's looking forward to her coming home,' I said. 'Her nephew is almost two now. She'll notice a big change in him.'

'She told me that,' Paula said, nodding her head. And then she smiled. It wasn't a spontaneous smile. It was forced. She was trying to cover the fact that she might have made a mistake. I'd taken her off script again and she wasn't sure whether she'd ad-libbed correctly or not.

'The three monkeys—'

'—belong to Lucy.'

'What did you mean about the brass being proof?'

'Proof that I know Lucy. Because she's always taken it everywhere with her. She told me that if you'd been talking to her dad you would know that.'

'But why would I need proof? Why didn't she just come and see me herself? You came to my house, didn't you? To post it through the letter box.'

'You don't understand. She's afraid. When you live on the streets, you learn not to trust anyone. It's tough, you know. *Fucking* tough. You have to look out for yourself.'

She said this with feeling and I knew she was talking about herself, not Lucy, who by now I doubted Paula had even met.

'And how did you get my address?' I asked.

'I looked you up.' She began scratching her arm.

'How? I'd never even told you my name.'

She shook her head. 'You did.'

If she'd been thinking straight she could have said she'd looked in my handbag when I was down on the ground, after Brian Laidlaw had half-strangled me. But she couldn't think straight because she was the puppet not the master.

'I didn't give you my name or number or address. The old lady, Min Fraser, she told you who I was, didn't she?'

'I don't know what you mean. I don't know why you're asking me these questions!' Her voice grew louder. 'I'm only trying to help you find Lucy! I felt sorry for you when you were mugged, and I'm trying to help.'

'Shh.' I put my hands over hers. 'Calm down.'

'You're making me feel bad about myself.'

'I'm not meaning to do that, Paula.' The pool-playing pricks stared in our direction. 'I'm simply trying to get to the truth.'

'I am being truthful.' She used her eyes again. Her pupils were huge, and swam with sincerity. 'I am.'

'I know.' I smiled. 'I just have to be sure.'

'I don't have to help you.'

'I know.' I swallowed some juice. 'Just one more wee thing. The mobile you called me from, is it yours?'

She nodded.

'My brother called your number the day he came to Glasgow.'

She frowned. 'I don't know your brother.'

'Then why did he call you?'

'Other people use my phone. It might have been Lucy.' She snapped her fingers. 'But probably it was Jimmy. He's always taking my mobile.' She looked around as if she expected Jimmy to be standing behind her. 'I'm sure it was him. It will have been him. Definitely it will have been him.' She continued to scratch her arm, made contact with a scab and pulled her nails through it. Instantly fresh blood spotted her skin. I pulled a paper handkerchief out of my pocket and pressed it over the bleeding.

'You should really consider seeing a doctor, Paula. Your arms . . . That cut could become infected.'

She looked down at herself, interested but unconcerned, as if the limb belonged to someone else. 'Lucy will know what to do. She always looks after me when I'm in trouble.' Her eyes caught hold of mine. 'You do believe me about Lucy, don't you?' she said. 'And about my mobile?'

'Of course I do.' The pool players were moving towards our table.

'You will come with me to meet Lucy then, won't you?'

'Yes,' I said, lying through my smile. 'I'll come with you.'

12. Wiser Than Monkeys

Paula told me where to meet Lucy the next day, and then we left the pub quickly, Paula slinking off into the shadows like a cat. A couple of the men had followed us out, their heckling biting at my neck. I'd parked your van far enough away to not draw attention, but close enough for me to signal to Tania if I was in trouble. I walked the fifty or so metres towards it, holding the key fob in my hand, hovering over the rape alarm button in case one of the men decided to follow me. When Tania saw me coming she started the engine. 'I won't ask you anything until we get back to the room,' she said.

I nodded my appreciation. I felt elated and depressed at the same time. Elated because I'd managed to get through the evening with a clear head, and depressed because I wasn't sure I was any closer to finding out what had happened to you.

Back in the room, Tania was buzzing, 'First things first.' She waved the room-service menu at me. 'Let's get something to eat.'

'I'm okay.' I sat on the edge of the bed and took off my shoes. 'You go ahead, though.'

'You need to eat something,' Tania said.

'Paula needs to eat something,' I said. 'I've never seen anyone so skinny.'

'She won't be hungry for food,' Tania told me, reading

the menu. 'I'm going to order a burger and chips. Sure you don't want anything?'

'Is there any soup?'

'Tomato and basil. It'll be out of a packet.'

'Just get me some chips and a bottle of water.' I undid my jeans. 'I'll take these off. It'll be easier to plug the cable in.'

'Did you use the watch as well?'

'I forgot about recording until I was sitting down, and then I thought it might be too obvious.' I went into the bathroom. 'I'll have a quick shower and then we can listen to the playback.'

The water was hot and stung my skin, although there was less power in the shower than in an average tap. Still, I scrubbed away at myself as if all the intensity of my feelings were stored on the surface and could be washed down the plughole along with the dead skin cells. I longed for a clean emotional slate where I could stand back and observe, reflect on the past and on the present, and come up with a clever solution. Emotional arithmetic. I was never any good at it.

By the time I came out, Tania had the button cam plugged in and was pacing in front of it. 'You took your time.'

'We might as well wait until the food comes.' I tipped my head upside down to towel dry my hair. 'We'll only be interrupted.'

'I'll hurry it along.'

'I don't think they'll appreciate you turning up in the kitch—' I stopped talking because she'd gone out of the door. She'd accused me of being jittery, but in fact she seemed more on edge than me. I pulled on my pyjamas and dried my hair, and by the time I was finished Tania was back with a young lad pushing a trolley. He arranged the food with haste and left before I could tip him.

'Let's get this going,' Tania said, switching on the playback. She focussed all her attention on the tiny display, pointing at the screen. 'What's that? Paula's legs?'

I peered at the screen, but couldn't see much. The underside of the table cast such a complete shadow that almost nothing was visible. 'We might as well forget visual,' I said.

Tania sat forward, her mouth open as she focussed on simply listening. Background noise drowned out some of what was said, but mostly it was surprisingly clear. Paula's voice sounded more robust than I remembered, until we got to the point where she suspected I'd trapped her and she began to talk in a higher, louder pitch.

'What's made her nervy?' Tania asked, hitting the pause button.

'She's worried she's dropped herself in it because I took her off script by mentioning Lucy's sister.'

'Why's that bad?'

'Lucy's an only child. If Paula was that much of a friend she'd know that.'

'Crafty,' Tania said, admiration on her face.

'Alec taught me how to trip up insurance claimants. Get them talking and lob in a question that catches them unawares.'

Tania began the recording again, and we listened through to the end.

'I don't think Paula knows where Lucy is,' Tania said, taking a mouthful of burger. 'I think she was playing you.'

'I agree. She wasn't a good liar.' I ate a chip. It tasted dry and powdery, and almost made me gag. 'She was shaky and freezing, and her arms are covered in cuts and track marks.' I swallowed some water. 'I don't think

Dougie called her. I think she's using someone else's phone, probably Min Fraser's. She didn't seem to know who Dougie was, never mind the fact of his death. She used the present tense when she spoke about him.'

'I don't know your brother,' Tania said, repeating Paula's exact words.

I nodded. 'And she was panicking by then. If she'd known about his death she would have automatically used the past tense. She lives in a squat that's controlled by Min Fraser. I think she's working for her and her nephews, surviving the only way she knows how.'

'Don't buy the sob story. I bet her mum was no more a nurse than mine was,' Tania said. 'She'll know the score. They use her to lure you onto their patch, and in exchange she gets her fix. If it had all gone tits up and you'd marched the police into the pub, Paula would have been the fall guy.'

We fell into silence as Tania ate her burger and I forced down a few more chips. It was almost midnight by now, and, apart from an electrical hum from the lights, the hotel was completely quiet. I wondered who ended up staying in a place like this. It was too grubby for the average businessman, but not cheap enough for young travellers. It felt like a no man's land, a way station for people on the climb up or the slide down.

'This place needs a refurb,' Tania said, staring at the ceiling. 'That stain looks like it's been there for years.'

'I was thinking much the same,' I said.

We both contemplated the stain, and then she stood up and shook out her limbs. 'So, what are we thinking? Min Fraser had Paula pretend she knew Lucy in order to get you onto their patch?'

I nodded. 'Assuming she's as much of a criminal as her nephews.'

'Keeping it in the family.'

'I don't know how long I was passed out on the ground, but I expect it was long enough for Min Fraser to tell Paula and Jimmy to go outside and be there when I woke up,' I said. 'The search for Lucy and the debt Dougie was paying off have never really fitted together. Unless Dougie was paying for Lucy's release or something.'

'Who from? Slave traders?' Tania laughed. 'That doesn't happen.'

'Now you're sounding like Gavin.'

'Well, have you ever heard of that?'

'I think so. I don't know! I'm not exactly familiar with this sort of world.'

'Well I am and . . .' She shrugged. 'Kids who've been brought up in care, Russians and Eastern European women are trafficked and held as sex slaves. Nobody looks for them. They have no power. But a Scottish girl whose father's been all over Scotland publicising his daughter as a runaway, leafleting here there and everywhere.' She gave a dismissive shake of her head. 'It's not worth the criminals' trouble. They can get women way easier. Lucy is one of the disappeared. She'll be living in London, or dead, or . . .' She took her cigarettes out of her pocket. 'I'm gasping for a fag.' She glanced back up at the ceiling. 'Do you think the smoke alarm works?'

'Probably.'

'I'll be back in a tick.'

While Tania was gone I scrolled through the photos I'd taken on my mobile. I wanted to comfort myself by looking at Caitlin and Fin's faces, remind myself that I was a mum and I had a life that was waiting for me beyond the hotel. There were half a dozen photos from last summer, when you, me, and the kids had gone into town. The festival was on, and we had walked down the Royal Mile enjoying the street performers. We'd ended up on Princes Street, and I'd taken a photograph of you and Fin standing in front of the National Gallery, Edinburgh castle in the background. You had your arm around Fin's shoulder and he was smiling up at you. Green eyes and freckles met green eyes and freckles. Marie had inherited Mum's fair colouring, but you and I took after Dad, with our green eyes and curly brown hair, tinged with red, and Fin had inherited the same. We'd asked an American tourist to take a photograph of the four of us pointing up at the castle. We were all making silly faces and laughing.

Happy times.

Tania came back, wafting in on a gust of cigarette smoke and sharp air. 'I got this in the machine along the hallway.' She held up a can of Coke. 'Did you want one?'

'No thanks.'

As she walked to her bed her eyes flicked sideways at the minibar, a furtive glance as if she was afraid of waking a sleeping Rottweiler.

'If the booze is too tempting, we can take it down to reception,' I said.

'That won't work. I'll just counter it with another move.' She lay back on the bed. 'Okay . . . so, where were we?'

'I doubt that Lucy has got anything to do with the debt, or Dougie's death, and so neither, I suppose, does Gordy.'

'What have we got left?'

'I could see whether Alec can find out who owns the phone Paula used.' I looked at my watch. 'It's a bit late now though.'

'Chances are it'll be a pay-as-you-go.' Tania swivelled onto her stomach, elbows bent, chin on her hands. 'You're not planning on going to meet Lucy, are you?'

'Of course not. I'd just be walking into a trap.'

'We have to get ahead of them.'

'I know.'

'How?'

I didn't answer her straight away. I hoped that divine intervention would strike and that words would come out of my mouth, wise words that would reveal the clever thing to do. But after a few seconds, when nothing struck me, I shrugged my hopelessness. 'I don't know,' I said. 'I really don't.'

Tania rolled onto her back again and gazed up at the ceiling, her expression thoughtful.

I dreamt about the bike ride, but this time we never made it home because the road lengthened before our eyes. And darkness was chasing us, grabbing at our legs with giant, birdlike claws, making me wobble and almost fall. You were throwing your voice behind you, shouting 'Keep up, Isla! Hurry!' and I was trying my hardest, straining to pedal faster and faster as we cycled towards home. We were almost there, just a few more metres, two more wheel lengths, and then, 'Isla!' you screamed, and I saw you crushed by a wall of water, your body tossed into the air like a discarded doll.

I woke up in the hotel room, my heart pounding like a navvy's hammer on nails. My T-shirt was stuck to my back, and I was boiling hot. I sat up and practised deep breathing: in through my nose, hold for five seconds, and out through my mouth. When I was calmer, I swung my legs over the edge of the bed and onto the floor. Tania's bed was empty, and I could hear the muffled sound of her voice coming from the bathroom. The minibar fridge was open, and the light shone across the room spotting a pathway across the carpet. I got up to close the fridge door and noticed that the miniature bottles of spirits were missing. Every last one of them.

Shit.

I walked to the bathroom door and knocked, 'Tania?' I didn't wait for an answer. I turned the handle and found her inside. She was perched up on the faux marble sink surround, her feet on the loo, her mobile in the crook of her neck. The bottles were scattered in the bath. They were all empty.

'Tania?' I expected her to be drunk enough to fall over, but she looked perfectly alert.

'It's okay, I haven't drunk them,' she said. 'I tipped all the alcohol down the sink.'

'Eh?' My first thought was expense. 'Now we're going to have to pay for them! We could have returned them to reception like I said.'

She held her hand over the mouthpiece. 'I couldn't. I had to empty them out or I would have drunk them.' She spoke back into the phone. 'Simon, we'll talk tomorrow, yeah?'

'Why didn't you wake me up! I'd have taken them away.'

'I needed to speak to Simon.' She finished the call and slid down onto her feet. 'He knows me. He understands.'

'Well that's great then!' My second thought was about waste. 'Let's all go around willy nilly, tipping bottles of alcohol down the drain.'

'And what do you know about addiction?' Her eyes were frosty. 'More than would fit on the back of a postage stamp?'

'No, but—'

'Up there on your pedestal,' she shouted. 'Lording it over the rest of us.' She pushed past me. 'Some of us live our lives, Isla. We take risks. We make mistakes. Life can be messy.'

'There is such a thing as *choice*.'

'Dougie always said you lived too safe a life.'

I took a step away from her. 'I don't believe he said that.'

'He did.' She looked smug. 'Marrying Gavin, working in insurance when you were clever enough to do better.'

'I'm not defending myself to you, Tania.'

'And then there was that railway trip across Russia you wanted to go on.'

'Dougie talked me out of it!'

'He said you talked yourself out of it.' She was smirking now. 'That you didn't really have the balls for it. You were just winding your dad up.'

That hurt, Dougie. It was a low blow, and one I wasn't expecting. Why did you even tell Tania about that trip? Why the hell would you? Did you often talk about me? Have a laugh at my expense?

'Home truths are hard to take, aren't they?' Tania said. She had a look of triumph on her face. My hands twitched. The urge to throttle her was an allergic itch in my fingers. The thought of unleashing all my anger and frustration on her was a heady and delicious one, but I settled for pushing her out of the way.

'What are you doing?'

I was pulling on my clothes, detaching the cable from the button cam, and doing up my jeans.

'Where are you going?'

I slung my jacket over my shoulder and left the room. She followed me along the corridor.

'It was a joke! Stop being so sensitive!'

'You know what, Tania?' I whirled back around to face her. 'I *am* sensitive. I have barely slept in a month. My dad is in hospital. I fell in love with a liar. My brother is dead. D-E-A-D. Gone. *For ever.*'

'You fell in love? How did I miss that? Who is he?'

Cold air smacked me in the face as I walked out through the front door.

'Isla?' I think she would have followed me, but for the fact her feet were bare. 'For fuck's sake! Just come back!'

Five degrees higher would have been invigorating, but this was just plain freezing in that insidious, damp way that seeps into your bones. I buttoned my jacket, pulled up the collar, and pushed my hands deep into my pockets to stop my fingers from going numb. I walked through patchily-lit, deserted streets and down to the river, crossing over at the Clyde Arc. Chain-link railings were rattling with the wind, making music that sounded like Christmas, sleigh bells without the sleigh. I didn't turn right towards the Science Centre, but went straight up onto Govan Road and into the streets beyond.

A lone jogger with a light on his forehead ran past me, and I pounded the pavement behind him, keeping pace until I ran out of breath and took shelter in the shadow of a shop doorway. I was still cold on the outside, but a fist of anger warmed my insides. You had the cheek to call me safe! To talk to Tania about me. To criticise me behind my back. Well, Douglas McTeer, know-it-all, here are some home truths for you.

You should have dumped Tania years ago. Yes, really. You let her pussy whip you until you'd shrunk to half the man you were. Tania is, was, and always will be a spoiler. A self-serving little bitch who puts herself first. You could have married a girl who deserved you. You should be living in a semi-detached in Balerno with a couple of skippy, happy, wee kids and a Labrador.

Admit it, Dougie. There were times when you let other people dictate your life. Why were you even dead for God's sake? *Why?* Why would you take on someone else's debt? Was it for Marie? Or was it going to turn out to be Tania after all? The woman whom you'd pandered to since you met? Because she seemed incapable of staying in the hotel room for any length of time, and it wasn't just about smoking.

Snow began to fall, light as dust. It meandered down from the sky, in no particular hurry to reach the earth. I put my anger to one side and moved out of the doorway, opening my mouth to let the flakes melt on my tongue. I stayed like that until my teeth were chattering and my feet were numb, and then I stepped back into the relative warmth of the doorway. The shop was close to a junction, an ideal position for customers you might think, except that the windows were boarded up. There were posters plastered across the chipboard, layers and layers of advertising shouting out to passers-by, publicising bands and dance lessons and newly opened restaurants.

Every so often a car drove by, and once a group of young people, oblivious to the weather and to me, stumbled past, laughing and holding on to one another, their faces loud and bright under the street lights.

Do you remember, Dougie, that Mum used to say coincidence was God's way of giving us a nudge? I was about to cross the road to head back to the hotel, when I noticed a car stopped at the traffic lights to one side of me. The car was a green Golf. And the man at the wheel had a bald head, a tough jaw, and tattoos reaching up around his collar.

Brian Laidlaw.

I forced my hand over my mouth to bottle up the shock, and pulled back into the doorway so I couldn't be seen. My eyes were wide open and my breath held until I heard his car accelerate away.

Fuck.

I hadn't been imagining it then. Back in Edinburgh, Laidlaw had been following me. He knew where I lived. He knew where I dropped the kids at the bus stop. He'd even followed me to visit Dad at the hospital.

I stood in the alleyway and thought about this, alert to every small sound, every movement in the air. At one point I was spooked. I could swear there were footsteps creeping towards me and I swung out onto the pavement with my arms raised, but there was no one there. Eventually, my mind made up, I set off at a run, not back towards the hotel, but in the other direction. Laidlaw had been driving towards Glasgow city centre; I headed for the squat.

I half expected to find a guard on duty, or if not that, then the fire exit door back on its hinges and locked against intruders, but there was nothing and no one to stop me letting myself into the squat. I walked along the litter-strewn passageway and straight into the communal space, the dilapidated function room. I was met by a chorus of breathing, loud and soft, deep and shallow. The air was fuggy with booze and bad breath. I used the torch app on my phone to inch my way through the huddles of sleeping bodies on mattresses, making sure I didn't step on anyone. I went into the passageway leading to the abandoned bar where I'd met Min Fraser for the first time, and tiptoed along the tiled floor, stopping just short of the open door. People were talking inside the bar room, too quietly for me to hear the whole conversation, but odd words and phrases carried on the air . . . 'in the drawer' . . . 'before he left' . . . 'I told you I would' . . . Snippets that meant nothing, but did allow me to gauge how many people were there. I could make out four distinct voices: Min Fraser, Paula, Jimmy, and a woman whose voice I didn't recognise.

I'd been listening for about five minutes when I felt brave enough to shift position. I switched on the button cam and stretched my neck around the door surround. Min Fraser was sitting on her chair. She was wearing the same soft knits and ankle boots, and had an open book on her lap. Paula and Jimmy were less than two metres away from her, their eyes fixed on the fourth occupant. She looked about fifty but she could have been younger. Her skin was grey and lined, and, like Paula, she was super skinny. She was holding a huge, expertly-rolled spliff. She inhaled a lungful then passed it to Min Fraser, who laid it in the ashtray on the small table next to her.

Super-Skinny took a package from her pocket and tipped the contents onto the small table. She began mixing powder with water, using a small metal bowl, the sort you'd find in a doctor's surgery. Jimmy passed her a lighter, and she applied heat to the base of the bowl before drawing the solution up into a syringe.

Paula and Jimmy were quivering, the expressions on their faces nothing short of ravenous. They looked more wolf than human. I had the feeling that even if I jumped out and waved my arms in front of them they wouldn't notice, because they were so intent on what Super-Skinny was preparing for them. Paula's jaw was slack and drool dribbled from the corners of her mouth. Jimmy's eyes snatched at Paula. I didn't need to look at the photo of Jimmy Piercy again to recognise that this was a different

Jimmy, one with no connection to Lucy. His nose was larger, his eyes deeper set and his hairline was low on his forehead.

'Me first,' he said yanking down his trousers as if desperate for sex, but his penis was flaccid and of no interest to Super-Skinny, who searched for a working vein in his groin.

All the while this was going on, Min Fraser had been sitting with her eyes closed as if she'd fallen asleep. But then, 'I know someone's there,' she called out. 'Whoever you are, you're welcome to come in and join us.'

My stomach turned over, but my feet propelled me forward as if they'd been waiting for the go-ahead.

'I thought it might be you.' She smiled up at me. 'Isla McTeer. From Edinburgh.' She angled her head towards the spliff in the ashtray. 'Help yourself.'

'No thanks.'

'Perhaps you'd like something stronger?' She opened the drawer and took out a brand new syringe and needle. 'You want to try some?'

'No.'

'You sure? Even Queen Victoria liked her opium.'

I turned away and stared across at Jimmy, who had slid down onto one of the floor cushions, his head thrown back, his spine arching to the ceiling. Super-Skinny turned her attention to Paula, who was moaning and swaying on her feet like a lost drunk. Paula's veins were easy to find, and within seconds Super-Skinny was injecting the drug into her arm. I watched Paula's eyes flood with an opiate-sweet kiss, and then she too lounged backward onto a cushion.

Min Fraser watched me watching them. Calculating. Her milky-blue eyes were sharper than a mountain vulture's. 'Sit down,' she said.

I sat down.

'You come here and you think to yourself – not me, not my children. My children could never end up in a place like this,' she said quietly. 'My daughter is a good girl. My son won't be a criminal.'

I hadn't been thinking any of those thoughts. Fin and Caitlin, my precious children, the two people in the world I would die for, existed in another realm, in an Edinburgh that was a world away from here. This place? This was a temporary stop, an out-of-body encounter, a means to an end.

'Have you read this?' She took the book from her lap and held it towards me.

I glanced at the title but didn't recognise it. 'No,' I said.

'Have you heard the phrase memento mori?'

That I did know. 'It's Latin for "remember you will die".'

'Clever girl.' She leant across and patted my knee. 'You've been well educated.'

'Not especially.'

We were twenty-one. You were home on leave, and you had a funeral to go to. I came with you because Mum didn't want you going on your own. She was worried about you. You'd completed one tour in Iraq, and it had brought a dark colour to your eye, a sore look that said 'Don't ask'.

The funeral service was intense, the atmosphere tight with the mourners' grief. I never knew the dead marine and much as I empathised with his family and friends, for me the whole experience was a wake-up call because the marine who had died was no older than you. I asked you – I begged you – to leave the marines to go AWOL, buy yourself out, whatever it took.

*'We're always close to death,' you told me. 'Always.
All of us.'*

*And then you quoted me a poem. I don't have a
clear memory of the author or the words. What I
remember was the impression I got as you spoke. For
the length of the poem you weren't my brother. You
were a soldier, an archetype, a man who understood
what it meant to die for your country.*

*'The poem is called "Memento Mori",' you told me.
'Remember you will die.'*

*You got paralytic at the pub and I had to drive us
both home. Afterwards, when I thought about it, I
wasn't sure what surprised me more, the fact that you
were reading poetry, or the fact that you knew Latin.
But more than that, it was the first time I realised
that you'd been places I'd never go and seen things
you'd never be able to share.*

'I like to remind myself that none of this is permanent,'
Min said. 'Not the lamps, nor the cushions, nor me.'

Super-Skinny was now sitting on the floor next to
Min, staring up at her as if she were an aspirant at the
feet of her guru.

'Nor my brother?'

'Nor your brother.' Min drew more heroin into the
syringe, while Super-Skinny probed for a vein on the
underside of her elbow.

'Your nephew's been following me,' I said.

'I know.'

'Why?'

She cast her eye my way. 'You know why.' She slid
the needle into Super-Skinny's vein, drew back some
blood, and deftly injected her. I had to look away. I was
holding onto the arms of the chair to stop myself from

running back to the hotel. I'd never felt more on edge. Every so often the reality of where I was and what I was trying to do washed over me in a wave of heat and nausea. And the whole business of drug-taking was making my skin crawl.

Paula and Jimmy had drifted into a stupor that mimicked sleep, but while Jimmy was quiet, Paula was making tremulous, whimpering sounds as if she were in pain. Her face and one of her legs were twitching, and I wondered whether I should shake her awake. 'Leave her,' Min said, anticipating my move. 'She's not your concern.'

Anger flared inside me. 'I met Paula earlier. In the pub. I think you were behind that. Paula doesn't know Lucy O'Malley and neither do you.'

'You're sure?'

'No, I'm not sure. I'm guessing, because that's all I can do, is *guess*. I'm here because I need to find out what happened to my brother.' I met her eye. 'I need to know how he died.'

She nodded. 'I can understand that.'

I powered on. 'This is about money, isn't it?'

'That's right.'

'He's given you money. He emptied his savings account.'

'He's given us some.'

'But it wasn't even my brother who owed you the money, was it?'

'He took the debt on.'

'Whose debt?' I blurted out. 'Whose debt was it?' (Because if it was Tania's debt, Dougie, I was planning on throttling her with my bare hands.)

Min's eyes lit up. 'Whose debt?' she repeated, pleased I didn't know, and I cursed myself for being so keen.

'You give us the rest of our money and we'll tell you.'

'How much?'

'He gave us twenty-five and we're owed another seventy-five.'

A hundred grand? My mouth hung open.

'You're shocked?'

I nodded. 'How do I know that's true?'

'You don't. You just have to take our word for it.' She leant across towards me and gripped my sleeve. 'You really have no choice, my dear.'

Cruel women go against the order of things, and Min Fraser had threat and menace all wrapped up in a cosy, old-lady package. But that wasn't all she had. There was empathy there too, and vulnerability. 'We are all shaped by our circumstances,' she told me. 'You've lost your brother and that's brought you to me.'

Her eyes were persuasive, kindly. Evil I would have recoiled from, but she wasn't evil. I was a novice and she was one of the initiated. She tuned into me. 'We have to help each other.' She dragged at time's heels so that every second lengthened, giving her the opportunity to slip inside my skull and ferret around. I couldn't resist. I was swept along by a feeling of relief. 'That's right. We can be allies.' She was on my side. She understood why I was there. She would help me if I helped her. A transaction. Simple.

A door slammed along the corridor and Min pulled back, watching the entrance to the room, waiting for the herd of footsteps to reach us. Brian Laidlaw came in first, followed by his brother Gerry, who was marching Tania along beside him. I gave Tania a 'What-the-fuck?' look that she met with a 'So?' expression, and then I stood up, backing away from them, almost tripping over the whimpering Paula.

'Found her nosing around outside,' Gerry said, pushing Tania onto the floor in front of him.

'Now, now.' Min narrowed her eyes at her nephew. 'There's no need for that.'

'Please, let her go,' I said. 'She's nothing to do with this.'

Brian Laidlaw stared at me, and my hand automatically felt around my throat, remembering. I hoped he didn't notice how much I was afraid of him, but his expression told me that he did. His lips stretched across grey teeth, more grimace than smile. The bruising around his eye had faded to a dirty yellow, and tattoos spread up his bare arms in hectic, hardman fashion. And then I noticed the watch he was wearing. 'That's my brother's,' I blurted out.

'You want it?' He held his wrist towards me. 'Take it.' He paused to allow the absurdity of his suggestion to scare me even further. 'Take it,' he repeated.

'Just give it to her,' Min said, waving an arm from him to me. 'She's going to honour the debt. There's no need to make an enemy.'

Laidlaw came towards me. A low hum of energy leaked through the pores in his skin and reverberated through my bones. My teeth began to chatter, and I closed my jaw tightly. He took the watch cam from my wrist and tore the button from the waistband of my jeans and threw them across the room. They ricocheted off the mirror behind the bar and fell to the floor. He gave me a look that said 'Don't try that again', and then he removed your watch from his wrist and wrapped it around mine. It was too big and heavy for my wrist, but it was yours and that fact made me feel empowered.

Paula sat up and began to whimper more loudly than ever. Both the brothers and Min Fraser glanced in her direction. Gerry Laidlaw kicked her in the small of her back and the whimpering turned into loud groaning.

'Shut the fuck up!' Gerry shouted and kicked her again, harder this time, the toe of his boot making heavy contact with her thigh.

Tania was on her feet and I grabbed her arm. 'Let's go,' I said.

'No.' She moved towards Paula.

'You can't help her,' I said.

But that wasn't Tania's intention. As she walked the few paces towards the huddle of people, she pulled something from the back pocket of her jeans. I saw the blade glint in the light from the standard lamp and then she sank the sharp end into Gerry Laidlaw's chest.

13. Real Life is Bad For You

Gerry Laidlaw must have had a sixth sense for danger, because as Tania lunged for him, he turned to one side and the knife made contact with his left shoulder rather than his heart. At the same time, his right hand struck out, knocking Tania off her feet. She was on the ground for less than a second when she came back for more, charging towards him with her head down.

'Tania!' I shouted, but she ignored me and he hit her again. This time she fell backward on top of Jimmy, who didn't even budge, and as she flailed around, Brian Laidlaw grabbed the back of her neck with his left hand and caught hold of my hair with his right. He forced our heads into a collision, knocking them together with a force that made the air between us evacuate the space in a whooshing sound. I felt my brain shake inside my skull. I felt my forehead split. I felt a shaft of pain fragment off in all directions, punching into every corner of me.

The last thing I saw before blood trickled down into my eyes was Min pressing a rag into the hollow of Gerry Laidlaw's shoulder.

When I woke up, I was lying face down. I lifted my head and looked around me. The room was almost completely dark, but I guessed that I was in the pub cellar. The floor was made of cold, uneven stone, and the air was stale with the smell of old beer and blood.

'Tania?' My voice was a whispery croak. 'Tania?'

I concentrated on listening out for her reply, trying to hear beyond the tinnitus inside my own eardrums and the loud *drip-drip* of water somewhere off to my left. But there was nothing. No other human sounds. I was down here on my own.

Tears ran down my cheeks, combining with the blood to form a sticky stream that leaked into my mouth and made me retch. 'Stop . . . stop . . . *stop!*' I ordered myself.

I stopped crying and sat up, staying as still as I could. There was no part of me that didn't ache. Breathing was the worst of it and I felt sure I'd cracked at least one rib, because every inhalation was a sharp pain in my chest. I took time to practise shallow breaths, found the angle where my ribs hurt the least – head back, neck tilted to the right – and kept myself in that position.

There was only one point of light, a thin, horizontal strip that was several metres away from me and well above eye level, like the light coming from beneath a door at the top of a flight of stairs. My way out.

I got myself up onto my hands and knees, and then very slowly to a standing position. Every so often a tsunami-tremor passed through me, flooding me from head to toe, and I had to ride it out. I thought of those posters that are everywhere now, variations of Keep Calm and Carry On. Keep Calm and Drink Champagne. Keep Calm and Call Batman. Fin had a pencil case that said Keep Calm and Get the Ball in the Net.

'Keep calm and find your mobile,' I said out loud. 'Do it. Just do it.'

My hands fumbled for my back pocket. Several of my fingers were swollen and couldn't bend, but I managed to extricate the phone by using both hands at once, one hand pulling the pocket outward while the other grasped the phone. Once retrieved, I held the phone up to my face and pressed the button to activate it.

No signal. Fuck. I felt the onset of panic again and immediately my breathing deepened. 'Don't, don't,' I whispered to myself. 'Go to the top of the stairs. You need to find Tania and get out of here.'

I used the torch app to shine light ahead of me to the foot of the stone staircase, but between me and the stairs Tania was lying in a heap.

'Tania! Jesus . . .' I knelt down beside her, groaning with pain as I bent my head towards her face. 'Tania? Can you hear me?' I listened at her mouth. She was breathing. Thank God! 'Tania, wake up.' I hadn't done any first aid since I was at school, and the main thing I remembered was that you could cause someone more damage if you moved them. She was partly on her side, her legs and arms twisted underneath her, but what was worse was the awkward angle of her head. That couldn't be good. I balanced the light close to us and gently moved her head into alignment with her spine. 'Please wake up. Please wake up.' I shook her shoulders. 'Tania. Come on.'

Nothing.

I stood up again and took the light with me to climb the stairs. My right ankle was throbbing. My left hip ached with an intensity that made childbirth seem a dawdle. I held onto the wooden handrail and half-dragged myself up the stone steps. The door at the top was made of metal. I turned the handle. It was locked. I banged on the door. 'Please. Help me!' I shouted. 'My friend needs help. Please.'

I thought about all the people asleep on mattresses. They might not hear me shouting, but they would hear the rape alarm. I didn't consider Laidlaw and what he might do to me if I drew attention to myself. I was only thinking about Tania. I took my keys from my pocket and pressed the red button on the fob. The sound was a high-pitched wail not dissimilar to a car alarm. I kept the button depressed for almost a full minute until I heard an answering bang on the other side of the door.

'You have to stop that.' It was Paula's voice. 'He'll come back . . . hit you again.'

'Paula, listen to me.' I pressed my mouth up against the doorframe where there was the merest of gaps between the metal and the wooden surround. 'My friend is unconscious. She needs a doctor. She might be bleeding internally. You have to help us.'

'Can't,' Paula said.

'Have they gone to the hospital?'

'No,' Paula replied. She leant in towards the door, her mouth just inches from mine. 'He's bleeding . . . Min's . . . Shut up! You don't know.' She let out a whimper. 'No more noise.'

'Paula? Paula? Please.' I put my ear to the gap and listened to the sound of her retreating footsteps. 'Fuck.' I stepped back from the door. What now?

'I'm not unconscious.'

My heart bounced. 'Tania?' I stared down into the black.

'You've woken me up with all that racket.'

I made it down the stairs as fast as I could and found Tania awake and sitting up, clutching the back of her head. 'I feel like I've been kicked by a horse.'

'You and me both.' I shone the light onto her red hair. It was matted and stuck to her scalp with the darker red of blood. And I could see more blood running down her neck onto her top. 'You're still bleeding, Tania. Let me see if I can find something to press against it.'

The cellar was about fifteen feet square, with masses of junk stuffed into nooks and crannies. Empty bottles, old magazines, beermats, and squashed cardboard had been dumped and left to rot. The dripping sound was a tap in the corner where water leaked out and dribbled towards a grate in the floor. I found a pile of old towels, the oblong sort used to clean up beer spills, lying on top of some packing cases. I held the cleanest one against Tania's head and pressed as hard as I could without hurting her. 'I think you'll need stitches in this,' I said.

'Is Gerry Laidlaw dead?'

'No. I don't think so.' She slumped with disappointment. 'What possessed you to run at him like that?'

'I want him dead.' She held my eyes. 'He killed Dougie, Isla. He killed him.'

'Are you sure?'

Her face paled and she closed her eyes. 'Shit. I feel really dizzy.'

'Let's lie you down.' I fashioned a makeshift pillow from the rest of the towels and settled Tania's head on it. 'You mustn't fall asleep though.'

'I'm tired.'

'I know, but you have to stay awake.'

'You'll have to talk to me then.'

'I will.' Anger and fear washed over me, chilling the sweat on my back. I was trying to stay calm, Dougie, but if the man who killed you was in the room somewhere above us, then I wanted five minutes alone with him.

And do what, Isla? I heard your voice say. *Kill him?*

'What will we talk about?' Tania asked.

'Whatever you want.'

Who was I kidding? I wasn't brave. I wasn't confident. I could never have been a soldier. I wanted to be a mum at home with her kids. I doubt I could stick a knife in someone, even for you. But I could have him arrested. I could do that.

'Dougie loved this watch.' Tania took hold of my wrist and we both stared at your watch as if it might tell us something. 'The glass is scratched.'

'I can get it replaced. Listen.' I pointed to my mobile. 'I'm worried about the battery running down. I think I should switch the torch app off for a bit.'

'It'll be dark.'

'I know, but we should save the battery for when we need it.'

'Okay,' Tania said. Her hand came out and grabbed onto my sleeve. 'Don't leave me.

'I won't.'

I turned out the light and let darkness take control. In the absence of sight, the *drip-drip* grew louder, and the smell of beer grew more pungent. I thought about home and all the mundane things that would slip through the net if I never returned. There was the key for the garden shed. Last week I'd dropped it down the back of the washing machine, and I hadn't had the time to retrieve it. They'd never be able to get out the mower unless they broke the lock. A voice told me that would be the least of their worries, but still my mind persisted. I'd ordered Fin new football boots and I'd promised to collect them next week before his match against Newcastle. The living-room curtains needed to be taken up. Myrtle was due her injections. And then there was your house to sort. Marie would have to come across from Norway. And what about Dad?

'No one knows we're here,' Tania said, pulling on my sleeve. 'We didn't tell anyone, did we?'

'Alec will work it out,' I said, sounding more sure than

I felt. 'He knew I was lying when I said we were at Loch Lomond.' I leant in towards her. 'How did you know where to find the squat?'

'I checked your phone when you were asleep,' she said.

'Why?'

'Because you have kids and a life. I'm the one who should be putting myself in danger.'

'How do you know it was Gerry Laidlaw?'

'I asked him. He admitted it.'

'Fuck.' I breathed in too deeply and my ribs caught with a sharp, burning pain. I placed my hand over one of my sides and tried to hold myself still. 'But Why? Why did he kill Dougie?'

'I didn't have the chance to ask that. He grabbed hold of me and brought me into the squat.'

'Tania,' I took a shallow breath, 'if we get out of here – *when* we get out of here – we can go to the police. It's good you didn't kill him. He'll be imprisoned. We can make sure of it.'

'Men like that are scum,' Tania said, her tone low. 'My mum died when I was ten, but I always remember her saying, "Real life is bad for you, Tania. Get yourself away from all this. Find a different way to live".'

'What did she mean by "real life"?'

'Violence, power struggles, drugs. The shit that men get up to.'

'Not just men.' I put my hand out into the air and felt my way to her forehead, stroking her hair away from her eyes. 'I think Min Fraser's the leader.'

'Maybe you're right.' She took my hand from her head and held it on her chest. 'Tell me about the man you're in love with.'

'I'm not in love with him any more.'

'Tell me anyway.'

Ritchie. I visualised him standing at the top of the stairs. 'I like his voice. I like his hair.' I paused. I imagined him coming towards me in the dark. 'He's friendly and kind.' I paused again. 'He has lovely hands. He looks at me like . . .'

'Like what?'

'Like he loves me.'

'You might be better telling me what you don't like about him.'

'Lies.' I told her about the file Gavin had shown me.

'It doesn't sound like that big of a deal to me.'

'You think it's all right to start off a relationship with lies? He knew the police were investigating him. He should have told me before Gavin did, but he didn't. Bloody Gavin, of all people.'

'What bothers you more, the fact that he lied to you, or the fact that you feel humiliated?'

I thought about that.

'Be honest,' she said.

'Both. Fifty, fifty.'

'So forget the humiliation part. It doesn't matter what Gavin thinks, or the whole Scottish police force for that matter.' She pulled herself around on the floor, groaning as she went. 'I think you're making too much of the lies. Real life isn't Walt Disney. People make mistakes. I can't believe you're not going to give him another chance.'

'Yeah . . . well.'

'True love doesn't come along very often. You need to hang on to it. No one knows that better than me. I am queen of the screw-up.' She coughed. 'Could we have the light on again?'

'Okay.' I switched on the torch app. At first my eyes cramped against the light, and then I focussed on Tania.

She looked paler than ever; blood had seeped through a layer of towel. 'We need to make this tighter,' I told her, adjusting the pressure pad on her head so that she flinched. 'I'm sorry, I'm not very good at this.'

'It's okay,' Tania said. 'You're doing better than most people would.' She leant her shoulder against me. 'Dougie would be proud of you.'

'You think?'

'Yeah.'

'It's a shame we were never friends when he was alive.'

'I was a bitch and you were Judgezilla.'

'Judgezilla?' I felt the birth of laughter, but my ribs fired back a warning shot of pain.

'Dougie didn't like me calling you that, but . . .'

'. . . if the shoe fits.'

Her smile was weak.

'He'd be mad as hell, wouldn't he?' I said. 'If he could see the danger we've put ourselves in.

'Just a bit.' She sighed. 'It felt good, though, stabbing the fucker.'

We talked for hours, Dougie. About everything and nothing. About our upbringings, about the men we'd slept with and the men we hadn't, about the best place in Edinburgh to buy a coffee (the wee place in Stockbridge), about films and books and eye make-up.

And of course, you. We talked about you.

'Why did Dougie even tell you about the time I wanted to go to Russia?' I asked.

'We were listening to David Bowie, and he said you were a fan.'

'That's true. The year I was born, Bowie travelled on the Trans-Siberian railway.'

'You wanted to follow in his footsteps?'

'I believed I'd meet him one day and I'd be able to say we had something in common. I'd be as cool as he was.' I sighed. 'As if . . . It was a crazy idea. I probably did talk myself out of it.'

'It's okay to change your mind.'

'I didn't want to be ordinary, live an ordinary life, never go anywhere or see anything. But I ended up being so bloody ordinary.'

'Yeah, because checking into a cheap hotel in Glasgow with your brother's alcoholic ex-wife in tow and ending up injured and locked in a cellar—' She paused for effect. 'That's really ordinary.'

'You're not an alcoholic any more.'

'Once an alcoholic, always an alcoholic.' She shifted position again. 'I need to stand up.'

'Are you sure? You've lost a lot of blood.'

'It must be morning by now.'

I checked my phone. 'Ten past seven.'

'We should try again with the alarm, bang on the door and see if Paula might open it this time.'

'You're right.'

'And listen to me, Isla,' she clutched my arm tightly, 'if those two arseholes come back in here, you're going to let me do the talking. I know how to handle that sort of man.'

It took us a while to climb the stairs. We had to take it one step at a time, resting in between each lift of Tania's left leg. 'Sit down on the top step,' I told her when we finally made it to the metal door. 'Take a breather.'

Her face was ashen. She sat down on the step and immediately closed her eyes, her back against the bannister, her hands holding on to the struts.

'Help!' I banged on the door again. 'Please. Somebody

help us.' I could hear activity beyond the door, shouting and screaming and a loud crash that shook the building's foundations.

'What's going on?' Tania asked, her voice sleepy.

'I'm not sure but—'

The door swung open with a clatter and Paula stood there, glazed eyes, dribble escaping from one side of her mouth. 'Police raid. It's all kickin' off.'

'Thank you.' I helped Tania onto her feet again. 'Thank you, Paula.'

She stood aside to let us hobble by, her fingernails tearing at her arms, drawing blood to the surface of her skin. 'Turn left at the end.'

I turned myself and Tania left along a passageway I didn't recognise. We must have been a sorry sight, the pair of us, caked in dried blood, our bones aching and, as it turned out, in some cases, broken. Tania seemed to be in a state of semi-consciousness, but despite the pain in my arm and my ribs I was feeling euphoric. There had been moments when I thought we'd never see daylight again. And moments when I was afraid that Tania would die down there. I had imagined Collette becoming Fin and Caitlin's mum. (She would have done a good job – but not as good as me. No one loved them like I did. No one.) And I'd imagined seeing you again, Dougie. In the afterlife. If there is such a thing.

Tania and I left the pub through the front door, and the first thing I noticed was the smoke. It took me a moment to get my bearings. While the River Clyde bordered the north side, there was a huge patch of waste ground bordering the south. People had dumped their rubbish there. Old mattresses and broken buggies, empty fridges and smashed televisions. There was even a milk float that looked as if it had been abandoned some time in the last century. In the centre, a towering pile of old tyres had been set on fire, and acrid smoke mushroomed into the air. It stank of petrol and rubber, and immediately Tania started coughing.

'We'll move away from here and then we can rest,' I told her, half-dragging her over to one side.

'I parked the van . . .' She waved her hand around. 'Somewhere.'

We sat down on the edge of a wall and watched the spectacle unfold. Three fire engines arrived, blue lights flashing. Firemen leapt out, moving quickly despite their heavy suits, spooling hose through their hands to begin fighting the blaze with a jet of water that seemed to arc as high as the sky.

Three police vans were parked close by, and there were officers in riot gear everywhere, cuffing addicts and reading them their rights. Super-Skinny was shouting and bawling, marching up and down and generally causing a disturbance, a diversion even, because Min Fraser and Brian Laidlaw were nowhere to be seen, but I was pleased to see that Gerry Laidlaw, with his damaged shoulder, hadn't been able to slip away. The police had him cuffed, hands behind his back, his chin fallen onto his chest. He had bandages tied around one shoulder and anchored under his arm. His white T-shirt was scarlet-stained with splashes of blood.

Tania stood up, swayed, and then steadied herself. 'I just want to tell the policeman something.'

'We can do that later Tania,' I said. 'Don't worry, they have him now. He won't get away with it.'

She wasn't listening. She walked towards the policeman and Laidlaw. I was about to follow her, but changed my mind when I saw an ambulance arrive. I was sure I was thinking straight, Dougie. I thought we were through the worst of it. When the paramedic climbed out I asked him to follow me. 'My friend's concussed, I think,' I said. 'We were both attacked and thrown down some stairs.'

We were only a couple of feet from Tania. Gerry Laidlaw hadn't noticed her approach. The policeman had registered her, but dismissed her as a non-threat, and it was obvious why. She was dragging her left leg. She was bleeding. She couldn't have looked less hostile if she'd tried. I was barely an arm's length away when she took a knife from inside her shoe and stuck it in to Gerry Laidlaw's windpipe.

'Tania!' I screamed.

'Always carry two knives.' She smiled at me. 'That was something else my mother told me.'

Her head lolled backward and she collapsed into my arms.

14. The Truth is Overrated

I parked the car and joined a dozen other visitors walking into Corton Vale Prison. The wind and rain were charging through the trees, busy, blustery weather that drew attention to itself.

After she had killed Gerry Laidlaw, Tania spent twenty-four hours in the hospital, handcuffed to the bed, a police officer by her side. When her leg and arm were plastered and her head had been scanned for damage, they had carted her off to prison. I visited her twice a week, no matter what. We fell into the habit of beginning with banter.

'Did you pay for those miniatures when you checked out of the hotel?' she asked.

'Of course.'

'The difference between you and me is that I'd have filled the bottles up again. Water for the vodka and gin. Pee for the whisky.'

'I'd rather just pay.'

'Why?'

'Because it's dishonest to try to get away with it.'

'The hotel is owned by some mega corporation with fat shareholders who have two or more homes.' She pulled at her nails. 'And yachts on the Med.'

'And what if it had come out of the cleaner's wages? What if she'd been fired and she was a single parent with no other income?'

'You're over thinking it. That was another thing Dougie always said about you.'

'Yeah, yeah.'

We both smiled, and then she reached across the table and took my hands. 'Tell me about the kids.'

To say that I felt like I owed her is an understatement. I know you won't be surprised by what she did, Dougie, and I shouldn't have been either. She was facing at least a decade in prison because I'd been too stupid to register that she would have her own agenda. It wasn't as if she didn't give me any clues – her anxiety in the hotel, her turning up at the squat instead of just calling the police. I knew she was a loose cannon. I knew she did and said exactly the wrong thing at exactly the wrong time, but I had still asked her along.

'She's an adult,' Gavin told me. 'She could have said no.'

She couldn't though, could she? Because she owed you, Dougie. Because you'd stood by her through all her misery and strife. Yes, you divorced her, but that was never the end of it. She called; you responded. She was always going to avenge your death, with or without me.

It fell to me to tell Tania about Gerry Laidlaw's innocence. Her lawyer would have done it, but he was a speedy guy who barely sat down before he was up and gone, and I didn't want her hearing it from him.

Gerry Laidlaw had a watertight alibi. He was in a police cell in Middlesex the night you died, Dougie. This was confirmed by CCTV and by his fingerprints. There could be no mistake.

After I told Tania this news she sat very still, and then she said, 'But he told me he'd done it.'

'He was lying.' I shrugged. 'Bragging.'

'So I stabbed the wrong brother?'

We were sitting on either side of a plastic table, other women and their visitors all around us. Privacy was impossible, but still I leant in towards her. 'Tania . . . I'm not sure it was either of them.'

'Brian Laidlaw also has an alibi?'

'Yes.'

'Who? What?'

I told her he'd been ID'd by a cop in Kilmarnock on the night of your death.

'Could the cop be lying?'

'Unlikely.'

'So it was Min Fraser, then?'

'Maybe . . . but Tania . . . It doesn't make sense that they would kill him, because he was getting them their money.'

'These people aren't rational like you and me, Isla. They kill folk who look at them the wrong way. If Dougie was refusing to pay what was left of the loan, they could have him killed to teach him a lesson, then come after the family for the rest.' She started coughing, and clutched her ribcage. 'I can't shift this bastard cough.'

'Have you been to the prison medical centre?'

'No. I'm going to go private.' Her tone was sarcastic, her stare aggressive. 'How can you come here and tell me all this? It's like you've given up! Are you just going to let these fuckers carry on with their lives?' She slammed her hands on the table top, then stood up and walked away from me. I saw one warden glance at the other, and then they lead Tania back inside the body of the prison.

Before my next trip to Corton Vale they called me to say she'd been denied visiting rights. She'd been caught with drugs. I emailed her, but she ignored me. I left messages for her to call me, but she didn't. This went on for three weeks, and then she phoned me one evening when I was making tea for the kids.

'I've been thinking, Isla,' she said, launching straight in. 'You are going to find out who the debt belongs to, aren't you?'

'Laidlaw says he'll tell me when I give him the rest of the money.'

'Good. I reckon whoever's debt it is will know what happened to Dougie.'

'Maybe. Yes. I hope so.' I put a smile into my voice. 'Listen, Caitlin and Fin would like to come and visit you.'

'No.'

'Are you sure? Because it's not so bad in the Visitors' Centre, and I think they're old enough.'

'No.'

'It might be nice for you, you know, to see them . . .' I trailed off, sensing the breaking of her temper.

'Nice? Nice?' She laughed. 'What would be *nice*, Isla, would be for you to focus on finding out who killed Dougie. I can do *nothing* from in here. I go over it and over it in my head. But I can't do shit from here. We need answers.'

'I understand.'

I spent the rest of the phone call making promises. Not empty promises, but promises that I knew I might be hard pushed to fulfil.

Those first couple of weeks, my wrist in plaster and my ribs taped, I had to listen to no end of criticisms.

Gavin and Collette made it plain what they thought of me. 'I can't *believe* you didn't think of Caitlin and Fin,' Collette said, wearing her sternest, most teacherly expression.

'They were safe with you,' I said. 'I was thinking of my brother.'

'Your children deserve so much more.' She moved aside to let Gavin have a go.

'I've a good mind to sue you for custody, Isla,' he said tersely. 'You've lied. You've been deceitful. You've behaved—' He shook his head. 'You couldn't have been more irresponsible if you'd tried.'

I knew he wouldn't sue me – there was no way he wanted the kids full-time, and there was no way he would get them either – and while Collette was genuinely upset on the kids' behalf, Gavin was annoyed with me for not listening to him.

'The time I spent explaining the investigation to you. The favours I called in with my colleagues in Glasgow. Did that mean nothing to you?'

'Of course it meant something, but—'

'But *what*? But everyone else is wrong and you are right? Only you are capable of seeing clues? Only you . . .'

I let him rant.

Alec couldn't stay in the same room as me. When I returned to work, still in plaster, he ignored me for a week, and when I went through to his office to have it out with him, he let rip. 'Why, Isla? *Why?* What the fuck possessed you?'

'I had to—'

'We had an agreement.' He towered over me, wagging a finger in my face. 'You said you'd be careful.'

'I thought I was.'

'Why didn't you tell me where you were going?'

'I knew that if I told you, you'd have stopped me.'

'Damn right I'd have stopped you! *Damn* right. Tania wouldn't be in prison, and a man wouldn't be dead.'

'I know.'

'And did you find anything out? Did you? *Did you?*'

'No.' I shook my head. 'But . . . You know how I asked you to pull a few strings for me . . . Well, did Marie call Dougie the evening he died?'

'What?' He drew away from me, flabbergasted. 'Let it go, Isla!'

'But did she?'

'No. She didn't call him.' He ran a stressed hand across his forehead. 'Now listen to me, Isla. Listen hard. You know perfectly well that Dougie would be the last person to agree with the way you've been behaving. And frankly, lassie, if I was your father I'd tan your hide for being such a bloody, irresponsible fool.'

By the time Dad learnt the ins and outs of what had happened, over a week had gone by, so he was a bit easier on me. He was slowly recovering from the chest infection, and he didn't have the energy for a fight. He gave me a melancholy look and said, 'God knows what Douglas or your mother would say. I know none of us were exactly fond of Tania, but I wouldn't wish prison on her.'

Marie had a different point to make. She wasn't concerned with any danger I might have been in. She wasn't concerned about Caitlin and Fin. She was annoyed because I'd left her out, because I was playing 'hero' without her.

'I tried to tell you,' I said. 'But you didn't want to hear me.'

'You should have tried harder! And what did you find out anyway? What have you achieved? I mean, I can't say I've ever cared about Tania, but Dougie did, and now look where she is!'

'I know exactly where she is, Marie. I visit her twice a week.'

'Anyway, it's the final straw. We're moving back to Scotland. We're leaving Norway and coming to live in Aberdeen.'

'*What?* That's sudden, isn't it?'

'No. We've been thinking about it for ages, but I just haven't mentioned it. Erik can fly to the rigs from Scotland just as easily as he can from Norway. And quite honestly, after everything that's gone on, I think you could do with having me a bit closer.'

Lucky me.

Caitlin and Fin saved me. I played the whole thing down. I lied, to protect them and to protect myself. I told them that Tania and I had gone to see where you had died, and we'd got mixed up with some rough men, but that I'd never go there again. They were concerned for Tania, but she'd never been a large part of their lives so they weren't as upset as they might have been. I told them that she loved you, and that she'd thought the man she killed might have had something to do with your death. That she'd made a mistake, and was going to have to pay for it with her time and the loss of her freedom.

'We can visit her with you, Mum,' Fin said. 'Otherwise she'll get lonely.'

I got on with the business of selling your house. I showed people around. I threw my back into gardening and fixing and sorting. My left wrist was broken, but I still had full use of my right hand, and I pushed myself to my limits. I ended up with cut fingers and sore muscles, but it all paid off when a family of five put in an offer in November and we'd completed by January.

Brian Laidlaw and Min Fraser never let me forget that they were waiting for their money. They reminded me of it, if not daily, then every other day. Min Fraser would call me, 'Just checking in,' she would say. Or else

I'd see Brian Laidlaw sitting in his car at the top of the lane. I worried about reprisals against Tania, but they seemed to take Gerry's death in their stride. 'He was an eejit,' Brain Laidlaw told me. 'He'd been living on borrowed time for years.'

I had lost my fear of Brian Laidlaw. I could look him in the eye and talk to him without panicking. 'But he was your brother,' I said.

'He was still a fuckin' eejit.'

Only Tania knew that I was planning on giving them the rest of the money. I could have told Gavin, I could have rallied the might of Police Scotland behind me, but I wasn't about to fight them over it. You were dead, and Tania was in prison. I just wanted to give them their money, find out whose debt it was and how you'd died, and try to move on.

In January, just before your house sale was finalised, I went up to see how Marie was settling in. Aberdeen was hardly close by, but it was still do-able in a day. It was Martha's third birthday party, and there were a dozen little girls and boys running up and down the stairs in pirate and princess costumes, screaming and giggling.

'You've made friends quickly,' I said.

'It's easy with kids, isn't it?' She stacked some plates in the dishwasher. 'Thank God the pregnancy was a false alarm. I couldn't have coped with a fourth.'

I finished off my piece of cake and handed her the plate. 'Is Erik missing Norway?'

'A bit, I think.'

'You think?'

'He doesn't talk about his feelings. As long as we're happy, he's happy.'

I leant my back against the fridge and said quietly, 'There never was any boat, Marie, was there?'

'Kind of.' She shook her head. 'Well, not really, I suppose.'

'Why did you lie?'

'I don't know.' She met my eye. 'You have that disappointed look that Mum used to give me.'

'Marie.' I put my arms around her. 'I wish we could be better friends.'

'We're sisters. We don't need to be friends.'

'But I want us to be friends.'

'Like the way it was with you and Dougie, you mean?'

'No . . . it could never be like that.'

She stepped away from me. 'Why not?'

'Because we were twins! We had so much in common. We were together all the time, all through school and . . . whatnot.'

'And there we have it!' Marie said, her arms folded tightly against me. 'Your exclusive club.'

'I don't mean it like that!'

'You're no longer special, Isla.' She tossed her mug into the sink and I heard a crack as it broke in two. 'Welcome to my world.'

I left her at teatime and began the drive home. The sun was already setting, the sky the colour of blood-orange flesh. I remembered that you'd driven up to Aberdeen just before you took the money out of your account. You'd visited Gordy's wife, and I could have done the same, but she had recently died and Gordy was down in London speaking to one of the homeless charities, passing around Lucy's photo, ever hopeful. I admired him for that. What do any of us have if we don't have hope?

I was right in thinking that Paula had never known Lucy. It was me who had invited the pretence of a connection. I had shown Min Fraser the flier with

Lucy's photo and the details about the three wise monkeys on it, and she had used the information to have Paula lure me back to Glasgow. I had jumped to conclusions and made connections that didn't exist. But soon . . . soon, I would know how you'd died. I was living for that moment, anticipating how I would feel, praying for a measure of understanding, maybe even peace.

I drove back from Aberdeen on the A90, and when I got to Dundee I thought I might as well pop in and see Dad. The kids and Myrtle were with Gavin for the weekend so there was no rush to get back to Edinburgh and an empty house.

The lights were on in his living room, but the front door was opened by someone I didn't recognise.

'I'm looking for my dad.'

'George?'

'That's right.' I held out my hand. 'You're Dorothy's son, Mark?'

'Yeah.' He gave my hand a perfunctory shake and turned his back to lope off into the living room. 'Your dad will be back in a minute.' He put his feet up on the coffee table. 'He goes to meet my mum from work.'

In the alcove by the window Dad had created a corner for you: memorabilia, photographs, certificates. Your life condensed into snapshots of success. Special memories that grew more important with time, from your raggedy old teddy to the candlestick you made in third year. Most of it, though, focussed on your time in the marines. Commendations, pictures of you in the desert next to smiling children. You with a rifle in your hand, looking serious. You and Mum at your passing out parade.

I walked over to the window to close the curtains, but

stopped before I pulled them to. 'My dad didn't mention he'd replaced his windows.'

'It was after that time they got smashed.'

'What time?' I said.

'Few months ago now, eh? End of the summer.'

The air around me thickened. I tried to breathe in but was met by resistance, and from that point on my breathing became snatched and shallow.

'Was it before he broke his leg?'

'Just, yeah.'

'Before my brother died?'

'Yeah. Like a couple of days before. Bad luck comes in threes, though, eh? First the windows, then your brother, and then your dad's leg.'

I felt light-headed and leant both hands on the sill. 'Did the police find out who smashed them?'

'Couple of big guys with Glaswegian accents. That's what the neighbour said, anyway.'

We were seventeen. I came home from my Saturday job at Boots in Princes Street. I'd bust a gut to get the earlier bus because I was going out with my boyfriend, Davy Leach, him-of-the-sweaty-hands, and I needed time to get ready. As soon as I opened the door, I heard the shouting. You were in the living room, standing watching television, your hands in your pockets.

'What's going on?' I said.

'Nothing much. They're just having an argument.'

'What about?'

'Dad wants to start a new business, but Mum won't let him have the savings book.'

I stood at the new windows and watched Dorothy and Dad walk back towards the house, arms entwined. Dad had been left with a limp, and he was leaning in to Dorothy. He saw me at the window and waved. I didn't wave back and his hand dropped down to his side, uncertain. When he came into the living room I turned towards him. 'Dad?'

Guilt.

Guilt, Dougie.

Guilt.

It flashed across his face and then he covered it up with enthusiasm. 'What brings you here?' He hugged me, avoiding my eye. 'Great to see you. Isn't it great to see her, Dorothy?'

'If you'd told us you were coming I'd have got something special in for tea.' She moved towards the windows, swift as a busy mouse, and closed the curtains. 'We've only got sausages and mash, but Mark will give up his share, won't you Mark?'

'Yeah. Course.'

'Dad?'

He was whistling through his teeth.

'Tell me about the windows.'

'Nothing to tell, really.' He laughed. 'It was time to make the double-glazing salesman happy.'

'Tell me about the men who smashed them.' My ribcage swelled with air and emotion: anger and fear, expanding to fill the space. 'Tell me it wasn't the Laidlaws.'

'Isla . . .' he sighed. 'Now don't go getting yourself in a paddy.'

I moved closer. 'Did. You. Or did you not—' I tried to breathe. '—borrow money from the Laidlaws?'

'Where is this coming from?'

'Just answer the *fucking* question.'

'What are you doing getting all bossy with your father?'

Dorothy said. 'Take the weight off your feet and I'll get you a hot drink.'

'*Did you*, or did you *not*, borrow money from the Laidlaws?' I shouted.

'Isla? Jesus! Calm yourself.'

'I *am* calm.' I was raging. 'Tell me. Tell me *now*.'

'All right! All right!' He gave me the sort of smile he used to give us when he'd let us stay up late, watching television we weren't allowed to see – conspiratorial, in the nicest possible way – not deceit, not treachery, just oh-look-at-us! Haven't we been naughty? (Don't tell your mother.)

I smiled back. A wee girl to her dad.

'George, don't,' Dorothy said, plucking at his sleeve. 'Let's just leave it be.'

'It's fine, Dorothy. Isla will understand.' He steadied himself with a reassuring breath. 'Dorothy and me, we started a business, a garden centre. It was a sound idea, but the stock was destroyed by rain and the temperature gauge in the polytunnels was faulty, and if it hadn't been for the recession we would have made a go of it. The banks weren't lending and—'

I punched him, hard. Hard enough to split his skin. He reeled backwards, clutching his cheek. Dorothy screamed and Mark stood up.

'Now, now,' Dad rubbed his face then held out his arms in surrender. 'Calm down everyone. I deserved that. I absolutely deserved that. No doubt about it. No doubt at all.'

'My *brother*,' I whispered. 'Your *son*.' I was incensed, Dougie. Horrified, saddened, gutted. 'You got him *killed*.'

'Hit me again.' I didn't move and he turned his fists on himself, bashing his face. 'I'll hit myself, if you want.

It's no more than I deserve. Don't you know I'd swap places with him? Don't you know that? I told him not to get involved. I told him, but he wouldn't listen.'

'Don't you blame this on him,' I said quietly. 'Don't you fucking dare.'

'I'm not, Isla! I'm not!' He tried for a laugh, but swallowed it down into his chest. 'He was on his way back from Aberdeen and he came to see me. The Laidlaws had been around and smashed a couple of windows. Nothing I couldn't handle, and Dougie wanted to know what was going on. And God help me I shouldn't have told him, but I did, and then he took it upon himself to try and sort it out for me.'

'You knew he would sort it for you. *You knew that.*'

'I wanted to have a successful business and make you all proud and I thought if your mother's watching from upstairs, she'll—'

'Upstairs? *Upstairs?* Mum's dead, Dad. She's *dead.*'

'I let her down when she was alive. She kept it from you girls, but she confided in Dougie. He was her lad really. He was never my lad.'

'That's bullshit, Dad. Fuck!' I pressed my fingers against my temples. 'I can't listen to this.'

'You're not going to tell Marie, are you?' He followed me into the corner. 'You know how judgemental she can be.'

'Get me a bin bag.' I was looking at Mark.

'What?'

'Get. Me. A bin bag!'

In the minute Mark took to get it, I gathered together the pieces in the alcove. 'I'm taking all of this.'

'Why?'

'Why? *Why?* Because you don't bloody deserve it, is why. Because you've set up a *shrine* to a son who didn't die in Iraq or Afghanistan. No, he died in bloody Glasgow, *Glasgow*, and whose fault was that, Dad? Whose fucking fault was that?' Mark was back, and I grabbed the bin bag from his hand, dropping the pieces in, one by one. When I lifted the photo of you and Mum at your passing out parade off the wall, my breath caught at the sight of you both, happy and alive. 'You can't have this. You can't have any of it.'

'Isla!'

'Don't Isla me! And don't you dare give me the doe-eyed look you gave Mum for years, because it's not fucking working on me. How dare you? How dare you involve my brother in your crappy schemes?'

'You shouldn't be talking to your father that way!' Dorothy moved forward, her arm circling Dad's as if he were a child needing protection. 'You don't know the half of it.'

'Then tell me, Dorothy! Go on. Tell me what could possibly justify a loan of one hundred thousand pounds and then my brother's life?'

Dorothy started crying, and then Mark waded in and told me to, 'Fuck off back to Edinburgh.'

'He's right. You need to leave now,' Dad added, sounding haughty and self-righteous.

I don't remember the drive back to Edinburgh. I only know I made it home. I brought all the memorabilia into the house and then I sat with it on my knee: photos and cards, good-luck charms, and a pile of postcards and letters that you'd sent home. It was in that pile that I found a large Manila envelope with four smaller, white envelopes inside. One of the letters had my name on it. The other three were addressed to Mum, Dad, and Marie. My heart chilled when I realised what they were: 'In the event of my death' letters that you'd written when you were a marine.

I sat staring at the envelopes, and then hid them at the back of my wardrobe. I couldn't open the one addressed to me.

Not yet.

15. Now That You're Gone

I understand now, Dougie. I see why my name was in your diary. I see why you said to Tania you were going to Glasgow for me. You didn't want me to think less of our dad. You were handling it. You were saving him from himself and protecting me from the truth.

I don't have your powers of forgiveness. For a man who behaved with honour and integrity, you understood weakness in others. While you were alive you had enough compassion for both of us, but now? I'll never be able to forgive Dad. His bad decisions killed you. I know. I know. You didn't need to fix it for him, but were you really going to let Dad deal with his troubles alone? Of course not, and I bet he knew that too.

Over the following few days, he left a couple of messages. There was no remorse, no apology. Most of the messages revolved around Dorothy's feelings. 'Dorothy has been extremely upset by this,' he said. 'I think you're being very selfish.'

??

What the fuck??

I told no one. I couldn't bring myself to speak the words. *My dad was responsible for my brother's death.* I was so sore inside, Dougie, that I struggled to behave normally. I grew detached. I said words that didn't feel like mine, and made my mouth smile in all the right places. I walked and talked and went through the motions, but only the kids could bring a real smile to my face.

I spent all my child-free and work-free time outside with Myrtle. Winter barley was a foot high in the fields as we trudged the pathway and up the hill, leaning into the wind like determined travellers. Mossy stones, thorns and thistles, brambles and sharp sticks, rain, wind and sleet – no matter how inhospitable the ground or the weather – I kept going until I'd worked it all out.

My thoughts were like footsteps, and every one of them led me to you. I reflected on our shared history, and on what you meant to our family. I realised that when all the heat and chat, the what-ifs and maybes, had been boiled off, what was left was this: we all depended on you too much. If I had been a better sister, more mature, more emotionally capable, you would have told me about Dad and we would have dealt with it together.

That's the truth as I saw it.

That's the truth as I will always see it.

'You've come to accept that Dougie's death was an accident, haven't you?' Gavin said to me, and I lied, told him I had. We were standing at the window in my kitchen watching Collette and the kids fixing Christmas lights around the old apple tree.

'I think you should try to have your vasectomy reversed and let Collette become a mother,' I said.

'What?' He made a face at me.

'I'm just saying.'

'Yeah? Well don't.' He grabbed his car keys and opened the door. 'When I need your advice, I'll ask for it.'

At the beginning of February, Alec called me into the office. I hadn't spoken to either Dad or Marie about the deal you struck with Alec, but made my own mind up to go with your decision to buy a stake in the company. I was now part owner of the business, but I had yet to play any part in the running of it. I came in to work and functioned on automatic pilot. Did my job as well as ever I had, and went home again.

'Isla, we need to . . . not replace Dougie, but we need to find someone to do the job he did.'

'I thought you had someone.'

'I was trialling a bloke, but he's not a patch on your brother. Ex-marines have a way about them. They carry themselves well.'

'They do.' I nodded, then said casually, 'I know an ex-marine.'

'Richard McFadden?'

Just hearing his name made something inside me soften.

'I approached him, but he said he wouldn't work for us,' Alec said. 'He thought you might not like it.'

'Is the Prendergast case over?'

'Aye. Evidence gathered, and Ritchie was squeaky clean. If there was any mud, it would surely have stuck by now.'

'Let's employ him then,' I said. 'If he's willing, that is.'

'Are you sure about that?'

'I am.'

'I thought you had a falling out?'

'It was nothing, really.' I opened the door. 'Just a misunderstanding.'

I'd been thinking about Ritchie a lot. Thinking and dreaming, but not doing anything about it. And then Caitlin came to talk to me and I was pushed to act. She had her very serious face on. 'Mum?'

'Yeah?'

'There's something I've been meaning to tell you for a while.' She bit her lip. 'You know how you and Ritchie split up?'

'Yeah?'

'It's all my fault, isn't it?'

'No. Of course not!' I pulled her down on the couch beside to me. 'Why would it be your fault?'

'I mean . . . because I called him. When you were away with Tania. Because I was worried, and you said you'd call me and Fin, and you did but you sounded strange and Dad said it was because Dougie was dead but I knew that wasn't it. And so I called Ritchie and I told him where you were.'

'How did you know where I was?' I asked, amazed.

'Because of location services on our phones. We set it up, remember?'

'Vaguely.'

'So I looked, and you were in Glasgow. In a hotel. And I told Ritchie that's where you were, and is that why you split up, because I told on you?'

'No, Caitlin. No.' I hugged her. 'That wasn't the reason.'

I met Brian Laidlaw in a lay-by on the road to Livingstone. The air was fresh with frost, and for once he was wearing more than just a white sleeveless vest. I used the money from your estate that was meant for Dad to pay Laidlaw off. I'd sent Dad a letter telling him as much, daring him to fight me on it. He didn't. That was a step too far even for him.

I passed Laidlaw a sports bag full of cash and he checked it in front of me, then nodded his head, satisfied. 'Questions?' he asked.

'The debt belonged to?'

'Your dad.'

I nodded. 'Who killed my brother?'

'No one.'

'I don't believe you.'

'*No one* killed your brother.' Laidlaw climbed back in his car. 'It's my patch. If someone had killed him, I'd know about it.'

He drove off. I haven't seen him since.

Did I believe him?

No, I didn't.

It was ten o'clock on a Saturday morning when I made my way to Ritchie's. I'd prepared myself for the fact that he might have another woman in his bed, but the girl who opened the door was about fourteen, and she looked like her dad.

'Leonie?'

Her eyes widened. 'Are you Isla?'

'Yes.'

'I heard about you.'

'I heard about you too.'

'All bad, I hope?' She turned away and shouted, 'Dad!' at the top of her voice. When there was no answer she said, 'He might be in the garden. You know your way?'

'Yes.'

'I'm Skyping a friend in Oz.'

'Don't let me keep you.'

She padded off along the hallway and I went inside, closing the front door behind me. I was about to see Ritchie again, and anticipation set my heartbeat off on a run. I was still standing there several minutes later when he came in through the patio doors and spotted me.

'I hope it's okay,' I said. 'Your daughter let me in.'

'Of course.' He started walking to the kitchen, calling over his shoulder, 'Coffee?'

'No . . . I . . . um . . .' My feet were glued to the mat. 'I have a couple of things I want to say.' He turned to face me. 'Caitlin told me that she rang you.' He nodded. 'The police came to the squat, and without that . . . I don't know.' I tried to breathe in. 'Was it you who called them?'

'I thought you might need a hand. There's nothing like a police raid to empty a place.'

'How did you manage it?'

'Just someone I used to work for.'

'Well . . . thank you.'

'Pleasure.'

There was an awkward moment when we both just stood there, and then I heard myself say, 'I'm sorry I was a bit over the top. I've had a long time to think about what I said to you, and Tania made me realise I'd been harsh and I want to apologise.' I looked him in the eye. 'I am apologising. I'm sorry.'

'Accepted.' He smiled. 'Are you okay?'

'Not really.' My eyes filled up. 'My dad's the reason Dougie's dead.'

'Fuck!' His head jerked backward. 'Are you sure? How?'

'I'm as sure as I can be. There I was thinking up all sorts of complicated scenarios and it was really very simple. My dad and his friend Dorothy, who I was stupid enough to think was a good influence on him, borrowed the money.'

'Isla, I'm so sorry.' He moved towards me, but I held up my hand to stop him coming too close because I wasn't ready to let him touch me.

'I keep thinking that as time goes by the shock will lessen, but it doesn't.' I sighed. 'Anyway, you know Alec wants to offer you work?'

'I won't take it if you don't want me to.'

'You should take it. He's good to work for. He pays well.'

'But you own half the business now, don't you?'

'Technically, yes. But Alec still runs it.' I opened the front door. 'I have to go home.'

'Kids waiting for you?'

'No. They're with Gavin.' I glanced at my feet, then up at the sky. 'I have a letter to read.'

'Do you fancy getting the dogs together some time?'

'Yes.' I started walking to my car, then turned back for another look at him. 'Definitely,' I said.

I took the letter from the back of the wardrobe and sat down on the sofa. It was handwritten and was dated 15 July 2002, a couple of months after the party Mum and Dad had thrown for your fifth wedding anniversary, the one where Tania dropped the abortion bombshell. My hands were shaking as I started reading . . .

Dear Isla,

If you're reading this, it's because I've been killed in action. What can I say? No wailing and moaning and trying to find out exactly what happened to me! (I know you, remember?)

Celebrate my life.

Celebrate your life.

And your kids' lives.

Especially your kids. You're a dead good mum, Isla. I was watching you with Caitlin and you've got another baby on the way and – well, tell them

about their uncle, won't you? Let them steal each
other's chocolate and lie to their parents. Let them
run free. Let them be like us.

Be kind to Tania. And Dad and Marie. I don't
have to tell you to be kind to Mum because you'll
do that anyway.

Be patient, yeah? Or I'll come back and haunt
you.

Remember sis – memento mori.

Love you always,

Dougie xx

Acknowledgments

Special thanks to Detective Inspector Paul Matthews for his help with police procedure, and to the private investigator who let me into his world (you know who you are).

To my editor Laura Macdougall and my agent Euan Thorneycroft for their sound advice and guidance – I couldn't have got there without you.

My friends, Mel, Ellie, Jo, Jackie, Cristina, Neil and George for reading scenes from earlier drafts and for listening to me talk through plot and character.

And, as ever, my three sons, Mike, Sean and Matt, your love and support keeps me going.

If you were hooked on *Now That You're Gone*, why not try more of Julie Corbin's novels?

What Goes Around

**If someone took away your perfect life
How far would you go to get it back?**

Ellen's family is her world. So when her husband leaves her for another woman, she is almost destroyed. But not quite, because Ellen has a plan, a way to make those who have hurt her suffer.

Leila is the other woman. She finally has everything she ever wanted. But Leila's brother has come back into her life, raking up a past that needs to stay buried.

One of them will pay for their actions with their life, but which one?

Out now in paperback and ebook.

HODDER

Tell Me No Secrets

They say that everybody has a secret. Mine lies underground. Her name was Rose and she was nine years old when she died . . .

Grace lives in a quiet, Scottish fishing village – the perfect place for bringing up her twin girls with her loving husband Paul. Life is good.

Until a phone call from her old best-friend, a woman Grace hasn't seen since her teens – and for good reason – threatens to destroy everything. Caught up in a manipulative and spiteful game that turns into an obsession, Grace is about to realise that some secrets can't stay buried forever.

For if Orla reveals what happened on that camping trip twenty-four years ago, she will take away all that Grace holds dear . . .

Out now in paperback and ebook.

HODDER

Do Me No Harm

When her teenage son Robbie's drink is spiked, Olivia Somers is devastated. She has spent her adult life trying to protect people and keep them safe – not only as a mother, but also in her chosen profession as a doctor.

So she tries to put it down to a horrible accident, in spite of the evidence suggesting malicious intent, and simply hopes no-one tries to endanger those she loves again.

But someone from the past is after revenge.
Someone closer to her family than she could possibly realise.
Someone who will stop at nothing until they get the vengeance they crave.

And, as she and her family come under increasing threat, the oath that Olivia took when she first became a doctor – to do no harm to others – will be tested to its very limits.

Out now in paperback and ebook.

HODDER